W9-BYE-111

LOVE AND DEATH

LOVE AND DEATH

Edited by

Carolyn Hart

BERKLEY PRIME CRIME, NEW YORK

LOVE AND DEATH

A Berkley Prime Crime Book
Published by The Berkley Publishing Group,
a division of Penguin Putnam Inc., 375 Hudson Street,
New York, New York 10014
The Penguin Putnam Inc. World Wide Web site address is
http://www.penguinputnam.com

First edition: January 2001

Library of Congress Cataloging-in-Publication Data
Love and death / edited by Carolyn G. Hart.
    p. cm.
    Contents: Bridal flowers / Dorothy Cannell—Away for safekeeping / Susan Dunlap—A girl like you / Ed Gorman—Company wife / Jean Hager—Secrets / Carolyn Hart—The first one to blink / Gar Anthony Haywood—The tunnel / M.D. Lake—Til 3:45 / Margaret Maron—A night at the love nest resort / Robert J. Randisi and Christine Matthews—Tea for two / Nancy Pickard—April in Paris / Peter Robinson—The people's way / Eve Sandstrom—Love at first byte / Kathy Hogan Trocheck—The collaboration / Marilyn Wallace.
    ISBN 0-425-17805-6
    1. Detective and mystery stories, American.   2. Love stories, American.   I. Hart, Carolyn G.
PS648.D4 L675   2001
813'.087208—dc21   00-033692

PRINTED IN THE UNITED STATES OF AMERICA

10 9 8 7 6 5 4 3 2 1

CONTENTS

FOREWORD

Carolyn Hart

L ove is the wellspring of life. Without love, life is cold, barren, and unforgiving, as sterile as a crater on the moon. Every heart must have love, and every heart seeks love in a different way.

In this collection of stories, readers will experience joy, intimacy, sadness, triumph, and despair. These stories reveal the core of life. These stories tell of crimes of the heart:

Therese can't keep her mouth shut about her husband's transgressions . . .

Peter will never forget Nora . . .

Marcie was the perfect company wife . . .

Gretchen saw love and loss everywhere she looked . . .

Celia did everything right until . . .

Sam heard the crackle of the flames, and he knew they'd blame him . . .

Mara dialed the number and listened as it rang and rang and rang . . .

Stephen heard the man and woman in the room next door . . .

Heather is young and blond and beautiful, as Claire once was . . .

Professor Dodgson sat in the café, and the years fell away . . .

Amaya watched as Rogar walked into the water with the baby . . .

Brett wanted money, and he wanted love . . .

Gloria held her baby tight. She'd made up her mind . . .

Welcome to *Love and Death*—a chilling exploration of love sought, love found, love lost.

LOVE AND DEATH

BRIDAL FLOWERS

Dorothy Cannell

*Dorothy Cannell first introduced her unlikely pair of private de-
tectives—the Misses Hyacinth and Primrose Tramwell—in the
pastoral mystery novel* Down the Garden Path. *They subse-
quently made appearances in* The Widows Club *and* Mum's
the Word, *Cannell's series featuring Ellie and Ben Haskell.
"Bridal Flowers" is a response to readers' frequent requests for
a return of the Tramwell sisters. Cannell's novels and short
stories are most often set in her native England. "The Family
Jewels" won the 1994 Agatha in the best short story category.
Her latest book is* Bridesmaids Revisited, *published by Viking
in June 2000. She lives in Illinois with her husband Julian and
two Cavalier King Charles spaniels named Bertie Woofster and
Jeeves.*

"That obnoxious woman!" Hyacinth Tramwell set
down her cup and saucer with a bang on the coffee
table. "I ran into her last year at the church bazaar, and
she bored me for an entire hour. What on earth can she
want?"

"Probably come collecting for one of her pet projects."
Her sister Primrose gave a fluttering sigh. "And the bother
of it is that I'll probably agree to make a donation to a
group I despise simply because she intimidates me so."

"Nonsense, Prim. You will square your shoulders and remember that you are a woman in your sixties and a private detective to boot, not a child to be ordered to hand over a bag of sweets."

"Yes, dear."

Before either woman could say more, the sitting room door opened and their butler, a man of uncertain age and nondescript appearance, entered. "Mrs. Smith-Hoggles," he intoned, as if informing them of an outbreak of bubonic plague in the village. Behind him loomed a shadow, which took on form and substance when he bowed and retreated.

"Does he always do that?" The woman in the brown felt hat and camel coat was slimly built but she had a large voice.

"Always do what?" Hyacinth raised an eyebrow.

"Pad about the place in his socks."

"Certainly. He is an ex-burglar, excellent training for his present job. We could not ask for a more unobtrusive butler."

"But aren't you afraid he'll pinch the silver?"

"Dear me, no," twittered Primrose. "His passion is eighteenth-century clocks, quite single-minded about it. His brother specialized in sundials before his retirement. And there is a sister who I believe still deals in pocket watches. Quite the family business one might say. But I must not rattle on, pray do sit down, Mrs. Smith-Hoggles, and tell us what brings you here on such an inclement morning."

Their visitor hesitated before taking a seat. She had met the Misses Tramwell on several occasions at village functions but had not previously been to Cloisters, their ancestral home. She had passed it numerous times in the car and occasionally on foot, and although she preferred modern dwellings, she had conceded that its mellow brick and pigeon gray roof were charming. The same, she now admitted, must be said of the interior. The hall had been imposing with its walnut paneling and family portraits, and this room, whilst small, whispered of old money. The sisters sat on chintz sofas facing each other on either side of a fireplace whose mantel displayed brass candlesticks and several pieces of Minton china. A grandfather clock stood in one corner, two floor-to-ceiling bookcases housed leather-bound volumes, and Mrs. Smith-Hoggles was herself seated on a striped Regency chair. Indeed, nothing could be faulted, from the silver tea service on the rent table under the window to the time-muted colors of the needlepoint rug. Even so, she winced as she settled her handbag, a recent purchase from Harrods, on her knees.

Hyacinth Tramwell had not, in Mrs. Smith-Hoggles's opinion, aged gracefully. Indeed, she looked as though she had battled the process every inch of the way. Her improbably black hair was plaited into a coronet on top of her head, which in itself might not have been so outré if it had not been poked around with stick pins that flashed with a variety of colored stones. Mrs. Smith-Hoggles suspected that there might be genuine emeralds and rubies among them. But that only compounded the absurdity, when offset by a pair of dangling, dagger-shaped earrings and the ankle-length dress of some gauzy red material topped by a black lace shawl. With her sallow complexion and dark eyes, the woman could have been a gypsy come in from hawking clothes pegs and bunches of wax flowers door to door. Mrs. Smith-Hoggles had a well-bred distaste for gypsies along with a great many other things that she did not consider to be top drawer. And for all her bizarre appearance, Hyacinth Tramwell was from among the country's leading families.

The sister Primrose was definitely more what one might hope to expect. Her silver curls, periwinkle-blue eyes, and crumpled petal complexion reminded one of a sweet little aunt whose days were mainly spent knitting or writing beautifully penned letters to beloved nieces and nephews. The only perceivable oddity was that she wore a long Mickey Mouse watch and—Mrs. Smith-Hoggles noted, looking down—a pair of frilly socks instead of stockings. But eccentricities, even in Hyacinth Tramwell's case, should perhaps be overlooked, given what was rumored to be their vast wealth and the cousin several times removed who was either a duke or an earl. Besides, if they weren't the least bit untraditional, they wouldn't have entered the private detection business, and she wouldn't be sitting here.

"May we offer you some tea? We can ring for Butler," Hyacinth indicated a tasseled bell rope, "and have him bring you a cup."

"No, thank you, I had one just before leaving home." Mrs. Smith-Hoggles replied in her oversized voice. "How curious that he should be called that!"

"Butler?" Hyacinth picked up her own teacup. "It's an alias. As with all self-respecting criminals, he had dozens when we first met him hiding in the wardrobe in Primrose's room."

"After all those years spent looking for a man under my bed." Her sister's eyes twinkled at the folly of it. "Life never turns out the way we expect it to, does it? I had the idea that you had come collecting for some charity, but I have a presentiment that an unexpected turn of events in your life is what has brought you to us. In other words, you seek the services of Flowers Detection."

"That is the case," said Mrs. Smith-Hoggles.

"You have a daughter." The dagger earrings sliced

against Hyacinth's neck as she leaned forward. "Could this be a matter touching upon her? Has she disappeared?"

"No, it's not that."

"Then you fear some danger threatens her."

"How astute of you." Mrs. Smith-Hoggles drew a deep breath. "To think immediately of Emily."

"You are sadly a widow." Primrose adjusted the cuffs of her lavender cardigan. "Therefore there is no husband to be a cause of distress. Also, you have no other children. And if it were anything other than a personal matter, you would presumably have contacted the police."

Mrs. Smith-Hoggles eyed her thoughtfully. She was clearly more astute than those guileless blue eyes would indicate. "It is so difficult when one is in the position of being both mother and father to an impressionable young girl. And one feels the burden most astutely at a time when one's darling child is about to make the greatest mistake of her life." She reached into her handbag for a monogrammed handkerchief and dabbed at her eyes.

"What sort of mistake?" asked Hyacinth.

"She wants to get married."

"And how old is Emily?"

"Twenty-five."

"Hardly a child; unless," Primrose paused delicately, "the poor dear is simpleminded."

"Certainly not!" Mrs. Smith-Hoggles balled up the handkerchief and returned it to her handbag. "Emily is an intelligent girl. She went to the very best schools and has had every possible advantage. I sacrificed my own social life to be there for her every possible minute. I still tuck her into bed at night. Still cut her bread and butter into soldiers for her when she has a boiled egg. And now this!"

"You have something against the young man. Dear me!" Primrose patted her silvery curls. "I remember how grieved my parents were when I expressed an interest in an insurance salesman. My father did not approve of insurance. He considered it a form of gambling."

"If only it were that simple! Not that I think much of James Watson's means of making a living. He writes articles for a small newspaper. Worse, Emily says he wants to write books. So thoroughly irresponsible. But that is nothing against the fact"—Mrs. Smith-Hoggles shuddered—"that he is the grandson of a man suspected of poisoning his young wife in 1947. Surely you remember the case, seeing that it was a local one?"

"Here in Flaxby Meade?"

"No, in Longbourton, but that is only twenty miles away. The trial was widely reported at the time."

"I do seem to remember." Hyacinth sat ramrod stiff on her sofa. The dagger earrings hung still against her neck. "It was referred to as the Black Hearted Murder because that was the name of the accused: Black. And wasn't his Christian name also James?"

Mrs. Smith-Hoggles nodded. "He and his poor murdered wife had a daughter who is James Watson's mother. That surely tells you what sort of a woman she is, to have named her son after her villain of a father. And this is the family into which Emily is intent on marrying! When there is that perfectly delightful George Hubbard, who is so fond of her and has an irreproachable background and a house with a granny flat already in place."

"But if I recall correctly," said Hyacinth, "James Black was acquitted of his wife's murder."

"Because he'd been clever enough to have her body cremated."

"Before people started fanning the flames of suspicion." Primrose looked pained.

"They didn't take much fanning." Mrs. Smith-Hoggles

gave a snort that hadn't been taught at her finishing school. "The poor woman was barely disposed of before James Black married his pretty blond secretary. But from what I've heard, there was talk even before that of the first wife, whose name was Elizabeth, being violently sick after meals and being afraid to eat until she languished away to skin and bone. The housekeeper gave evidence that she once saw James Black pry her mouth open when she refused to touch her soup and force her to swallow a spoonful. There were days—weeks—when she never left her bedroom and would see no one, or more likely was not permitted to receive visitors." Mrs. Smith-Hoggles looked as though she, too, had been given a dose of poison. "And my poor, foolish Emily wants to marry into that family. I have told her it will be over my dead body, but you know how young people are." She stared mournfully at the sisters. "They don't look ahead."

"What of the grandson's character? Is he a reprehensible person?" Hyacinth roused herself from several moments of reflection.

"Not on the surface, although I can't say I appreciate the way he encourages Emily to 'be her own person,' as he calls it. The other day she came home with her ears pierced—something she would never have done without talking to me about it first. Knowing, as she must, how upset her dear father would have been. And of course it led to a row with Emily in tears and Jim, as she calls him, making a great big fuss of her. But I don't see that he needs to have robbed a bank or hit an old lady over the head for me to oppose this marriage. The stigma is bad enough, but bad blood will out. And I have not only Emily to think about but also my future grandchildren." Mrs. Smith-Hoggles reached again for her handkerchief. "Who knows what horrible criminal tendencies they will display as they mature! But I have endeavored, in the midst of my heartbreak, to be fair. As you said"—addressing Hyacinth—"James Black was acquitted of murder, and I suppose there is the remote chance that he was indeed innocent, which is why I have come to ask you to investigate the case."

"One that is more than fifty years old?"

"Oh, but only think, Hy." Primrose pressed her hands together. "What a delightful challenge. One can hardly wait to begin. It is to be hoped"—she eyed Mrs. Smith-Hoggles—"that some of those on the scene are still alive."

"James Black has been dead for more than thirty years."

"That would make him unavailable for questioning." Primrose's face crumpled. "What about the doctor who attended his first wife?"

"Deceased."

"And the housekeeper."

"Succumbed to old age."

"Let us not forget the blond secretary who became the second Mrs. Black," said Hyacinth.

"Died at a health spa," replied Mrs. Smith-Hoggles with another of her less-than-refined snorts. "There was a maid, Kathleen somebody, who lived-in, and gave evidence at the trial, but she left the area immediately afterward. She was young, only seventeen or eighteen years old, so she very likely married. I think she may have immigrated to Australia. So I am afraid that really only leaves the daughter—Jim's mother—as a candidate for questioning. He's very fond of her, I will say that." She returned the handkerchief to the handbag for what the Tramwell sisters hoped was the final time and snapped it shut. "Quite devoted in fact. But, as I said to Emily, that's not always such a good thing. She could end up living

with both of them. Unlike dear George Hubbard with his
pots of money and impeccable pedigree, I can't see Jim
ever having the financial wherewithal to spring for a
granny flat."

"Does Emily know you have come to see us?" Hyacinth's eyes were on her teacup, which she had picked
up.

"Of course. I wouldn't have dreamed of acting behind
her back. She was upset, just as I expected, but I stressed
my hope—faint as it is—that you will bring something to
light that will set my maternal fears at rest. You will then
agree to take on the case?" Mrs. Smith-Hoggles rose to
her feet and pulled on a pair of gloves that matched her
handbag.

"If you are sure this is what you want," said Hyacinth
to the teacup.

"I have thought the matter over carefully and see no
alternative course of action."

"Some of our clients are not pleased by what we uncover."

"I have already told you that I don't hold out high
hopes of a reassuring outcome."

"Precisely." Hyacinth jangled the bell rope and the sitting room door opened instantly. "Ah, Butler," she said,
"our guest is leaving; kindly attend her outdoors with an
umbrella. I see"—her black eyes turned to the window—
"that it is raining."

"Very good, madam."

"We have not yet discussed the matter of your fee,"
Mrs. Smith-Hoggles pointed out.

"Oh, I am sure you will not find it unreasonable, but
should you do so," responded Primrose at her most fluttery, "we will be only too happy to adjust it. And do not
worry; we will be in touch with you the moment we have

something to report. Timeliness is the byword of Flowers Detection. Which is not to say that any stone will be left uncovered. That maid you mentioned . . . it may be possible to trace her. We have our ways. And James Black's daughter, of course . . . no, do not bother to delay yourself giving us her address. Those clouds look quite menacing. Was that not thunder I just heard?"

Mrs. Smith-Hoggles found herself out in the hall with an ex-burglar, and when he withdrew the umbrella from its stand, she wished for a moment that she had not come. But when he did not cosh her over the head and make off up the stairs with her handbag, she left the house feeling that she had made a good morning's work of it.

"So," said Hyacinth to Primrose, "we await a visit from Emily."

"And in all likelihood her young man."

"Possibly on their lunch hours."

"Yes, I don't think they will allow us much time in which to set about our inquiries." Primrose looked at the clock. "Time for a little something, as Pooh would say. But I can't say I fancy either condensed milk or honey. That Dundee cake Butler made yesterday would, I think, do very nicely with a fresh pot of tea."

"My thoughts precisely." Hyacinth smiled at her, but her black eyes held a glitter that did not bode well for whoever occupied her thoughts. Before she could again pull the bell rope, Butler slipped silently back into the room with a loaded tray.

"Wonderful man. You anticipate our every whim," she informed him.

"Certainly, madam. I made sure that I took the umbrella that leaked." He appeared about to say more when the doorbell rang, and he vanished back into the hall to return a few moments later with a fair-haired young woman of a pleasantly plump build and a dark, handsome man in his early thirties.

"Miss Emily Smith-Hoggles and Mr. James Watson," he announced before again disappearing.

"Mother's been here already, hasn't she?" The girl's lips quivered. "I can always tell when she's been in a room. She takes something out of it, leaving it somehow horribly blank. No matter who's left in it or how much furniture there is."

"Em, darling, don't do this to yourself." The man was helping her off with her damp raincoat. He was, Primrose noted with a maidenly flutter, extremely handsome. Dangerously so, some might have said, but she liked the way his eyes lingered on Emily Smith-Hoggles's flushed face, and she thought his mouth kind.

"Yes, do get out of those wet coats, that's right—I'll take them." Hyacinth did so and tossed them on the settle in front of the fireplace. "And now sit yourself down on that sofa and unburden yourselves to my sister Primrose and me."

"But you've already talked to Mother," Emily protested, "which means you're bound to be on her side. She'll have told you the whole lurid story about Jim's grandparents. Only I don't see it that way any more than Jim does. He told me all about it, soon after we first met at a party—neither one of us realizing at first that we came from the same part of the country. Well, Jim hadn't ever lived around here, but it's where his roots were, and I wasn't horrified to think that his grandfather had been tried for murder. Not in a grisly sort of way. The whole thing seemed to me so very sad. A terrible tragedy, but not something that alters who Jim is. It was Mother who went and put her dreadful spin on it. Scolding and nagging day in and day out that I was putting my head in a noose by wanting to marry him. Such rubbish"—her eyes filled with tears—"because he is the dearest man in the entire world."

"I wouldn't go that far." Jim stroked back a lock of her hair.

"Your only fault is that you're too modest." Emily gave him a watery smile. Her hand reached out to the plate filled with the slices of Dundee cake, but she immediately drew it back.

"Please have some," urged Hyacinth.

"No, thank you, I mustn't really. I'm not the sort who can get away with eating between meals."

"Go on, Em," said Jim. "Your mother's not here to pull that face at you. And it looks like excellent cake."

"Oh, indeed it is." Primrose beamed as she handed them each a plate. "I intend to have at least three slices myself."

"You can afford to," replied Emily dolefully, "you're so dainty; I don't suppose you ever gain an ounce."

"And you, my dear, are so young and pretty it won't matter if you do. Now, eat up while I pour you and Mr. Watson each a cup of tea and then we will discuss your side of things. Sugar?"

"No—"

"She likes two spoonfuls and plenty of milk," Jim told Primrose while looking tenderly at Emily.

When the cups and saucers and cake plates had been handed out, Hyacinth rearranged the black lace shawl around her shoulders and leaned forward so that her dagger earrings swung in a wide arc. Her face might have been an engraved invitation, and the couple seated on the sofa across from her and Primrose began talking, adding to each other's sentences as they went along.

"Mother has involved you ladies for one reason only.

To cause pain to Jim by injuring his widowed mother. And Lizzie has been through enough already." Emily bit into a slice of Dundee cake.

"Em's not just talking about my father's death," Jim explained. "She suffered terribly growing up, as you might imagine, from being branded the daughter of a murderer. And she doesn't deserve to have the business raked up after all these years.

"She's such a darling." Emily swallowed a second mouthful of cake. "One of the most loving, caring people in the whole world, just as you would expect Jim's mother to be. But she's emotionally fragile."

"Under a strong exterior."

"That's exactly it. Lizzie—she was named after her mother, Elizabeth—has shouldered so much through the years that most people who know her think she's invincible, but she isn't. I realized that as soon as I met her. She deserves cosseting. Breakfast in bed and flowers and lots of hugs."

"And the thing is"—Jim put another piece of cake on Emily's plate—"my mother loved her father. If she hadn't, she wouldn't have named me after him, would she?"

"Lizzie never believed he was a murderer."

"Or that anything was going on between him and his secretary before his wife's death. It developed afterward, when he was going through the grief and the ugly rumors being spread around. She was the one person who stood by him through it all. My mother grew very fond of her over the years."

"Surely you can see what Mother's doing?" Emily appealed to Hyacinth and Primrose. "She doesn't for one moment think you will uncover anything of significance either way. What she's counting on is that I love Jim too much to put him through this and will break it off with him. That's why she told me she was coming to see you. Playing fair with me had nothing to do with it. She can be diabolical."

"Not a nice thing to say about one's mother." Primrose replenished their teacups. "But one does tend to agree with you, my dear."

"Then you did see through her?"

"That surprises you?" Hyacinth raised a black-painted eyebrow.

"Well, yes, it does in a way because . . ." Emily resorted to more cake.

"What Em is trying to say," Jim grinned engagingly, "is that we're convinced Mrs. Smith-Hoggles made you her first choice for the job at hand because she had you pegged as a pair of well-to-do women playing at being private detectives. The Sam Spades of this world would very likely have ushered her out the door before she was five minutes into her nonsense."

"Whilst a pair of eccentric elderly ladies would leap at the chance to interrogate your poor mother." Primrose nodded her silvery head. "But you young people put your faith in the possibility that we might also be kind. There is a fly in the ointment, however, my dears. If we get back in touch with Mrs. Smith-Hoggles to say we have rethought the matter and will not be taking on the case, I very much fear that she will find someone else willing to take her money. As in all professions, there are those in the private detection business who will do pretty much anything for the money."

"Despicable, but there it is," agreed Hyacinth.

"So Mother gets what she wants." Emily set down her plate as if the sight of the cake crumbs on it revolted her. "Oh, darling." She turned to Jim and caught up his hands.

"You do see we can't take our happiness at the expense of Lizzie's pain. But I do promise you that I'll never marry George Hubbard. That's one thing about which Mother won't get her way."

"We'll find a way out of this mess, Em."

"That goes without saying when Flowers Detection is on the job." Primrose looked genteelly smug.

"Don't worry your heads about it." Hyacinth readjusted the black lace shawl, setting the earrings in motion. "It is as well that my sister and I did not show your mother the door within five minutes of getting into her old murder story because that was all it took to make the case entirely clear to myself and—"

"Absolutely, Hy," Primrose concurred. "Nothing could have been more obvious than who caused the first Mrs. Black's death, and it was not, let me reassure you two nice young people, her husband. Of course it must needs be said that he made things hard on himself by having her cremated, but men don't always think ahead. A woman would have been far more alert to the possibilities that doing so would stoke the fire . . . if you will forgive the unfortunate pun."

Jim looked astounded. "Do you mean to say that you sorted out what really happened just sitting here, using your little gray cells like Hercule Poirot?"

"Oh, we wouldn't dream of putting ourselves in his elevated category," remonstrated Primrose. "The man was sheer genius. God rest his soul."

"But I thought he was a fictional character." Emily looked confused.

"Correct." Hyacinth inclined her head. "But my sister believes that if one lives and breathes on the printed page, one is entitled to go to one's heavenly reward when the time comes. She has not discussed the matter with our vicar, who holds to more conventional views."

Jim looked suddenly less cheerful. "The trouble is, I don't see that your knowing will be enough for Mrs. Smith-Hoggles. She will want proof."

"Very little in life comes stamped with a seal of authenticity." Hyacinth got to her feet and plied the bell robe. "The best we can offer is compelling evidence of the sort that it will be difficult for her to refute. There is one question I have for you. Did your mother ever mention the maid who worked for her parents? Mrs. Smith-Hoggles said that her Christian name was Kathleen."

"Yes." Jim's brow furrowed. "But what was her surname? I could ask Mum, but she would wonder why I wanted to know. Give me a moment . . . I've got it! It was Rose. I remember because Kathleen Rose sounded like two first names, but Mum said it wasn't that way."

"That should be helpful," said Hyacinth.

"Jim has a marvelous memory." Emily looked adoringly at him. "It's what makes him such a wonderful writer. One day he could be famous, but even if he isn't, we're going to be blissfully happy. If all goes as you promise." The two young people were on their feet when Butler appeared in the room.

"We'll be in touch in a couple of days," Hyacinth assured them. When she and Primrose again had the room to themselves, she said, "Having but a few minutes ago maligned other members of our profession, I fear we must take an unethical step in this proceeding."

"No need to say more!" Primrose beamed at her. "Our minds work as one, although I prefer to regard our methods as creative rather than as a breach of the code. Ah, Butler!" she said as he padded toward them, his expression at once deferential and inquiring.

"I sensed that I might be needed."

"You are in tune as always." Hyacinth regarded him fondly. "As a reward you may take the Louis VI clock up to bed with you tonight. Meanwhile, Miss Primrose and I wish you to locate a maid."

"My services aren't up to snuff?"

"Dear me, your grammar does go out the window when visitors go out the door." Primrose fluttered back to the sofa. "We're not looking for a maid to work for us. Sometimes I wonder why we need the services of Mrs. Brown three times a week when you leave so little for her to do. But sit yourself down, and we will explain exactly what we require of you. I am sure it will present you with very few difficulties."

"I should 'ope not." Butler settled himself on a chair and flipped open the cigar box on the side table. "Go on ladies, fill me in. What's it you want me to wangle for you this time?"

Even Primrose could be succinct when she set her mind to it, and Hyacinth rarely waffled.

"So them's me orders." Butler tapped ash into a saucer. "A piece of cake. I'd say you can have your meeting with that nasty Mrs. Smith-Hoggles the day after next. I could get things done sooner, but I've got eight dozen pots of jam promised to the Women's Institute for tomorrow. And they'll have me underpants for garters if I lets them down."

"No need for that," replied Hyacinth crisply. "We don't want to make this look too easy. We'll set up the meeting for three days from now. That will be Thursday." Hyacinth went over to the secretary desk in the alcove by the window and made a notation on the calendar she took from one of its drawers. You're sure that will give you enough time to produce Kathleen Rose?"

"H'ample."

He was not a man to make a promise he couldn't keep, and Hyacinth and Primrose went about the business of the day unruffled by qualms. On the following day, he delivered the jam to the church hall. The day after, he went up to London on the early train. And on Thursday evening, he ushered Mrs. Smith-Hoggles into the sitting room where she met with the unwelcome sight of her daughter and James Watson seated hand in hand on a sofa. She had been told that they would be present. It was the coziness to which she objected.

"Good evening, Mrs. Smith-Hoggles." Jim got to his feet.

"Hello, Mother," said Emily.

"Why don't we all sit down." Hyacinth entered the room just as Butler exited it.

"Yes, do let's." Primrose came in behind her, appearing more fluttery than ever as she moved toward a chair. "We do believe, Mrs. Smith-Hoggles, that we have information for you that will lay to rest all your worries on your daughter's behalf and encourage you to embrace her fiancé with open arms."

"They are not yet engaged," came the icy reply.

"Oh, yes we are." Emily held up her left hand on which a diamond ring sparkled.

"I'm afraid you're going to have to get used to the idea," said Jim.

"Nothing will induce me to do anything of the sort." Mrs. Smith-Hoggles remained standing.

"Not even the news that James Black did not murder his wife?" Primrose responded in a soothing voice. "I thought you said . . . but never mind, we don't expect you to take our words at face value. We have a witness for you. Someone who was in the house during Elizabeth Black's final months. It is the maid, Kathleen Rose."

"And I suppose she is going to say it was the house-keeper who did the poisoning, now that the woman isn't alive to defend herself." Mrs. Smith-Hoggles gave one of her inelegant snorts. "All I can say is that this Kathleen person must have been in on the murder. Perhaps she hoped to marry that wicked man, but he dumped her for his secretary, when he no longer needed her."

"Why don't you hear what she has to say?" Hyacinth opened the sitting room door to a pleasant-faced woman in a shabby coat and a hat that looked as though it had been sat on more times than it had been worn.

"Oh, Mr. Jim!" She clutched at her black plastic hand-bag as he stood. "How very like your grandfather you are! I'd have known you anywhere, and that's no lie! Such a nice man he was, always so kind and thoughtful to me, and him with all his troubles. And I'm speaking about when his wife was sick, not that awful business after she died. The worst was over for him then, poor Mr. Black. It was watching her suffer that was so hard for him to bear."

"I thought you went out to Australia," Mrs. Smith-Hoggles interrupted in her oversized voice.

"It was a nice place to visit, but when it came to it, I didn't want to live there," said Kathleen. "I'd had all these fantasies, you see, about kangaroos hopping around in the back garden and handsome young men lying out there on beach towels. But it was just like Brighton, if you ask me. Only hotter. And I perspire something awful at the best of times."

"But weren't you supposed to get married?"

"My fellow let me down at the church gate, so to speak. And I never did meet anyone else that seemed worth the bother."

"This is the right Kathleen Rose." Hyacinth eyed Mrs. Smith-Hoggles austerely.

"I'm not saying it isn't."

"Well, I can't see why I'd come pretending to be someone I'm not." Kathleen looked hurt. "It was a shock when my employer told me there was a firm of private detectives looking for me. It's not the sort of thing a decent woman expects. But when it was all explained to me, I was glad of the chance to have my say. The police and those lawyers in their silly wigs only wanted me to say what they wanted to hear. About Mrs. Black being sick so often after she'd eat. And her losing all that weight till she looked like a skeleton, poor soul. Of course, I didn't understand at the time. Such things weren't talked about in them days. I don't think anyone even knew what it was."

"What *what* was?" asked Emily.

"This anorexia business. And that's what was wrong with Mrs. Black. I can see that now plain as day. When I said I'd hear her making herself sick in the toilet, no one wanted to listen. And most of the time she wouldn't eat at all. I remember her husband getting so upset once he tried to force some broth down her. Course, he didn't understand, either. It's a sickness in the mind, isn't it?"

"That explains it." Jim gripped Emily's hand.

"Explains what, darling?"

"Mum said that when her mother was hours away from dying, she made her promise to eat—not just her vegetables to make her hair curl, but everything. Including lots of cake."

Mrs. Smith-Hoggles sat down heavily. "So perhaps your grandfather didn't murder your grandmother. But there's still instability in your family. And I refuse to allow Emily to . . ."

Hyacinth cut her off. "I think you might do better to concern yourself with the fact that your daughter could end up with an eating disorder, given the fact that you nag her about what she eats."

"You said that?" Mrs. Smith-Hoggles glowered at Emily.

"No, I did," said Jim. "And it's going to stop."

"Don't worry, I don't intend to visit if she marries you." The outraged mother rose to her feet in a swirl of camel coat. "Don't even think about building a granny flat!"

"It never crossed our minds," replied Emily serenely. "Lizzy is going to live with us, under the very same roof. She's earned herself lots of love, and she is going to get it. And if you try to hurt her or Jim ever again, you'll have to answer to me."

She was talking to an empty space. Her mother had stalked from the room. A few moments later, after gratitude had been expressed, Kathleen Rose said she would go and have a cup of tea in the kitchen with that nice Mr. Butler before leaving to catch her train.

"So," Hyacinth said when she and Primrose had Emily and Jim to themselves. "I hope you are satisfied with the results of our investigation."

"Lizzie will be so relieved." Emily gave each sister a hug. "It's awfully sad about her mother, of course, but at least she no longer has to live with questions about what really happened. I do hope you will get to meet her."

"Of course they will." Jim took her hand. "They'll do so at the wedding. You will come, won't you?" The smile he gave them was enough to turn their spinster heads.

"Oh, you must," exclaimed Emily. "You'll be our bridal flowers."

"What a lovely thing to say." Hyacinth's black eyes

sparkled suspiciously. "And please don't spoil it by mentioning our fee. There is none. To have allowed you two fine young people to be kept apart would have been a crime of the heart."

"Very true," Primrose assured her after they left, "but don't you feel the least bit guilty, Hy, about having Butler produce that shoplifting acquaintance of his to pose as Kathleen Rose?"

"Not a petal!" came the crisp response.

Away for
Safekeeping

Susan Dunlap

*Susan Dunlap is the author of seventeen novels, encompassing
all three categories of mystery protagonists: private eye, police
detective, and amateur sleuth. For her short stories, she has
twice won Anthonys, awarded by the Bouchercon World Mystery Convention, and once won the Macavity, awarded by Mystery Readers International.*

*Her protagonists include former forensic pathologist turned
detective Kiernan O'Shaughnessy; Berkeley, California, police
detective Jill Smith; and public utility meter reader Vejay Haskell
in the Russian River area north of San Francisco.*

*She has completed the Berkeley Police Department's Civilian
Academy course and was a speaker at the Investigation Semi-
nar of the National Association of Legal Investigators.*

*Dunlap was a founding member and president of Sisters in
Crime, an international organization of 3,600 members that
supports women's contributions in the field of crime writing.*

"I keep feeling like I've forgotten something," I blurted out.

The woman in the next deck chair—Delia Hammond, she called herself—nodded in sympathy. "I never leave home without worrying whether I've left the stove on or shot the dead bolt in the back door." She nodded in silent chorus with herself, like she was used to keeping up both ends of a conversation all on her own. "Couple of times I had the air porter wait, with four other people already on it, and I ran back into the house. Course, the door was bolted and the stove was off. Still, you know, you do worry. Can't be helped." She nodded again, and I pictured her nodding her too-blond head at her fellow travelers as she climbed into the van's remaining seat, reiterating her rationale until all four heads nodded, too.

She'd meant it to sound comforting, but there was no way that could calm the turmoil in my stomach. I steeled my face and forced myself to look slowly, appreciatively around this magnificently luxurious hotel. I've always wanted to travel but I had only dreamed of a place like this. The mature palm trees grew tall and elegant around the pool as if they, like the guests here, were too important and decorative to be expected to do anything so mundane as create shade. Gaudy tropical flowers were crowded thick beside the paths, as if the ground were carpeted in oriental rugs. The ocean lapped at our private beach. Towels and bathrobes, almost too thick to bend, draped over every empty deck chair lest a guest walk down from his cottage unprepared. And those wonderful little thatched cottages, each protected by blossoming hedges, thick-leafed trees, and steep cliffs; each was so private that when you sat on your patio you felt like you were alone in paradise. I inhaled slowly, drawing in the sweet air around the pool, tinged with salt and suntan oil and gin.

I knew sooner or later I'd run into someone like Delia Hammond. I haven't traveled much of late, but I remember that when you're a woman by yourself, eventually you end up stuck with someone who doesn't cling but never quite leaves you alone, either. I might have been wise not to talk to her at all, certainly not about this trip. *Silence,* I'd instructed myself on the plane from LAX to Honolulu. But silence is not my style now, and after three days of talking to no one but the check-in clerk and the waiters, I might as well have been in prison; admittedly a better prison than Frontera—that's where they send women in southern California. A lot better. I had that thought as I'd been sitting beside the pool here yesterday. I'd made a point of raising my hand, not so high that I had to lift my elbow, not that great an effort, a ladylike movement, the movement of the monied. And before I could consider the full extent of my ease, the lei-laden waiter was at my side smiling as if my order of a second mai tai was just the thing to end his perfect day. "You don't get service like that in Frontera."

I hadn't realized I'd been speaking out loud, not again. I almost leapt out of my deck chair.

Delia stared at me, and it was a moment before she pulled herself together enough to focus back on the hotel. "You're right about that; the waiters here are great. You don't even get this kind of service at the Waikiki Grande."

I was too unnerved to answer. This was bad. Maybe George was right all along, maybe I couldn't manage without him keeping an eye on me. I hadn't been a chatterer before I met him. I'd been too quiet, too wary. But when I married him, I'd determined to become just what was expected from a flea marketeer's wife. I stood at the booth weekend after weekend and chatted up everyone who stopped. I made myself learn to natter on about prices and freeway congestion around San Bernardino and

weather and how hard life was till I could do it in my
sleep. Which was just about what I was doing now.

By the time I had recovered, Delia had already laid out
the tribulations of her stay at the unappealing Grande last
year and was into the shortcomings of the previous year's
lodgings. She was a natterer par excellence.

So no harm done. I couldn't go through the rest of my
life in silence. I was thirty-eight years old. Two of my
great-aunts lived to be over a hundred. No way was I
going to make it through sixty-two wordless years. Okay,
so I'd speak, but I still had to make myself some rules,
though not the kind of rules George was so big on—just
show some common sense, take precautions. People like
Delia here were going to ask about my life, so I'd better
decide what to tell them.

A breeze riffled my hair. Trade winds? I was probably
the only person who found that term annoying. It didn't
remind me of South Seas islands, just of George and his
flea market stall. Even my hair reminded me of him, this
tight brown perm that had so horrified him when he realized it cost thirty dollars. It fit right into the flea scene,
but here among the beautifully coiffed, I looked like I was
wearing birthday-gift ribbon on my head. Even Delia with
her tomboy cut looked levels better than I did.

I took another sip of my mai tai and concentrated on
its sweet sting as it eased down my throat. People would
ask me about myself. What a pleasure it would be to create a new and much better life for them, make it up out
of whole cloth. The first thing I'd choose would be a new
and better husband. Well, that would give me a range,
wouldn't it? Better than George? A man who dressed in
clothes no one else had already thrown out? A guy who
yearned for hotels like this one, instead of night after night
in his double-wide trailer? Already better than George. A
jet-setter with a fat trust fund? Well that was just about

the polar opposite of George, the universal miser, the black hole of all possessions. What I would create was a man who had never set eyes on a flea market.

"Yeah, Therese, I've stayed in some flea-holes, too."

Delia's reply shocked me. Again I hadn't realized I was speaking out loud. This was very bad.

"But not this hotel, huh?" she went on. "This is really top notch. I just love this pool with the bar in the middle. Makes me thirsty just to look at it. I just may have to dip my tootsies in the pool."

"You go right ahead, Delia," I said with some relief. I really was going to have to get myself under control. Thank goodness the woman didn't pay close attention.

"You'll watch my stuff?"

I nodded.

"Thanks. And maybe while you're doing it you'll remember what it is you forgot." She sprang up—there was no other term for it, she really did remind me of a spring coming through the upholstery of an old chair. She had to be at least my age, probably older, but she was toned and tanned and she had the sense not to stretch her good fortune to wearing the skimpiest of bathing suits. Hers was a conservative two piece in a gold that just matched her hair.

She sat back down. "You know, Therese, they have some nice things at the hotel shop."

I followed her gaze to my own suit. "Replace this? I guess you could make a case for that." How could I not have done that? Now that I looked down at it, it stood out like the one black smudge in this whole sparkling poolside. It was the same old black one I'd had before I married George, and I was lucky to have held onto that. For once Delia wasn't nattering on into another topic. She was focused on my miserable suit and she was waiting, as if she expected something revealing from me. I was

going to have to give her some explanation about this and
pronto. "My husband's a trader at the flea market. Living
with George, there was no call for attire intended for lolling around a swimming pool, believe me. When I had a
spare moment there, George would eagle-eye me and repeat his slogan: 'A trader's work is never done.' Then
he'd start in on the litany of tasks: 'The take from last
week's flea market needs to be sorted into piles, one for
the antique store circuit, another for the next weekend's
flea markets, one for the self-storage containers.' Then
there were the piles for our own use or the trash. We
worked the stall eight hours a day, all day Saturday and
Sunday, and most of our haul could have gone directly
into the trash pile. I pointed that out to George; every
week I pointed it out. And every week he agreed. I don't
know why I bothered using my voice for it each week.
The conversation was always the same.

"Me: 'We might just as well take the whole load to the
dump.'

"Him: 'Yeah, yeah, yeah. Lousy weekend. We could
just as well shovel it all into the truck. All but this lamp.'
The item varied from week to week, Delia, but you get
the point. 'This lamp,' he'd say, 'you know, I think I saw
one like this in an antique shop in Santa Monica a few
years ago. In the window it was. And they were asking a
good price. I'll run this down to some of the shops in San
Berdoo tomorrow.'

"By this time I'd be carrying a load of stuff to the
truck. And he'd be walking beside me, grabbing a candlestick or a velvet scarf out of my load. 'Oh, now look
at this candlestick,' he'd be saying like he just discovered
a hoard of gold doubloons. 'This is brass. Won't bring a
fortune, but it'll take us to dinner tomorrow. I'll put that
into the antique pile. Oh, and this dress. A secondhand

shop in San Francisco had one like this. . . .'

"Maybe if I'd parked the truck closer, I could have gotten at least some of the stuff into it. In fairness, some weeks there were a couple items even George was willing to call garbage. But most weeks I might as well have labeled the entire take "antique." Not that George ever actually sold any of it to an antiquer. Oh, no. 'Twenty-five dollars!' he'd exclaim as he returned from an afternoon of visits to his buddies. 'Nate offered me twenty-five bucks for a magnificent lamp like this. And after I told him about the one that Santa Monica shop was asking eight hundred for! Imagine!' He'd be cradling the lamp against his flannel-shirted breast like it was a prodigal son.

"After the first couple times, I pointed out that he just thought maybe a store in Santa Monica had a lamp something like his prodigal, and even if it did, he had no idea what they were asking, much less what they actually got for it. But by that time George was entirely in the prodigal lamp's corner, and no amount of money would have made him part with it. By then the only question was whether the lamp would move into our trailer for a while or go directly to one of the storage boxes."

Delia sat openmouthed, clearly shocked by the tirade from this woman she barely knew. I took a deep breath. The chill that shot down my back was so cold I was shivering here in the middle of the day beside the pool in Waikiki. How could I have blurted out so much? I had never, ever intended to do that. "You never can keep your mouth shut, Therese," George had said plenty more than once. "That's why I don't tell you things. Trust you to blab to anyone."

"I don't blab to just anyone, George. I choose who I talk to. I talk to people, other people, because their interests are not limited to bartering castoffs in parking lots all weekend."

But now, I wondered. I certainly wasn't about to accede to George's opinion on that or anything else, but hearing my thoughts out loud was making me very uneasy. It was like talking in my sleep, only worse.

"So your husband's hooked on self-storage?" Obviously she had been paying closer attention than I'd realized.

The truth; go with the truth, I told myself. Just be careful.

"There was no way George could keep all the stuff he couldn't bear to part with in our trailer. It was a double-wide, but even so . . . So he rented a storage container, just one, at first. It's really easy to do these days. A truck arrives at your house with a box the size of a big Porta Potti—'Well, that's appropriate!' I'd told George the first time one arrived."

George, of course hadn't seen the humor. But Delia did. Something between a giggle and a snort gurgled in her throat.

I laughed, too, and said, "Anyhow, you pack the thing full. Or rather, George did. George never let anyone near his storage containers. He said he was worried that the load would go over two thousand pounds—that's the limit—and he had to weigh every item and keep a running list, and only he could do that."

"Did you believe that?"

"Only partly. The limit could have been a million pounds and he still would have mother-henned his precious cargo. Whatever, he stuffed those boxes full, and then the company wrapped them in some kind of plastic and carted them back to the storage lot. You pay them sixty bucks a month and they'll keep it forever."

"And if you don't?"

"They sell it sight unseen to the highest bidder at the flea market. That's where . . . George . . . got . . . a lot of his stuff."

I let out a gasp. "Oh my God, the storage payment! That's what I forgot!"

"Oh good!" said Delia. "Now you don't have to keep wondering what—" She stared at me in bewilderment as I moaned, "Oh, God, the payment!" Then she patted my hand comfortingly, "Don't worry, Therese; you're not the first person to send in a payment late. So they charge you a service fee, so what? Look, if your husband's a good customer, maybe the company will cut you some slack. I don't see why it's you making the payment, anyway. Why couldn't George do it himself? Just call him and tell him to hightail it over there."

"I can't."

"Well, why the hell not? I mean he's just sitting back there in the flea market in Hinsdale, isn't he?"

Hinsdale, had I mentioned Hinsdale? Oh, Jeez, I'd said way way too much. I was way beyond the easy ground of truth here. I'm not a good liar, and I don't think well on my feet, and, okay, I do tend not to watch my mouth when I'm nervous, or so George kept telling me. But what choice did I have now? "I can't call George! He's not there anymore!"

"You mean he's—"

"Gone. He just left! After four years of marriage, four years of living like a ragpicker in the desert, after the promise that he was stocking up for a big sale, that we'd sell all the stuff he bought at the flea market, do it in one huge sale and then we'd take off for Hawaii." I couldn't hold back the tears. "Valentine's Day, that's when we were supposed to go! He had the airplane tickets and everything. I saw the tickets with my own eyes. He'd booked six spaces at the flea market—that's how much stuff he had to sell. He sent out notices to antique dealers all over southern California. I bought new clothes, not just new to me but actually from a store. We were all set to go!"

"And then what happened?" She was leaning so far over her chair toward me the whole thing looked ready to tumble. Her mouth was open, and her whole expression said *I'm waiting to be surprised.*

Her and me both. I hadn't intended to tell her the truth, but so far that's what I'd given her, after a fashion.

"Huh, Therese?"

I'm an action person, not a natural talker. I like to plan things out so thoroughly before I ever start that I don't have to deal with surprises. Like I said, I don't think well on my feet, so I went a bit farther with the truth. "I think he really was going to take me to Hawaii. Then he got an offer he couldn't refuse, like they say. Only in George's case, it was a buddy of his he'd been telling about our big trip to the islands and what a great Valentine's Day gift it was going to be and how it would make up for all the years George had made me live like a serf. This buddy of George's, he knew what our life was like and I guess he figured if a trip was good enough to compensate me for that miserable existence it must really be something. And he was having some problems with his own girlfriend. So he offered George a thousand dollars apiece for the tickets and three thousand for hotel and all."

"And George sold your vacation just like that?" Delia was so outraged it was downright heartwarming.

"Not only did he sell the vacation package, but since I was the same size as the buddy's girlfriend, for another thousand he threw in the new swimsuit and cocktail dresses and the rest of the clothes I'd bought."

"And then what?"

"Then he lost all interest in the great sale and put everything back in storage. And while I was dealing with the last customer—"

"But why were you still selling for the bastard?"

"Well, he wouldn't let me near his storage boxes, so I had to do something while I waited for him to load them up."

Delia nodded noncommittally. Too noncommittally.

I knew that last bit of caving in didn't make me look good. If I'd had time, I probably should have come up with a better lie for that. She was thinking about the storage containers, I could tell, waiting to lure me back to those boxes, their contents. I was still going without a decent plan, and it was scaring me silly. I could not say too much. I had to dig in my heels here and stop before I blurted enough to land me in the Frontera Grande.

"Why didn't you just leave the bastard?"

"I couldn't."

"Why the hell not?" Her contempt was just about more than I could stand, particularly considering how undeserved it was.

I swallowed and said, "He disappeared."

"With another woman?"

"Yes."

"You mean he just took off and abandoned his beloved stuff in storage?"

"His stuff . . . and his wife," I pointed out.

"Sure." Delia sat still except for her tapping fingers, all eight of them banging her thighs. She looked anxious to keep on prodding but unsure how to get around the fact that she should have had more sympathy for the wife than interest in the storage. Finally she said, "Why do you care if his stuff is tossed out of storage?"

Now there was the sixty-four-thousand-dollar question. I had better come up with one damned good answer, and not just for her. "When we got married, I brought some family albums and some of my mother's jewelry. Before I realized it, those things got mixed in with the rest of George's stuff and shipped off to storage. So I need to go through the boxes before they're just carted out to auction and some stranger hauls the boxes sight unseen back to his own driveway, which could be anywhere in southern California. There are things of great sentimental value in one of those boxes." I swallowed hard. At least the last line was true. For the last four years one of those items had been the center of my life.

Delia nodded. She started to speak but caught herself. She'd been about to make some sarcastic remark, I could tell. But professionalism won out, and she merely nodded.

I hadn't been sure before then. Delia could have been just what she seemed, a chatty lone traveler anxious for another woman to share a dinner table in the hotel restaurant or take the adjoining stool in the bar. She'd been careful not to ask pointed questions, but she did keep coming back to George and his abrupt disappearance and the storage unit boxes. I wondered if the sheriff had already opened them. It was possible. George always said I had no head for accounts, and I had let the storage bill go unpaid.

I took a sip of that second mai tai of mine and glanced at Delia over the top of my glass. I wondered if the authorities had found George yet, and if they had, what shape he'd be in by now. Not good, there was no question about that. He always had hated the idea of being confined in a small space.

I took another sip, a very small sip, and forced myself to sit back and wait quietly—definitely quietly—and see what tack Delia would take.

"Why'd you stay with him for four years?" she blurted out.

I sighed. "It doesn't speak well of me, does it? George said I couldn't get along without him and, well, it was true."

"Oh come on!"

"I know it sounds mealymouthed, but see, it was a very bad time for me, that year before George came along. I'd been in an accident, had a bad fall, broke my collarbone in two places. I didn't have medical coverage, and I didn't know how I was going to live, and then there was George offering me an opportunity to get on my feet." And that was the truth, too, after a fashion.

"So you felt obligated?"

I shrugged and offered another truth. "I felt like I couldn't survive without him."

She leaned back in her chair, reached for the tube of suntan lotion, and began re-lathering a leg. But it was the leg nearest me, the one she could look over and note my reaction out of the side of her eye. "Did George really make enough money at the flea market to support two of you?"

"I guess," I said, giving up on truth. "We didn't starve. Actually, we ate pretty well. I haven't had that much steak in years. And . . . I don't know how he did manage that." Then with a spurt of honesty, I added, "I mean, he did love to buy and he hated to part with anything. When I first married him he had one storage unit, and by the time he ran off he had six."

"So how could he possibly have made a profit?"

I just shook my head. He hadn't made much of a profit

from his standard flea market stock, but he had fenced enough to clear fifty thousand a year, which he happily stashed in storage unit number one. He would have been proud of me not giving voice to that.

I figured Delia was with the sheriff's department in San Bernardino, and it surprised me that they had spent the money to send an officer to Hawaii, much less pay for one to go undercover as a guest at a $300 a night hotel. Of course she wouldn't really need a room here, just an agreement with the management. But she was good at playing within her cover of poolside buddy. She didn't move right on to the issue of burglaries in San Bernardino. She eased into that only hours later when we were at dinner in the tropical rain forest motif hotel restaurant.

"Really?" I said, forking a shrimp and leaning forward so she could hear me over the Hawaiian music. "What kind of burglaries?"

"Daylight prowls." The music stopped, and for a moment she seemed to be shouting to the whole restaurant. In almost a whisper she added, "He carried a velvet bag of burglar tools. Careful, thorough, knew what he was looking for. Took jewelry, appliances, stuff that could easily be fenced."

"Really?"

She'd finished her satay appetizer and tapped her fork on the empty plate. She looked as if she was considering a significant move, and this time looks were true. She said, "Therese, I need to come clean with you. I'm not just a tourist here. I'm a private investigator working with the San Bernardino County Sheriff's Department."

I was so relieved I wanted to lift my drink and toast my stroke of luck. Not a sheriff; only a PI. I just caught myself before I let out a big sigh. "Really!"

"We've been watching your husband George for a year now."

"Really!" I let a moment pass. "I shouldn't be surprised. He did say he was worried about men eyeing his goods. But, you know, George was so caught up in his stuff. He wouldn't even let me near his sacred storage units. Kept the keys in his pocket in the day and under his pillow at night. I mean, like I was dying to go down to the storage place and spend even more time with used clothes and junk. It didn't surprise me that he figured people wanted to snatch it. I just figured that was part of his paranoia. But no, huh? The sheriff really was eyeing his stuff! You know that's almost funny. But wait, are you saying George was a burglar? There's no way George could break into a strange house and steal. Not George! I mean, I'm not his biggest fan, not since he ran off with some strange woman, but still, I can't see the man breaking and entering. Not George."

Delia reached out and patted my hand again. "We've seen the hot goods on his table at the flea market. We would have subpoenaed the storage units, but when the rent went unpaid, we just bought them, and you know what we found?"

I was holding my breath. I made myself exhale and ask, "What?"

"Burglar tools."

I stiffened. "Really?" Then I added, "You mean George really was burglarizing?"

She nodded.

I waited till the waiter had removed the appetizer dishes and set the mahimahi down before us. It was time to get to the big question, but I couldn't afford to look too pushy doing it. On the far side of the room the little band was making about-to-start noises. I waited till they hit their intro and let the music cover any sharp edges in my demeanor as I said, "Delia, I have to ask you what you're after. I mean, you've come a long way to check me out. So what do you want from me?"

"We need you to testify."

"Against George? No problem."

"By law, you don't have to, not as long as you're married to him."

"Like I said, no problem." She still hadn't mentioned if they'd opened the other storage containers. I swallowed and asked, "Has the sheriff found George yet?"

"Oh yes."

"Where?"

"In a casino in Las Vegas. With his lady friend."

Now I did let out a sigh; I couldn't help it. Las Vegas. I hadn't known. I'd known for months George was carrying on with Jan Shimmerling. I'd been furious, but I was too afraid to leave.

George had been right; I couldn't manage without him. I mean, without him, who would fence the goods? Who would take the jewelry to the antiquers or break down the necklaces and bracelets and bargain with the jewelers over each and every gemstone? Who would leave the incriminating trail the sheriff could follow? I would never have done that. Breaking into the houses, now that was my forte. I could plan every aspect of each job and handle them competently so there were no undue surprises. I did like my work, and if I do say so myself, I was very good at it.

Like I said, things were rough before I spotted George. When you fall out a second story window with a bag of necklaces in your hand, it's not as if you can make a claim on the householder's homeowner's policy. It's not like you can get unemployment because you can't climb up the ivy till your collarbone heals. But with George I had time to heal and to plot out the next two dozen heists.

Although I married George for his business, I was his wife, and I would have shared. But what's the point of burgling if you're married to a hoarder? George would have been happy to permanently stash our illicit cash in among his brass lamps and antique velvet dresses in those storage units. It got so bad I'd begun to envision him in the storage unit buried under the used clothing, wrapped in plastic. I really didn't know what to do about him. But then Jan Shimmerling had come along and solved the problem for me. After that, it was just a matter of waiting.

I glanced at Delia Hammond, sitting across from me, making notes in a small pad. She was all business now. I guess George could try to blame those burglar tools on me, but who was going to believe him? People in Hinsdale knew he never let anyone near his storage units. They'd laugh at the idea of George giving me the key.

As if I'd needed a key.

And even if Delia did wonder about me, so what? I had a couple hundred thousand I'd taken out of the storage box before I left. And I wouldn't be here on Waikiki long. I couldn't afford to stay. Like George said, I do lack self-control, and the locks on those charming little hotel cottages were just too easy. It's okay, though; I've always wanted to travel.

A Girl Like You

Ed Gorman

> *And hearts that we broke long ago*
> *Have long been breaking others.*
> —W. H. AUDEN

He knew they were in trouble, and he couldn't eat. He knew they were in trouble, and he couldn't sleep. He knew they were in trouble, and he couldn't concentrate.

Not on anything except his girl Nora.

His name was Peter Wyeth and he was eighteen, all ready to enter the state university this fall, and he'd met her two and a half months ago at a kegger graduation night. He'd been pretty bombed, so bombed in fact that she'd driven him home in the new Firebird his folks had bought him for graduation.

That first night, she hadn't seemed like so much. Or maybe it was that he'd been so bombed he didn't realize just how much she really was. The truth was, Peter pretty much took girls for granted. He could afford to. He had the Wyeth look. There was something Dartmouth about the Wyeth boys, even though they'd lived all their lives here in small-town Iowa, and something Smith about the Wyeth girls. Between them, they broke a lot of hearts hereabouts, and though they didn't seem to take any particular pleasure in it, they didn't seem to care much, either.

Nora Caine was different somehow.

He'd never seen or heard of her before the night of the kegger. But he asked about her a lot the next day. Somebody said that they thought she was from one of those little towns near the point where Iowa and Wisconsin faced each other across the Mississippi. Visiting somebody here. It was all vague.

He ran into her that night at Charlie's, which was the sports bar on the highway where you could drink if you had a fake ID. Or if you were a Wyeth. She was dancing with some guy he recognized as a university frosh football player, something Peter himself had planned to be until he'd damaged his knee in a game against Des Moines.

He didn't like it. That was the first thing he noticed. And he realized instantly that he'd never felt this particular feeling before. Jealousy. He didn't even know this girl, and yet he was jealous that she was dancing with somebody else. What the hell was that all about? Wyeths didn't get jealous; they didn't need to.

He watched her for the next hour. If she was teasing him, she was doing it subtly. Except for a few glances, she didn't seem aware of him at all. She just kept dancing with the frosh. By this time, Peter's friends were there and they were standing all around him telling him just how beautiful Nora Caine was. As if he needed to be told. What most fascinated him about her physically was a certain . . . timelessness about her. Her hairstyle wasn't quite contemporary. Her clothes hinted at another era. Even her dance steps seemed a little dated. And yet she bedazzled, fascinated, imprisoned him.

Nora Caine.

She left that night with the frosh.

Peter spent a sleepless night—the first of many, as things would turn out—and knew just what he'd do at first light. He'd go looking for her. Somebody had to know who she was, where she lived, what she was doing here in town.

He met her that afternoon. She was sitting along the peaceful river, a sleek black raven sitting next to her, as if he was keeping guard. Her apartment was only a block away. The landlady, impressed that she was talking to young Wyeth, told him everything she knew about Nora. Girl was here for a few weeks settling some kind of family matters with an attorney. The frosh football player a constant visitor. Nora listening to classical music (played low), given to long walks along the river (always alone), and painting lovely pictures of days gone by.

"You remember me?"

She looked up. "Sure."

"Thanks for driving me home the other night. How'd you get home?"

"Walked."

"You could've taken a cab and just told them to put it on my father's account."

"He must be an important man."

"He is." Then: "Mind if I sit down?"

"I sort of have a boyfriend."

"The football player?"

"Yes." She smiled and he was cut in half, so profound was the effect of her smile on him. He wanted to cry in both joy and sorrow. He felt scared, and wondered if he might be losing his mind. He'd been drinking too much beer lately, that was for sure. "The funny thing is, I don't even like sports."

"I'd like to go out with you sometime."

"I guess I'm just not sure how things're going to go with Brad. So I really can't make any dates."

A few weeks later—well into outrageous green suffocating summer now—Peter heard that Brad took a bad spill on his motorcycle. Real bad. He'd be in University Hospital for several months.

He'd tried to distract himself with the wildest girls he could find. He had a lot of giggles and a lot of sex and a lot of brewskis and yet and he was still soul-empty. He'd never felt like this. Empty this way. Empty and scared and lonely and jealous. What the hell was it about Nora, anyway? Sure, she was beautiful, but so were most of his girls. Sure, she was winsome and sweet, but so were some of the girls he'd dated seriously. Sure, she was—and then he realized what it was. He couldn't have her. That was what was so special about her. If she'd ever just give in to him the way the other girls did, he wouldn't want her.

She was just playing games like all the other girls (or so he'd always imagined they were playing games, anyway) and he was—for the first time—losing.

He did a very irrational thing one rainy night. He parked in the alley behind her apartment house and watched as she left the building. He climbed the fire escape along the back and broke into her room, and there he saw her paintings. They were everywhere—leaning against the walls, set in chairs, standing on one of three easels. As silver rain eeled down the windows, he stood in the lightning flashes of the night and escaped into the various worlds she had painted. They looked like magazine cover illustrations from every decade in this century: the doughboys of World War I, the hollow-eyed farmers of the Depression, the dogfaces of World War II, a young girl with a 1950s hula hoop, an anti-Vietnam hippie protester, a stockbroker on the floor, Times Square the first night of the new century. There was a reality to the illustrations that gave him a dizzy feeling, as if they were drawing him into the world they represented. He'd have to give up smoking so much pot, too. It obviously wasn't doing him any good.

Then she came home, carrying a small, damp sack of groceries, her red hair bejeweled with raindrops. The funny thing was she didn't even ask him why he was there. She just set down the groceries and came to him.

N ot long after that, the local newspaper editor, Paul Sheridan, came up to him on the street and said, "I see you know Nora Caine. She's going to teach you a lot."

As always, the white-haired, ruddy-cheeked Sheridan smelled of liquor. He was in his sixties. As a young man, he'd written a novel that had sold very well. But that was the end of his literary career. He could never seem to find a suitable subject for a second novel. His wife and daughter had died in a fire some time ago. He had inherited the newspaper from his father and ran it until his drinking caused him to bring in his cousin, who ran the paper and did a better job than Paul ever had. Now Paul wrote some editorials, reviewed books nobody in a town like this would ever read, and wrote pieces on town history, at which he excelled. There was always talk that somebody should collect these pieces that stretched back now some twenty-five years, but as yet nobody had. Sheridan said: "If you're strong, Peter, you'll be the better man for it."

What the hell was Sheridan muttering about? How did he even know that Peter knew Nora? And how the hell did anybody Sheridan's age know Nora?

It was two weeks before she'd let Peter sleep with her. He was crazy by then. He was so caught up in her, he found himself thinking unimaginable things: He wouldn't go to college, he'd get a job so they could get married. And they'd have a kid. He didn't want to lose her, and he lived in constant terror that he would. But if they had a kid . . . When he was away from her, he was miserable. His parents took to giving him long, confused looks. He no longer returned the calls of his buddies; they seemed childish to him now. Nora was the one lone true reality. He would not wash his hands sometimes for long periods; he wanted to retain their intimacy. He learned things about women—about fears and appetites and nuances. And he learned about heartbreak. The times they'd argue, he was devastated when he realized that someday she might well leave him.

And so it went all summer.

He took her home. His parents did not care for her. "Sort of . . . aloof," his mother said. "What's wrong with Tom Bolan's daughter? She's a lot better looking than this Nora, and she's certainly got a nicer pair of melons," his father said. To which his mother predictably replied, "Oh, Lloyd, you and your melons. Good Lord."

They avoided the places he used to go. He didn't want to share her.

There was no intimacy they did not know, sexual, mental, spiritual. She even got him to go to some lectures on

Buddhism at the university, and he found himself not en-raptured (as she seemed to be) but at least genuinely in-terested in the topic and the discussion that followed.

He would lay his hand on her stomach and dream of the kid they'd have. He'd see toddlers on the street and try to imagine what it'd be like to have one of his own. And you know what, he thought it would be kinda cool, actually. It really would be.

And then, one morning, she was gone.

Her landlady told him that a cab had shown up right at nine o'clock that morning and taken her and her two bags (they later found that she'd shipped all her canvases and art supplies separately) and that she was gone. She said to tell Peter good-bye for her.

He'd known they were in some sort of trouble the past couple of weeks—something she wouldn't discuss—but now it had all come crashing down.

A cab had picked her up. Swept her away. Points un-known.

Tell Peter good-bye for me.

He had enemies. The whole Wyeth family did. When-ever anything bad happened to one of the Wyeths, the collective town put on a forlorn face, of course (hy-pocrisy not being limited to Madison Avenue cocktail par-ties), and then proceeded to chuckle when the camera was off them.

A fine, handsome boy, they said; too bad.

He wasn't a fine boy, though, and everybody knew it. He had treated some people terribly. Girls especially. Get them all worked up and tell them lots of lies and then sleep with them till a kind of predatory spell came over him and he was stalking new blood once again. There had been two abortions, a girl who'd sunk into so low a depression that she had to stay in a hospital for a time, and innumerable standard issue broken hearts. He was no kinder to males. Boys who amused him got to warm themselves in the great presence of a Wyeth; but when they amused him no longer, held strong opinions with which he disagreed, or hinted that maybe his family wasn't all that it claimed to be, they were banished forever from the golden kingdom.

So who could argue that the bereaved, angry, sullen, despondent boy who had been dumped by a passing-through girl . . . who could argue that he didn't deserve it?

His mother suggested a vacation. She had family in New Hampshire.

His father suggested Uncle Don in Wyoming. He broke broncs; maybe he could break Peter, who was embarrassing to be around these days. By God, and over a girl, too.

Peter stayed in town. He drank and he slept off the drink and then he drank some more. He was arrested twice for speeding, fortunately when he was sober. And—back with his friends again—he was also fined for various kinds of childish mischief, not least of which was spray-painting the *f*-word on a police car.

Autumn came; early autumn, dusky ducks dark against the cold melancholy prairie sky, his friends all gone off to college, and Peter more alone than he'd ever been.

His father said he needed to get a job if he wasn't going to the university.

His mother said maybe he needed to see a psychologist.

He was forced, for friendship, to hang out with boys he'd always avoided before. Not from the right social class. Not bright or hip or aware. Factory kids or mall kids, the former sooty when they left the mill at three every afternoon; the latter dressed in the cheap suits they wore to sell appliances or tires or cheap suits. And yet, after an initial period of feeling superior, he found that these kids weren't really much different from his other friends. All the same fears and hopes. And he found himself actually liking most of them. Understanding them in a way he would have thought impossible.

There was just one thing they couldn't do: They couldn't save him from his grief. They couldn't save him and booze couldn't save him and pot couldn't save him and speed couldn't save him and driving fast couldn't save him and fucking his brains out and sobbing couldn't save him and puking couldn't save him and masturbating couldn't save him and hitting people couldn't save him and praying couldn't save him. Not even sleep could save him, for always in sleep came Nora. Nora Nora Nora. Nothing could save him.

And then one night, while his folks were at the country club, he couldn't handle it any more. Any of it. He lay on his bed with his grandfather's straight razor and cut his wrists. He was all drunked up and crying and scared shitless, but somehow he found the nerve to do it. Just at the last minute, blood starting to cover his hands now, he rolled over on the bed to call 911, but then he dropped the receiver. Too weak. And then he went to sleep . . .

He woke up near dawn in a very white room. Streaks of dawn in the window. The hospital just coming awake. Rattle of breakfast carts, squeak of nurses' shoes. And his folks peering down at him and smiling, and a young woman doctor saying, "You're going to be fine, Peter. Just fine."

His mother wept, and his father kept whispering, "You'll have to forgive your mother. She used to cry when you two would watch Lassie together," which actually struck Peter as funny.

"I'll never get over her," he said.

"You'll be back to breaking hearts in no time," his father said.

"She wasn't our kind, anyway," his mother said. "I don't mean to be unkind, honey, but that's the truth."

"I still wish you'd give old Tom's daughter a go," his father said.

"Yeah, I know," Peter said. "Melons." He grinned. He was glad he wasn't dead. He felt young and old; totally sane and totally crazy; horny and absolutely monastic; drunk and sober.

He went home the next day. And stayed home. It was pretty embarrassing to go out. People looking at you. Whispering.

He watched *Nick at Nite* a lot. Took him back to the days when he was six and seven. You have it knocked when you're six and seven and you don't even realize it. Being six and seven—no responsibilities, no hassles, no doom—is better than having a few billion in the bank. He stayed sober; he slept a lot; every once in a while the sorrow would just overwhelm him and he'd see her right in front of him in some fantastical way, and hear her and feel her and smell her and taste her, and he would be so balled up in pain that not only would he want to be six or seven, he wanted to go all the way back to the womb.

*   *   *

March got all confused and came on like May. My God, you just didn't know what to do with yourself on days like this. Disney had a hand in creating a day like this; he had to.

Peter started driving to town and parking and walking around. He always went mid afternoon when everybody was still in school. He never would've thought he'd be so happy to see his old town again. He took particular notice of the trolley tracks and the hitching posts and the green Model-T you could see all dusty in Old Man Baumhofer's garage. He sat in the library and actually read some books, something he'd never wanted to do in his whole life.

But mostly he walked around. And thought thoughts he'd never thought before, either. He'd see a squirrel, and he'd wonder if there was some way to communicate with the little guy that human beings—in their presumptuousness and arrogance—just hadn't figured out yet. He saw flowers and stopped and really studied them and lovingly touched them and sniffed them. He saw infants in strollers being pushed by pretty young moms with that twenty-year-old just-bloomed beauty that flees so sadly and quickly, and saw the war memorials of three different conflicts and was proud to see how many times the name Wyeth was listed. He looked—for the first time in his life he really looked at things. And he loved what he saw; just loved it.

And one day, when he was walking down by the deserted mill near the newspaper office, he saw Paul Sheridan leaving, and he went up to him and he said, "A while back you told me Nora was going to teach me things. And that if I was strong, I'd be a better man for it."

For the first time, he looked past the drunken red face and the jowls and the white hair and saw Sheridan as he must have been at Peter's age. Handsome and tall, probably a little theatrical (he still was now), and possessed of a real warmth. Sheridan smiled. "I knew you'd look me up, kiddo. C'mon in the office. I want to show you something."

Except for a couple of pressmen in the back, the office was empty. Several computer stations stood silent, eyes guarding against intruders.

Sheridan went over to his desk and pulled out a photo album. He carried it over to a nearby table and set it down. "You want coffee?"

"That sounds good."

"I'll get us some. You look through the album."

He looked through the album. Boy, did he. And wondered who the jokester was who'd gone to all this trouble.

Here were photographs—some recent, some tinted in turn-of-the-last-century fashion—of Nora Caine in dozens of different poses, moods, outfits—and times. Her face never changed, though. She was Nora in the 1890s and she was Nora today. There could be no mistaking that.

Goose bumps; disbelief.

"Recognize her?" Sheridan said when he sat down. He pushed a cup of coffee Peter's way.

"Somebody sure went to a lot of trouble to fake all these photographs."

Sheridan smiled at him. "Now you know better than that. You're just afraid to admit it. They're real."

"But that's impossible."

"No, it's not. Not if you're an angel or a ghost or whatever the hell she is." He sipped some coffee. "She broke my heart back when I was your age. So bad I ended up in a mental hospital having electroshock treatments. No fun, let me tell you. Took me a long time to figure out what she did for me."

"You mean, did *to* you?"

"No; that's the point. You have to see her being with you as a positive thing rather than a negative one. I was a spoiled rich kid just like you. A real heartbreaker. Didn't know shit from Shinola and didn't care to. All I wanted to do was have fun. And then she came along and crushed me—and turned me into a genuine human being. I hated her for at least ten years. Tried to find her. Hired private detectives. Everything. I wrote my novel about her. Only novel I had in me, as things turned out. But I never would've read a book or felt any compassion for poor people or cared about spiritual things. I was an arrogant jerk, and it took somebody like her to change me. It had to be painful, or it wouldn't have worked. I was bitter and angry for a long time, like I said, but then eventually I saw what she'd done for me. And I thanked her for it. And loved her all the more. But in a different way now."

"You don't really believe she's some kind of ghost or something, do you?"

"The photos are real, Peter. Took me thirty years to collect them. I went all over the Midwest collecting them. I'd show a photo to somebody in some little town and then they'd remember her or remember somebody who'd known her. And it was always the same story. Some arrogant young prick—rich or poor, black or white, didn't matter—and he'd have his fling with her. And then she'd move on. And he'd be crushed. But he'd never be his arrogant old self again. Some of them couldn't handle it, and they'd kill themselves. Some of them would just be bitter and drink themselves to death. But the strong ones— us, Peter, you and me—we learned the lessons she wanted us to. Just think of all the things we know now that we didn't know before she met us."

The phone rang. He got up to get it. Peter noticed that he staggered a little.

He was on the phone for ten minutes. No big deal. Just a conversation with somebody about a sewer project. You didn't usually get big deals on small-town newspapers like this one.

Peter just looked at the pictures. His entire being yearned for a simple touch of her. In her flapper outfit. Or her World War II Rosie the Riveter getup. Or her hippie attire. Nora Nora Nora.

Sheridan came back from the phone. "I didn't expect you to believe me, Peter. I didn't believe it for a long time. Now I do." He looked at Peter for a time. "And someday you will, too. And you'll be grateful that she was in your life for that time." He grinned, and you could see the boy in him suddenly. "She had some ass, didn't she?"

Peter laughed. "She sure did."

"I got to head over to the library, kiddo."

Sheridan said good-bye to the pressmen, and then they headed out the door. The day was still almost oppressively beautiful.

"This is the world she wanted me to see, Peter. And I never would've appreciated it if I hadn't loved her. I never did find myself another woman after my wife and family died, so I took to tipping the bottle a little more than I should. But you'll be luckier, kiddo. I can feel it."

They crossed the little bridge heading to the merchant blocks. Sheridan started to turn right toward the library.

"The next woman you love, you'll know how to love. How to be tender with. How to give yourself to her. I can't say that my life has been a great success, Peter. It hasn't been. But I loved my wife and daughter more than I ever could've if I hadn't met Nora. Maybe that's the most important thing she ever taught us, Peter." And with that, Sheridan waved good-bye.

*　　*　　*

Six years later his wife Faith gave birth to a girl. Peter asked if they might name her Nora. And Faith, understanding, smiled yes.

COMPANY WIFE

Jean Hager

Jean Hager is the author of two mystery series with a Cherokee cultural background, published by Mysterious Press. Her most recent Cherokee mystery is Masked Dancers. *She also writes the Iris House Bed and Breakfast series set in the Missouri Ozarks, featuring amateur sleuth Tess Darcy. The seventh in that series,* Bride and Doom, *was a 2000 release from Avon Books. She has twice been a finalist for the national Agatha mystery award in the short story category. Her story "Country Hospitality" was chosen for* The Best of Sisters in Crime, *published by Reader's Digest. Jean is an active member of Sisters in Crime and has been inducted into the Oklahoma Professional Writers Hall of Fame. She lives in Tulsa with her husband.*

As Mike Riley pulled into the garage and switched off the motor, he felt a weight of depression settle on his shoulders. It had become a familiar weight the past few months, and each time he came home, he dreaded even more getting out of the car and going in. The house that had once been his castle had become his prison.

Sighing, he squared his shoulders and got out. Circling around to the front door, he entered the foyer, threw his briefcase on the foyer table, and followed the smells to the kitchen. There, his heart sank and the weight on his shoulders grew heavier. His wife had set a small table near the bay window with lace-trimmed linen, the best china, and an elaborate centerpiece of roses and candles. A romantic dinner for two. The last thing he wanted to deal with at the moment.

Marcie greeted him cheerily as she took a brisket from the oven. She set the meat on the range and walked over to give him a kiss on the cheek. She was wearing perfume, and she'd had her hair done. *Wonderful,* he thought grimly. Well, she wasn't wearing a negligee. Thank goodness for small favors.

"Would you like to pour us some wine?" She indicated the Burgundy nestled in ice on the counter with two wineglasses beside it. "Then you'll have time to change into something more comfortable before dinner."

Wordlessly, he poured the wine and escaped to their bedroom upstairs with his glass. He changed into khaki slacks and a sport shirt, wondering how long he could keep up this charade. He dawdled as long as he dared and finally went downstairs with his empty glass. The food was on the table, the overhead light off, the candles lit. Marcie was already seated, sipping her wine. She gave him a seductive smile.

With an effort, he gathered himself together. "This looks great," he said, as he poured himself another glass of wine, then replenished his wife's glass before sitting down. One thing he could say for Marcie, she was a fabulous cook. Since he'd worked through lunch, he was famished. *Just enjoy the food,* he told himself, *and don't think about afterward.*

He picked up his fork and began to eat. After a lengthy silence, he realized that Marcie was watching him expectantly. "Excellent brisket," he muttered.

She seemed to expect something more. He had no idea what was up with her, so he ignored it, and she sighed and began to eat. After another brief silence, she said, "You haven't forgotten that our anniversary is Saturday, have you?"

Oh, hell. He put down his fork. "Marcie, I'm sorry. I have to go to New York this weekend."

She was obviously disappointed, but she managed a good-sport smile. "Oh, well, we can celebrate when you return. You're leaving on Friday?"

"That's right, and returning Monday."

"I wish you'd told me sooner." She paused, giving him time to invite her to accompany him. He remained silent.

"If only—"

He interrupted before she could finish the thought. "I didn't know I'd be going until today. There's a problem with one of our retailers."

"Can't somebody else take care of it?"

"I need to handle this myself." Which was a lie. What he needed was to get away.

"I'll make the flight and hotel reservations first thing tomorrow. The air fare will be higher than if I could've had more notice."

"Don't worry about it. My assistant already made the reservations."

"But—" She gave him the wounded look he'd seen a lot of lately. "I've always made your travel arrangements."

"I thought you'd appreciate letting somebody else take over. We're a big company now. We've come a long way since those early days."

"I miss those days when we worked together as a team. Sometimes, since the girls left home, I feel—well—useless."

"Nonsense. Only last week you threw that wonderful dinner for those out-of-town clients. They raved about the food. And you have your volunteer work."

He was braced for more complaints, but she let it go and began talking about her phone conversation that day with Connie, their younger daughter. He tried to look interested as he finished his dinner, which ended with chocolate cake, one of his favorite desserts. *Now,* he thought, *if I can just get through the evening.* Tomorrow he had an appointment with his attorney. He held on to that thought as if it were a lifeline.

M ike paced the office. "I thought you were *my* attorney, not to mention my friend!"

"I am your friend, Mike," said Lance Perkins. "And as your attorney, I'm giving you my best professional advice. Work it out with Marcie. You two have been married twenty-seven years. You have two grown daughters. That's a lot of history. Surely this relationship is worth saving."

"It's over, Mike! I don't love her. I want to cut my losses and get on with my life."

"Is there somebody else?"

Mike halted to gaze sternly down at Lance. "That's neither here nor there."

Lance grunted and leaned back in his chair. "So there is somebody." Mike started to speak, and Lance held up a hand. "I'm not judging you. I just want you to understand a divorce is going to cost you dearly."

Mike flopped back down in the chair across the desk from Lance. "By God, I *am* the company. I'm not giving half of it to Marcie!"

Lance leaned forward, propping his elbows on his

desk. "Listen to me, friend. When you started Unique Jewels out of your garage, Marcie was right there, working as hard as you and keeping the books. When you'd grown the company enough to move into a building, she still kept the books and worked as your secretary until the first baby came. Then she stayed home to raise your kids. She's hostessed an untold number of company functions, from small dinners to big parties. Last I heard, she was still acting as the company travel agent. She's played her part in building the company into a multimillion-dollar business. She's the quintessential company wife. Any good attorney can make the case that she's entitled to half the business. She can probably get the house, half of your 401K, and alimony, along with half the business. Stay in the marriage. That's my best advice. Think about it, pal."

Mike uttered a curse and got to his feet. "Do you mind if I get a second opinion?"

Lance threw out his hands. "Be my guest."

Outside on Oakdale's main mall, a brisk March wind whipped down Main Street. Mike hunched his shoulders against the chill and stuffed his hands into the pockets of his Italian silk slacks. All his suits were tailored especially for him and cost an arm and a leg. Since he'd become a success, he'd acquired expensive tastes. He and Marcie had built their dream home on top of a mountain south of town. He had a rustic cabin and a Jeep for the hunting and fishing trips he took several times a year with friends. Two years ago, he'd bought twin Jaguars for Marcie and himself. He liked his lifestyle and had no intention of scaling down to any great degree.

Walking toward the parking garage where he'd left his Jag, he thought about what Lance had said. As far as he was concerned, Marcie could have the house. Going there—to her—only depressed him now. He'd have to swallow hard to give up half of his 401K, but he supposed he could manage it—and the alimony. But half the company? No way. Yet, in spite of his question about getting a second opinion, he knew another lawyer would probably give him the same estimate of his situation as Lance had. Several of his business acquaintances were divorced, and they'd all been taken to the cleaners by their ex-wives.

So, divorce was not an option. He started trying to come up with Plan B.

Back at work, Lucille followed him into his big office with its massive teak desk and panoramic view of the city. She closed the door and came to him, put her arms around him, pressing her soft cheek against his. "You look like your faithful dog just died, sweetheart."

He held her for a long moment, inhaling the perfumed scent of her glossy blond hair. She was twenty years younger than he, just four years older than his elder daughter. She was smart and pretty—no, not just pretty, she was beautiful. And she loved him. He'd fallen for her like a ton of bricks the first time he saw her eighteen months ago, when she'd applied for the job as his executive secretary. A month later, he'd promoted her to executive assistant and asked her out to dinner. At first, she'd refused, saying she didn't date married men. But he'd persisted until she finally gave in.

They managed an occasional night together in her apartment, when he told Marcie he had to work late and would sleep on the couch in his office. And they'd traveled together on business trips several times. In fact, Lucille was going to New York with him. She'd booked them into adjoining rooms at the Waldorf, although one of the rooms would not be used. They had to keep up appearances. But he knew that Lucille was getting impatient with the clandestine affair. She wanted him to be able to squire her around town openly, to be with her every night. He wanted that as much as she, and he was still old-fashioned enough to want to legitimatize their relationship with a wedding ceremony. He didn't particularly want any more children at his age, but if that's what it took to satisfy Lucille, then they'd do it. Besides, if he didn't marry her soon, she'd conclude their relationship was going nowhere. Lucille would have no trouble at all finding a man who was free to marry her and give her the lifestyle Mike wanted to give her.

She stepped away from him to peer up into his face. "What did the lawyer say?"

"He's working on the details. I'll meet with him again in a couple of weeks. Meantime, it's essential that Marcie doesn't get wind of my plans." He didn't think there was much danger of that. Marcie had always trusted him. Until the last eighteen months, she'd had no reason not to.

"She came by the office while you were gone."

That startled him. She hadn't mentioned that she'd be in town today. "Marcie, here? What'd she want?"

Lucille shrugged her lovely shoulders in the slim blue dress. "She said she was in town shopping and thought she'd take you to lunch. I told her I didn't know where you'd gone or when you'd be back. She waited in here for twenty minutes or so, then said she'd take you to lunch another time and left. She mentioned that your anniversary was this weekend. She didn't seem too happy about your being gone."

"She'll get over it. She knows these things come up."

She frowned worriedly. "I don't know, Mike. She asked a lot of personal questions—where I'd worked before, if I'd ever been married, was I seeing somebody special."

"She was probably just trying to be friendly."

Lucille shook her head. "I'm thinking maybe I shouldn't go with you to New York. What if she calls the hotel and finds out we're in adjoining rooms?"

He tried to put his arms around her again, but she stepped away. "Didn't she used to travel with you quite often on your business trips? If you want to keep her from getting suspicious, maybe you should take her instead of me."

Alarm bells went off in Mike's head. Lucille urging him to take his wife to New York? "I need this weekend with you, darling," he said, and hated himself for his wheedling tone. This woman could turn him inside out. He didn't know what he would do if he lost her.

She frowned again. "Marcie left not ten minutes before you returned. Your lawyer's office is only a block from here. I hope she didn't see you coming out of the building."

"If she did, it's no problem. Lance handles some of the company business, so she'll just assume that's what it was."

"I don't know how long I can do this, Mike." He'd sensed her impatience with him lately, but this was as close to an ultimatum as she'd ever given him. "Now, I'd better get back to my desk. We don't want the whole office starting to think the two of us spend too much time in here together." She started toward the door, then turned back. "I love you, Mike, but I'm very uncomfortable about what we're doing. Before you, I never let myself get involved with a married man. I hate slipping around behind Marcie's back. It makes me feel cheap. Sometimes, I wish I'd never gone to dinner with you that first time."

He went to her and kissed her deeply. "Don't even

think that, darling. We won't have to keep our relationship secret much longer. I promise."

Alone in his office, he sat at his desk and gazed out over the city. He wouldn't be able to pacify Lucille much longer, nor could he blame her. Both his unmarried vice presidents had asked her out, and she'd turned them down. She'd laughed about it when she told him, but it troubled him. He wondered if she'd told him just to let him know she had other options. Both men were much younger than he and didn't have the baggage of a wife and two daughters. He'd figure out a way to get rid of Marcie, somehow, without breaking the bank. But she was very close to their daughters, and they'd blame him—and his new "trophy wife." He was sure Lucille was wondering what impact the disapproval of Marcie's daughters would have on her relationship with Mike. The longer he gave her to think, the more disadvantages she'd see. He didn't want to lose all contact with his daughters, but if it came to a choice, he'd choose Lucille. As selfish and dastardly as that was, he couldn't help himself. He had never been this madly in love with Marcie, even in those early years. He'd loved her, of course, but it had been a quiet, peaceful sort of love. More like a sister-brother relationship with sex, he thought now. He'd never known real passion until Lucille came into his life, and he would do whatever it took to hang on to her.

By the end of the day, he'd thought of several plans to shed his wife, but they were all very risky, and that scared him. He had to keep the company and be free to marry Lucille. Surely, there was a legitimate way to do that. He sighed heavily. If there was, he hadn't thought of it yet.

He remained at his desk until everybody else has left the office, dreading going home to Marcie. Finally, he decided to get a couple of drinks to bolster himself before making the drive.

He drove away from his building, looking for a bar where he wouldn't see anybody he knew. He was in no mood for casual conversation. In a seedy neighborhood north of the main part of town, he saw Budweiser in neon lights and pulled over.

The interior of Jack's Bar was dim—probably as much to disguise the grime as for atmosphere. From what he could see of the customers, Jack's was frequented by working-class guys. His was the only suit in the place. He took a stool at the bar and ordered a scotch and water.

A burly man next to him turned and said, "Hey, Mr. Riley, isn't it?"

It was a moment before he recognized the man who'd worked on his Jaguar at Greeley's Garage the last time it needed repairs. The guy was a mechanical genius, according to his boss. "Hello . . . ," the name finally came to him, "Greg."

"Haven't seen you in here before," Greg said. "You slumming today?"

He forced a laugh. "I needed a drink before going home."

Greg nodded as if he understood, and Mike wondered if he was married. The conversation he had with the garage owner when he took his car in was coming back to him. Greg was an ex-con. He'd served six years in the state pen for robbery with a firearm. Nathan Greeley had hired several ex-cons, he'd told Mike, because he felt they deserved a second chance. Sometimes it worked out, sometimes not. Some cons found it difficult to stay away from their old habits. Mike wondered if Greg was one of those.

"How's the job going?" Mike asked casually.

Greg gestured to the bartender for another beer. He didn't reply until his glass was filled and the bartender moved away. "I'm not working at Greeley's anymore."

"Oh, really? So, what are you doing now?"

"Drawing workman's comp and looking," he said shortly. "I think Greeley is giving me a bad reference. He accused me of taking money from the till."

"Did you?"

He gazed at Mike for a long moment. His eyes were so cold it made Mike shiver. "No." Mike suspected that was a lie. Greg's lip curled a little. "A guy like you, you got no idea how hard it is for guys like me."

"I'm sure I don't. But everybody's got problems, Greg. Mine may be different from yours, but I've got them."

"Yeah, right," he said disbelievingly.

"Actually, I'm trying to write a book—a novel. It's the hardest thing I've ever done."

Greg looked at him as though Mike were speaking a foreign language.

"It's a suspense novel," Mike said. "A mystery. You ever read mysteries?"

"Dozens of 'em, when I was in the joint. They're not very realistic, but it helped pass the time."

"Here's my problem. In mysteries, the criminal is always caught and sent to jail. But I want my character to get away with his crime. I need to figure out a foolproof way to commit the perfect murder."

Greg's eyes were still cold. "You suggesting I might know?"

"No, well, I was just thinking that—you being in the pen and all—you must've known some murderers."

"Yeah, and they got caught. They were all stupid."

"But my man's smart."

"Who's he going to kill?"

"His wife."

"The husband's the first guy the cops will suspect."

"I know, but he's going to be miles away when the murder happens."

"So how's he going to manage that?"

"I've given that a lot of thought, and I think the best way is to disable the brakes in her car, cut the brake lines, maybe. They live on top of a mountain, you see, and when she starts down the winding road, she won't be able to stop or make the curves. The only problem is, she's probably going to hit the brakes a time or two before she starts down the mountain—like when she backs out of the garage. She'll be on level ground then, but she'll hit the brakes before turning around, and she'll realize they aren't working. At that point, she can probably stop the car with the emergency brake, or even just coast to a stop."

"Whyn't you just have her park her car so she comes out of the garage going in the right direction. No need for her to hit her brakes until she starts down."

Mike scratched his chin and pretended to think about it. "Yeah, that might do. But I'd like to work it out the other way. It's a mental challenge, you know."

"You got a problem with cutting the brake lines then, even if she doesn't hit her brakes before she starts down the mountain. The car is going off a cliff, right?"

"Yeah."

"Unless it burns up, the cops will examine the car and notice that the brake lines have been cut."

"No way to make sure it burns up, I guess."

"Nope—not unless the husband's down there and throws gasoline on it. But the cops would probably figure that out, too."

"That won't work, anyway. It's essential for the plot that the husband be miles away when it happens."

"How steep is this mountain?"

"Very steep."

"Does she have to make several curves going down?"

"A dozen or so."

Greg nodded. "Your guy could loosen the bleed-off valves on the brake lines. The brake fluid would only leak out when she hit the brakes. After the first few times, it'd be all gone, and whammo—" He slapped his hands together and made Mike jump. Greg laughed. "Off the cliff she goes. No more wife."

Mike stared at him admiringly. "Wow, I envy people who understand how machines work. I've always been hopeless with mechanical things. And the character I've created—he's the same way. So it wouldn't be credible for him to know about those bleed-off valves, or whatever you call them. And there's still the problem of my hero needing to be somewhere else when it happens."

"He could loosen the valves the night before, after she's through using the car, and leave early the next morning before she decides to drive somewhere."

"I don't know." Mike shook his head. "I'd like for the husband to be gone longer than that before it happens. He wouldn't know a bleed-off valve if he saw it; besides, he's kind of squeamish."

Greg gave him a thoughtful sideways look. "Doesn't like getting his hands dirty, huh? In more ways than one, if you know what I mean."

"That's right." Mike clapped a friendly hand on his shoulder. "You're starting to understand this character." He noticed Greg's glass was empty again and ordered him another beer, telling the bartender to put it on his tab.

"Thanks," Greg mumbled grudgingly.

"Don't mention it."

They drank in silence for a moment. Then Greg said, "Why doesn't he hire somebody to do it?"

He didn't look around as he said it. Mike studied his beefy profile. "That's risky, too. It'd have to be somebody he was sure he could trust not to spill the beans—if, for some reason, he was questioned by the police."

"Somebody with no connection to the guy—or no connection the cops could find out about."

"But he still might tell."

"Not if he was paid enough."

Mike let that roll around in his head while he finished his scotch and ordered another. "Just for the sake of verisimilitude, how much would a job like that cost?"

Greg mulled it over, then shrugged. "Fifteen, twenty grand oughta do it."

"Not five or ten, huh?"

He still hadn't turned to look at Mike. "Not if the guy wants to hire the best—somebody who knows what he's doing and knows how to keep his trap shut."

"You sure the cops wouldn't get suspicious when they examine the car—just like they would if the brake lines were cut?"

"They might, but the valves could have come loose when she was going down the mountain. The cops couldn't prove they were tampered with." He turned to gaze at Mike. "You got a card?"

"Uh—" Mike hestiated. Was this some kind of trick? "Yeah, I usually carry a few. Why?"

"Let me see one."

After another hesitation, Mike pulled his wallet from his pocket, took out a card, and gave it to Greg.

"You got a pen?"

Puzzled, Mike took a ballpoint from his inside jacket pocket and handed it to Greg, who turned the card over to the blank side and scribbled on it. He handed it back. "Here's my phone number, in case you need to ask me any more mechanical questions."

Mike reclaimed the card and his pen. For some reason, his armpits had started to sweat. "Why, thanks, Greg. That's nice of you."

Greg laughed shortly. "I'm just a nice guy."

Mike downed the rest of his drink. "I have to go now. Great running into you, Greg. And thanks for your help."

"No problem."

Mike hurried from the bar and was relieved to find his car where he'd left it, undamaged. He drove off as fast as he dared, the card Greg had written his phone number on feeling as if it were burning a hole in his chest.

Mike finally talked Lucille into accompanying him to New York. During the weekend he managed not to think about Greg very much—except a little at night after Lucille had fallen asleep beside him. Had Greg really offered to disable the brakes on his wife's car, or was Mike's imagination working overtime? Half the time he believed Greg had said he'd do the job for fifteen or twenty thousand. The other half, Mike thought he was reading far too much into the exchange in the bar. Or that Greg was toying with him, stringing him along. Only one way to find out: Ask Greg outright. But did he dare? Surely there was another way—a way that didn't involve murder.

Although Mike had told Marcie he wouldn't be back in town until Monday, he and Lucille returned Sunday evening, and he spent the night in her apartment. The next morning, they left for work in separate cars. But before he walked out the door of her apartment, Lucille said,

"Mike, I don't think we should see each other for a while, at least until your divorce is final."

The words hit him like a knife in the chest. "Don't do this to me, Lucille. I love you. I have to be with you."

She studied him for a long moment. "Then get a divorce."

"I'll get Lance on it today," he said. "They should be able to serve the papers within a week."

She smiled then and kissed him. "See you at the office, darling."

Several times during the day, Mike reached for the phone to call his attorney and tell him to go ahead with the divorce, no matter what it cost. But each time, he pulled his hand away from the receiver, unable to make the call.

At four-thirty, he laid the card on which Greg had written his phone number on his desk and stared at it for several moments. Lucille came in to ask if he needed anything before she left—anything to do with business, she added with a provocative smile.

He said no, he'd see her tomorrow. When she was gone, he continued to sit at his desk and stare at that card. Finally, he realized that the office was quiet. Everybody had gone home. To make sure, he left his office and checked the other offices. He was alone on the floor. He went back to his office and dialed Greg's number.

On the third ring, a gruff voice answered. "Yeah?"

"Is this Greg?"

"Who wants to know?"

"This is Mike Riley."

"Yeah, Mr. Riley. What can I do for you?"

"I may have a job for you."

"What kind of job?"

"I'd need to explain it to you in person. Could you come to my office?"

"When?"

"Right now."

There was a brief pause. "Yeah, sure. It's not like I have a full schedule or anything. What's the address?"

Mike gave it to him, adding, "You can park in the alley behind and come in the back door." That way, the security guard wouldn't see him. "I'm on the sixth floor. I'll wait for you at the elevators."

"Be there in fifteen minutes, Mr. Riley."

L ess than twenty minutes later, Mike and Greg were closeted in Mike's office. "I've been thinking about our conversation in the bar," Mike said.

Greg just watched him and waited.

"That idea you had about loosening some kind of valves on a car to make the brakes fail."

"The bleed-off valves," Greg supplied.

"That's right." Mike hesitated. "Look, I have to be sure that this conversation is confidential. Can I depend on you not to repeat anything said here? It'll probably shock you."

He shrugged. "I can keep it quiet. But, Mr. Riley, I ain't stupid—like all those murderers in the joint. You ain't gonna shock me 'cause I already know what I'm here for. You ain't writing no book. You want me to fix your wife's car, loosen the bleed-off valves on the brake lines like we talked about, right?"

Mike swallowed hard before he said, "Let's say, just for the sake of discussion, that you're right. Are you interested in the job? For fifteen thousand, I believe you said."

Greg scratched his whiskery chin and seemed to think about it. "Yeah, I'm interested. But the price is twenty thou."

"You said—"

Greg interrupted. "Twenty thousand, Mr. Riley."

Mike sighed. "Okay. I'll give you five now, and the other fifteen when the job's done."

Greg shook his head. "Ten now."

There was a moment when Mike almost called the whole thing off. How did he know he could trust Greg? He didn't, but what other choice did he have? The unacceptable one of staying with Marcie and losing Lucille.

He went to the wall safe in his office and took out ten thousand dollars, leaving very little cash in the safe. He'd have to replenish it tomorrow. He handed the money to Greg, who counted it carefully, then stuffed it in his shirt pocket.

"I want you to do it late Saturday night, after midnight. My wife will be sound asleep by then," Mike said. "I'm planning to leave on a fishing trip Friday, about noon, and return on Sunday."

"You sure she'll use the car Sunday?"

"Positive. She always goes to the early service at her church. You sure the car's brakes will work the first couple times?"

"Yep."

Mike took out a plain sheet of paper and drew a map with directions to his house. "There's a double garage here, attached to the north end of the house. That's where I keep my car and my jeep, only I'll be using the jeep this weekend. The second garage is here behind the main house, attached to the guest house. My wife's Jaguar will be there, along with my golf cart. Don't try to open the overhead garage door. You'd need a garage door opener and, besides, it'd make too much noise. There's a door in back of this garage that's never locked. Go in that way."

Greg studied the map, then tucked it into his pocket with the money. "Anybody else live in your house besides you and your wife?"

"No, the housekeeper doesn't live in. She's off on the weekends, anyway."

He nodded. "Any dogs?"

"No, just a couple of cats, and they'll be in the house. There's a security system, but it only covers the main house and the garage attached to it. Oh, and park some distance away and walk in. A car motor might wake my wife." Mike realized that his heart had speeded up. Was he really arranging to have his wife murdered? What if he got caught? This Greg character could decide to black-mail him later. A million things could go wrong. But he thought about Lucille and only said, "Any more questions?"

"Yeah, when and where do I pick up the rest of my money?"

Mike thought for a moment. "How about Jack's Bar, Monday evening about six. It's so dark in there, I can slip you the money without anybody else being aware of it. And, Greg, after that, I don't want to see you again."

Greg stood and went to the office door. "I ain't gonna be looking for you after Monday, Mr. Riley. See you then."

As soon as Mike heard the elevator doors open and close again on the sixth floor, he phoned a couple of his friends and talked them into a fishing trip that weekend. He'd pick them up Friday afternoon and drop them back home on Sunday. *Okay,* he thought, as he prepared to leave for home, *I've set up my alibi.* He decided he wouldn't spring the fishing trip on Marcie until Thursday night. He'd tell her it was a spur-of-the-moment thing, blame it on one of his friends. Meantime, he'd plan a dinner out to celebrate their anniversary. He'd better get her a present, too. There was a boutique on the ground floor of the building next to his. Tomorrow he'd get a nice bottle of perfume. While he was at it, he'd get something for Lucille.

Full darkness had descended Sunday night by the time Mike had dropped off his two friends and headed up the mountain to his house. He was so nervous, his heart was beating like a jungle drum. The guardrail along the outside of the curving road would be broken in the place where Marcie's car went over, but it was too dark to see it. He wondered what her last thoughts were as she crashed to her death and, for a moment, he felt a stab of guilt. But he brushed it aside.

He punched the button on the garage door opener clipped to his sun visor, which opened the garage door and, at the same time, disabled the security system. He drove the Jeep into the garage and parked next to his Jaguar. He got out, leaving his suitcase and fishing gear to be dealt with later. Then he walked around behind the second garage, which was attached to the guest house, opened the door, and switched on the light. Marcie's car was gone. For several moments, he stood there as the full realization of what he'd done washed over him. He took several deep breaths to steady himself. It was done, and there was no going back now.

He went back to the house, entering via the door leading from the garage into the utility room. Feeling oddly like a stranger in his own home, he walked through all the rooms, satisfying a compulsive need to be certain Marcie wasn't there. Except for the cats, he was alone in the house. When he went into the bedroom he shared with Marcie he saw a folded piece of paper propped up on the dresser. He opened it and read:

Mike, It's Sunday morning and I'm about to leave for church. I've decided to drive over to Riverside after church and check into the spa overnight. I feel like being pampered—sort of an anniversary present to myself. I'll see you when you get home Monday night. Love, Marcie.

His hand was shaking by the time he got to the end. She'd never reached the church, not to mention the spa. It was sad, but he couldn't think about that. He'd planned to start calling people when he got home and found her gone, like a worried husband. But with the note, he couldn't start to act worried until Monday night. No, wait. If he could see where she went off the mountain on his drive to work tomorrow morning, it would be natural to stop and look down. He might be able to see her car. Even if he couldn't, the broken guardrail would be enough reason for a concerned husband to call the police.

He slept very little that night. His head was full of what he'd say, how he'd act when he was told his wife was dead. He'd have to play the grieving husband for a few months before he started seeing Lucille openly. But she'd understand that. And he'd still have the house, the company, everything to share with his true love.

He finally gave up trying to sleep and rose before dawn to make himself a big breakfast of bacon, eggs, and biscuits from a refrigerated can. Odd how nervous excitement affected people. Some would be unable to swallow a bite; as for Mike, he was as hungry as if he hadn't eaten in days.

After breakfast, he left the dirty dishes in the sink and got dressed. He waited until the sun came up to leave for the office. Where would he find the broken railing? On the first curve? Halfway down? No farther along than that, he felt sure—you had to brake numerous times by the halfway mark.

He tossed his briefcase into his Jag and backed out of the garage. He'd make the drive down the mountain even slower than usual so he wouldn't miss the broken railing. Briefly, as he reversed and circled to head down, he had a mental picture of Marcie's car diving off the mountain, her mouth open, her eyes wide with shock and terror. He gripped the steering wheel and shook the image away. Couldn't think about that. He made the first curve and was well into the second. This time, when he braked, he pushed the pedal all the way to the floor. For an instant, the car slowed, but then it gathered speed and he pumped the brake pedal furiously, with no effect. My God! What was happening?

He had enough presence of mind to switch off the engine, but the car still didn't slow. In a panic, he jerked on the emergency brake. It didn't hold. The Jag hurtled downward as he fought to make the curves without power steering and keep the car on the road. Damn Greg! He'd fixed the wrong car! But how could that be? He'd drawn a map for Greg, marked a big X on the garage attached to the guest house where Marcie's car would be.

There was no more time to think, as he started around another curve and couldn't keep the Jag away from the edge. Frantically, he fumbled with his seat belt. His only chance was to jump out of the car. He reached for the door handle, but it was too late. The Jag's back wheels left the road, and the car went into a nose dive. Sky and trees raced by and Mike realized he was screaming. Then came the impact and blackness engulfed him.

Silence. A faint antiseptic smell. He struggled to open his eyes. Where was he? He lay on his back, a white acoustical tile ceiling above him. He struggled to sit up and pain shot through his head. He groaned.

"Mike?"

Carefully, he turned his head toward the sound. Marcie rose from a chair beside his bed. *Where am I?* he tried to say, but nothing but a garbled whisper came out.

"Don't try to talk, honey." She straightened the sheet across his chest. "You're in a hospital. You've been sedated for three days. I need to go tell the nurse you've regained consciousness."

She left, and Mike tried to remember what had happened to him. How had he ended up in a hospital? He recalled arranging with an ex-con to have his wife murdered, and then he'd left on a fishing trip. When he came home, he found Marcie gone—dead in her car at the foot of the mountain, he'd assumed. He'd left for work the next morning, and that's the last thing he remembered. Except—he'd dreamed he was falling off the mountain in his Jaguar. Or had it really happened?

Panic rose in his chest. He had to get out of there! He tried to sit up, but he couldn't. He couldn't move! The panic threatened to choke him. *Just stay calm,* he told himself. He heard the noise of his own labored breathing and made himself take deep breaths.

Why couldn't he move? Did they have him in restraints? He tried to raise his hand to feel what they had him tied down with. But his arm wouldn't obey the mental command. In fact, he couldn't even feel his arms, his legs either. The only feeling he was conscious of was in his head, where a headache hammered relentlessly.

Oh, dear God, no! Please, no, no! I'm paralyzed!

He heard footsteps, and Marcie came back into the room, followed by a nurse and a man in a white coat. "Good morning, Mr. Riley," the man said heartily. "I'm Dr. Worth. You decided to return to the land of the living, I see."

Mike opened his mouth and struggled to speak.

"Take it easy now," Dr. Worth said. "You may have a little trouble with your speech at first, but it should come back."

With what felt like superhuman effort, Mike gasped out, "Tell me—" It sounded funny, not like his voice at all.

"Good!" the doctor said. "You're talking already."

"Tell me—" Mike managed again.

The doctor exchanged a glance with Marcie, who stared back for a moment and then nodded. The doctor said, "You lost control of your car on the mountain, Mr. Riley. Your spinal cord was severed. Your wife says you've always faced problems head-on, so I'll be frank. You're paralyzed from the neck down. But we can do amazing things in rehab these days. An electric wheel-chair will help you be somewhat mobile, so don't despair."

Don't despair? My God, he wanted to die!

Marcie placed a hand on his forehead. "I'll always be here for you, sweetheart. We'll handle this together."

Mike closed his eyes to shut out her face. "He needs to rest," the doctor said. "Mrs. Riley, I'd like to talk to you outside for a minute."

He heard them leave the room, heard the soft thud of

the door closing behind them. He was exhausted from the effort of speaking a few words and slipped immediately into sleep.

When he awoke, it was dark outside the window on the wall opposite where he lay, and somebody was standing beside his bed. "Mr. Riley?"

He squinted to make out the face. It was Greg! "You!" Mike whispered. "You fixed the wrong car!"

"I fixed the Jaguar in the garage next to the guest quarters, just like you said. There was a golf cart in the other space. You must've got mixed up and drove your wife's car."

"No, I didn't! It was my car—and the brakes failed!" Merely speaking took so much energy that Mike felt himself slipping toward unconsciousness again. He fought to stay awake.

"All I know is I went to the garage you marked on the map, and I fixed the only car in it. So you owe me ten thousand."

Mike stared at him with disbelief. "You owe me, you damned fool!"

Greg moved closer, so that Mike could see his face and those cold eyes. "I want my money, Mr. Riley."

"No! Now, get out of my room!"

"If I don't get my money, you'll regret it. The way you are, you're a sitting duck now. I could kill you any time."

A hysterical laugh bubbled up in Mike's throat. "Kill me? Go ahead! Do it right now! I'd rather be dead than like this."

Greg stared down at him for an instant, then went away, leaving Mike to ponder what he'd said. The man had fixed Marcie's car, yet Marcie was unhurt and Mike was worse than dead. He couldn't understand how it could have happened. But he was too tired to figure it out now.

His eyes drifted closed. He'd sleep, and maybe when he woke up . . .

"Mike?"

At the sound of Lucille's voice, his eyes flew open. She placed a hand on him somewhere—his shoulder, he thought—but he couldn't feel it.

"How are you?" she asked.

"Lucille?" he whispered. He wanted to touch her, but he couldn't.

"I haven't come before because Marcie was always here. But she's been in your office all afternoon. She's still there."

"At the office?'

"She says she's going to have to run the company now, so she better get started. Listen, Mike, there's something I need to ask you. After you left on your fishing trip, I found a voice-activated tape recorder behind some papers in the credenza in your office. Did you put it there?"

"No," he said wearily. What did a tape recorder matter now?

"Well, I didn't put it there, either. I checked Monday morning when I got to the office, and it was gone. So, if neither of us did it, it had to be Marcie, and while you were at the cabin, she retrieved it. I wish I'd taken the tape out when I found it, but I thought you must have installed the machine to record business conversations, so I left the tape."

"But, why—when?"

Lucille shrugged. "Maybe Marcie suspected something was going on between you and me; I don't know."

"Didn't you say she was alone in my office a week or two ago?"

She thought about it. "Yes, that must've been when she did it. She was in there fifteen or twenty minutes alone, and she was carrying a big shopping bag full of stuff. And that means—" Lucille expelled a long breath. "That means she heard us talking when you came back from your lawyer's office that day. She knows you were planning to divorce her, which is why she did what she did."

"What—what did she do?"

"She fired me this afternoon. She gave me a month's severance pay and told me to clean out my desk."

Mike tried to assimilate what she was saying. Marcie knew about him and Lucille? If so, then she also knew . . . Mike groaned and closed his eyes. Marcie had heard him arranging with Greg to disable the brakes on her car.

"Mike," Lucille was saying, "I'm going to move back to Phoenix, so I probably won't see you again. I'm so sorry about what's happened. I wish—" She shook her head. "No point in wishing. I have to go now." She bent over and placed a soft kiss on his forehead. "Good-bye, Mike."

Mike lay awake for some time after she was gone, trying to understand how his car, which had been parked in its usual place, had been the one to go off the mountain, but his brain didn't seem to be working as well as usual. He finally fell asleep at dawn.

They woke him up to serve breakfast. Marcie was there again, and she punched something on the side of the bed to raise him to a sitting position. Then she began to feed him.

"The girls were here right after—after it happened. They'll come for a visit after you leave the hospital." Mike didn't respond. She went on, "I've been trying to get things organized at the office. I met with your vice presidents today, and I'm sure, with their help, I can manage things. So don't worry about the business, dear. I can do a lot of the work at home, and I'll find a good live-in nurse to be with you when I'm gone."

He stared at her face as she talked. He had no clue what she was thinking. Sometime during the night, he'd figured out what must have happened. While he was gone fishing, Marcie had used her key to get into the company building and had retrieved the recorder and the tape that contained his conversations with Lucille over the past couple of weeks, as well as his conversation with Greg.

After she listened to the tape, she must have switched his Jag to her garage and put his car where hers usually was parked. Greg came late Saturday night and loosened the valves on the brake lines on the car parked in the garage next to the guest house—*his* car. Then Sunday morning, Marcie had switched the cars again. She could have driven his car slowly back to its usual parking place and she would only have had to tap the brakes once, when she stopped the car in the garage.

After arranging for her husband's plunge off the mountain, she'd gone blithely off to church—and then to that spa in Riverside, he supposed. When he didn't show up at the office on Monday, Lucille would have tried to find him. Perhaps she finally called the police or maybe somebody driving on the mountain road saw his car. Then Marcie returned home, learned he'd been taken to the hospital, and went into concerned-wife mode. She must've been disappointed to find out he wasn't dead. But he might as well be.

She smiled at him. "You're awfully quiet this morning, Mike." He wondered why he'd never noticed before that she had calculating eyes. "We have to look at the bright side, darling. We're going to be spending a lot more time together from now on."

He wanted to recoil from her, but he was at her mercy. He'd be at her mercy for the rest of his life.

SECRETS

Carolyn Hart

Carolyn Hart writes two mystery series. She shares her enthusiasm for all mysteries in the Death on Demand titles, which feature the detecting duo of mystery bookstore owner Annie Laurance Darling and her unflappable husband Max. Hart offers an exuberant view of age in her Henrie O series. Retired reporter Henrietta O'Dwyer (Henrie O) Collins has a talent for trouble and a taste for adventure. Hart's most recent Death on Demand mystery is Sugarplum Dead. *Her new Henrie O mystery is* Resort to Murder. *Hart is the author of more than thirty mystery and suspense novels, including several stand-alone titles that have recently been republished. Hart's books have won the three major awards for traditional mysteries: the Agatha, the Anthony, and the Macavity. She is a past president of Sisters in Crime and a member of the Authors Guild, the Mystery Writers of America, and the American Crime Writers League. For an update on her most recent books, click www.carolynhart.com.*

Gretchen slid onto the hard metal stool at the soda fountain. She held tight to her nickel, enough for a cherry fausfade, her most favorite drink in the world, especially on a hot July day when the red liquid in the old tin thermometer on Main Street edged over a hundred and the breeze rustling the cottonwoods felt like hot molasses against her skin. She opened her mouth to order, knowing Millard would answer in his precise way, "Cherry phosphate, Gretchen." It was a favorite joke, and she would say again, emphasizing the sounds, "Cherry fausfade." He would smile his sweet, gentle smile. She would grin and say firmly, "It sounds like "fausfade" to *me,*" in the same tone as Miss Carstairs calling home room to attention.

Millard was there all right, slumped on a high wooden stool behind the cash register, but his round head topped by tight red curls rested on arms folded on the counter.

Gretchen darted a quick look toward the back of the drugstore. Mr. Thompson must be in back filling prescriptions. Millard's dad was strict as anything, and if he caught Millard asleep behind the counter . . . She reached out and pushed on Millard's shoulder.

"Wha-wha-wha—" Millard's head jerked up and his eyes were as dull and glazed as the rheumy old hog out at Aunt Lela's farm.

"Millard!" Gretchen's whisper was sharp.

Millard blinked. His round, freckled face looked bone tired like pictures she'd seen in the newsreels of soldiers on Bataan before it fell. Grandmother cried the night they saw those pictures. They'd gone to the Bijou to see *Mrs. Miniver.* Gretchen knew Grandmother was thinking about Jimmy and hoping his face didn't look like that: dirty, with eyes dull as lumps of coal. Jimmy was in the South Pacific, and his last letter home didn't say much except thanks for the cookies and popcorn and he sure hoped the war would be over soon and he could come home. Gretchen and Millard had been friends for a long time, since Millard was seven and she was four, and they played together because their big brothers, Jimmy and Mike, were good friends and let them tag along when they took a .22 into the woods to pop tin cans.

Millard had turned sixteen last week, though he looked older because he was so big, already six feet tall and still growing. He'd be four years older for a little while until her birthday next month when she would be thirteen. She would start junior high this fall, and when she thought about it, she was pleased and scared.

Millard was always making funny drawings, and once he'd given her a picture he'd drawn of himself, a round pink face with bright red curls and big freckles and a grin big as a carved pumpkin mouth. This afternoon, his skin was as white as library paste and his plump cheeks sagged. There was no trace of his sweet smile.

"Are you sick?" Gretchen whispered, keeping an eye on the door to the back of the store. She'd seen Mr. Thompson mad once, and the memory still made her stomach curl into a hard ball. Ever since the fighting in Italy got so bad and no letters came from Mike, Mr. Thompson walked with his head down and his shoulders bunched. He'd stopped coming over to the café for lunch. Gretchen could remember him coming in for lunch ever since she was a little girl. Mrs. Thompson taught math in the junior high. In the summers, she worked at the store, too. Mike had always jerked sodas, but when he went to war, Millard took his place, learning how to make brown cows and Hobokens and black-and-whites. And cherry phosphates.

The war had changed everything, turned Grandmother's little café from the Pfizer Café to Victory Café, sent Gretchen's mom off to Tulsa to work in the Mc-Donnell Douglas plant, made Gretchen a girl-of-all work, able to peel potatoes, wait tables, mop floors, wash dishes, carry out garbage, whatever needed to be done, whatever she could do to take the burden off Grandmother. In the hot summer afternoons, if they didn't have a late rush of customers, Grandmother insisted Gretchen go to Thompson's for her cherry phosphate, and sometimes she'd get a copy of the new movie magazine. Her favorite actress was Jennifer Jones, and she was from Oklahoma, too!

Everything should have been just like always, the whirr of the ceiling fans, the smell of ice cream, she and Millard reflected in the shiny mirror behind the counter with its rows of Coca-Cola glasses and sundae glasses. Instead, Millard blinked, his eyes dull, and his voice had a hollow sound like a long distance call from her mother.

"No. I'm okay. Cherry phosphate?" He thudded off the stool, moved to the fountain and the big spigots.

Gretchen nodded. Seltzer hissed into the tall glass, turning the thick cherry syrup into dancing pink liquid. Millard placed the glass in front of her. Before the war, his big brother Mike would have slapped down a paper doily and announced, "One cherry phosphate," and plopped the glass in the center of the white mat. But for the duration, there were no more paper doilies. Every month there was a paper drive and another for tin cans. She and Grandmother kept all the newspapers left by customers and washed each tin can and peeled off the paper. Usually Millard kept the marble counter sparkling clean. Today he didn't notice the spatters on the counter.

Gretchen sipped, wrinkling her nose at the fizz, savoring the tart cherry taste. "Are you worried about Mike?"

Millard's round face swung toward her. He rubbed his eyes. "We haven't heard from him for a month. My folks are scared." He yawned.

The door to the back of the store banged open. Mr. Thompson poked his head out, the overhead light shining on his bald head. His bony face was long like a horse. Big, black, tufty eyebrows creased into a dark frown above pale, cold eyes. "Millard!" His voice was sharp.

Millard hunched his shoulders. Big as he was, he suddenly seemed smaller. "Yes, sir."

"Come here." Mr. Thompson sounded like a man staring at a wall cloud in a dark spring sky. He lifted a thin hand to rub against his forehead.

Millard closed the door when he stepped into the back, but the arched window for prescriptions was open.

"Millard," Mr. Thompson's voice wavered. "You said nobody came in the store this morning while I went to the bank."

"I didn't see anybody." Millard almost sounded like his old, precise self except for his voice, hollow as an echo from the bottom of a dry well.

Gretchen gulped at her drink, then pushed the half-full glass away. She slapped her nickel on the counter by the cash register and hurried toward the front of the store, covering her ears to block out Mr. Thompson's angry shout.

The booths were full and the counter, too. Gretchen worked fast. Somehow word had got around about meat loaf today. Often the butcher shop was full of empty trays, even if you had enough points in the ration book to buy. But today they had ground beef. Gretchen had chopped onions until her eyes watered and her nose itched, onions and green peppers and celery. Grandmother used fresh tomatoes for the sauce. The café had a holiday air. Talk was so loud, Gretchen strained to hear when she took orders. Everybody ordered the special, meat loaf with mashed potatoes and green beans (Grandmother added a dash of nutmeg to her beans), coffee or iced tea, and watermelon for dessert. Grandmother bustled from the kitchen to help serve, blond hair slipping from her coronet braids to frame her dumpling plump face, always a little pink and now flushed from the heat of the kitchen and the long morning's work.

Gretchen didn't try to lift a loaded tray. They were too heavy for her. Instead, she carried a plate in each hand and sped back and forth from the kitchen to the booths and the tables. Even though her legs were beginning to ache and she'd burned a blister on her left palm when she raised the lid on the big pot of boiling potatoes, she felt happy. Everybody loved Grandmother's cooking. Of course, the businessmen in town knew they could count on Grandmother. Gretchen saw the usual faces in booth three, everyone but Mr. Thompson. In booth one, even the serious-faced army officers from Camp Crowder were exclaiming over their lunch. Good food made everybody happy. Gretchen listened to the din of conversations, especially pleased when she overheard a compliment to Grandmother's cooking.

Booth one, the army men: ". . . best meat loaf I've ever . . ."

Booth two, a bunch of farmers over from the sale barn: ". . . always come here for lunch when I'm in town. Used to be called Pfizer's . . ."

Booth three, Mr. Kraft, the banker; Mr. Willet, the barber; Mr. Douglas, the insurance salesman: ". . . apparently Millard ran away last night . . ."

Gretchen was on her way to get coffee. She kept on walking, grabbed up the pot. She refilled the cups at booth one but strained to hear Mr. Kraft. ". . . Bert called to see if Julie knew where he could be. Millard's followed Julie around like a tail to a kite for years."

The other men nodded. The Thompsons lived on Jefferson across from the Krafts in a two-story white Victorian house. Jefferson was the best street in town. It had sidewalks and iron fences and big old elms. Julie Kraft was the prettiest girl in town, blue eyes soft as a spring sky and shiny blond hair that curled in a Ginger Rogers pageboy. All the boys looked at Julie, especially at Shady Grove Lake when she wore her Catalina swimsuit. Gretchen wished she could look like Julie instead of having straight black hair in pigtails and dark blue eyes and skinny legs. But that was as likely as she and Grandmother ever moving to Jefferson Street. Their street, Archer, was just a dirt road. An alley ran behind their house and the back of the Thompson house.

At booth two, Gretchen bent her head to listen to the businessmen in the next booth.

Mr. Willet swiped a piece of meat loaf through the tomato sauce. "Mighty good today." He gave a small belch. "Don't sound much like Millard. He's been in my Scout troop ever since he was little. Made Eagle Scout last year."

Gretchen reached booth three.

"Bert was real upset." Mr. Kraft held out his cup.

"What'd Julie say?" Mr. Douglas played golf a lot, and his face was as red as a summer sunset. When he walked down Main, he spoke to everybody he passed.

Mr. Kraft stared into the dark, hot coffee like it was a bubbling volcano, his jowly face as blank as the round stone statues in a *National Geographic*. "Julie," he spoke his daughter's name as if the syllables didn't fit his tongue, "don't say much anymore. Ever since that good for nothin' Lewis boy—" His thick lips pressed together tighter than a box turtle slamming shut his shell.

Mr. Douglas glanced at the banker with shrewd, kindly eyes and boomed, "Did you hear the report on the radio last night about the P-40s? They said . . ."

Gretchen moved to booth four, automatically refilled

cups, stacked four plates, and headed for the kitchen. She
looked up at the round clock behind the counter. At least
another hour before she could hurry down the sidewalk
to the drugstore. She worked faster than ever, her dark
brows drawn in a frown. Millard run away? She felt shivery to her bones, like stepping out of the hot kitchen into
a sleet-edged February wind.

The shivery feeling spread from Gretchen's bones to
her heart when she looked into Mrs. Thompson's red-
rimmed eyes. Gretchen stood beside the metal stool at the
soda fountain. Gretchen heard the faint drip of water in
the deep sink and the whirr of the ceiling fans and old
Mrs. McClure's hoarse voice complaining to Mr. Thompson about the taste of the cough syrup he'd fixed up for
her last week.

"Millard?" Gretchen was scared to ask, but she had to
know.

Mrs. Thompson usually had a sweet smile, too, just
like Millard's. Today her face was puffy and lopsided like
a stepped-on pincushion. Her eyes filled with tears and
her lips trembled. "He's gone, Gretchen. He's gone."

"But where?" Gretchen clung to the marble counter.

"We don't know. Oh, Gretchen, I didn't believe it. I
didn't. Not my sweet Millard. Not until we found the
money—"

"That's enough, Rose." At the end of the counter, Mr.
Thompson bent forward like a black crow. "There's nothing to be said. Millard's gone. Good riddance. If your eye
offends thee . . ." He turned away, tears edging down his
cavernous cheeks.

*　　*　　*

Victory Café was closed on Sundays. Grandmother always fixed Sunday dinner, even though it was just the two of them. Gretchen wished she wouldn't. The kitchen table in its Sunday best was surrounded by ghosts. Every time Gretchen looked at the third seat on the right, she saw Jimmy, winking at her and sneaking a piece of meat from his plate to hand under the table to Walter, his springer spaniel. Walter died last March. Gretchen thought he died of a broken heart because Jimmy was gone, though Grandmother said he was twelve and old for a spaniel. They hadn't told Jimmy, and in every letter he asked about Walter, said to be sure and make hush puppies for him since Jimmy wasn't there to take him hunting and sit around a campfire.

"Ve haf chicken today." Grandmother still wore her navy silk dress from church.

Gretchen looked across the table and tried to smile. But she hadn't been able to smile this whole long week.

Grandmother knew, of course. "I'm sorry, *mein schatz.*" Her kind face looked unaccustomedly stern. "I would not haf beliefed it of Millard. He should not so treat his mama and papa. And to do such a bad thing! No more do ve talk about him. Here Gretchen, haf a leg I fix so fine for you."

"Millard wouldn't do anything bad." Gretchen's voice wobbled. Tears burned her eyes.

Grandmother's face softened. "I know. He vas your friend so gut. Ve vill not speak more."

Gretchen didn't go to Thompson's anymore in the afternoons for a cherry fausfade. She didn't mind working hard. She liked the crackle of grease on the grill and the smell of fried meat—when they had any—and stewed okra and tomatoes and, occasionally, apple pies. She liked polishing the tables at the end of the day and rolling clean silverware in red-and-white checked napkins and pushing the wheelbarrow with trash to the incinerator. That was the last thing she did every day. It was so hot now as the days rolled into August that the glazed sky steamed, and it hurt to touch the metal of the wheelbarrow. Gretchen kept on working and listening to the snatches of conversation, like turning the dial on the radio:

". . . ought to take John L. Lewis out and string him up to . . ."

". . . Emma Whittle don't go anywhere now, not since they got word about Billy. Oh, you knew that, didn't you? Billy got killed at Kasserine Pass. She . . ."

". . . the murder of Sir Harry Oakes had to be an inside job."

". . . what will happen now that Mussolini's gone?"

No one talked about Millard, and every time someone played "Stardust" on the jukebox, she felt sad. "Stardust" was Millard's favorite song because Julie Kraft sang it at the Fourth of July picnic.

By the third week in August, the cicadas rasped so loud she couldn't hear the whine of the big trucks on Highway 66. It was Saturday night, and the pile of trash and garbage would take at least two trips to the incinerator. Little cracks and crevices ridged the yellowish dirt in the alley behind the café. Gretchen moved slowly. She'd started the day in a fresh white Ship 'n' Shore blouse and pink pedal pushers. Spatters of spaghetti sauce trailed across the front of her blouse. When she mopped the kitchen, water from the bucket left a big wet patch on her pants. Maybe there would be time to ride her bike out to Shady Grove Lake for a swim before supper. But she was so tired. She shuffled toward the wheelbarrow leaning against the back wall. The alley was empty and Grandmother was already home, so Gretchen didn't have to act like she wasn't tired. Ever since her mother had gone off to Tulsa to work in the war plant, Gretchen had taken over closing down the café.

Gretchen stood on tiptoe to pull down the handles, careful not to touch the hot metal sides. She swung the wheelbarrow around and squinted against the sunlight glancing off the metal bed. When she dropped the legs next to the garbage pail, she took cotton work gloves from her pocket and pulled them on. She grabbed the edges of the garbage can, tipped it toward the barrow. The refuse slid forward. A cloud of flies swirled around her. She glanced at the wheelbarrow and saw a piece of brown cardboard stuck to the bottom of the bed with white adhesive tape. Slowly she righted the can, flapped her hands at the buzzing flies.

Her mind felt dull. But somebody had put the brown cardboard there, made it stay with bandage tape. Puzzled, she reached down, pulled away the tape, picked up the irregular piece of cardboard. Letters were printed on one side: m Beam. She turned it over. The message was simple:

Gretchen, meet me at midnight at the Fort.

There was no signature, only the drawing of a round face with tight curls.

Car lights flashed over the hill. Gretchen jumped into the ditch and crouched there until the car chugged past. It would be bad if anybody saw her out on Purdy

Road and told Grandmother. But once she got past the
Hansen farm, she didn't have to worry about being seen.
She'd take the path that plunged into the woods. She held
tight to a flashlight, but the full moon was so bright, she
might not need the light.

The wavery cry of an owl made her skin prickle. She'd
never come this way at night. Before the war, when she
and Millard were little, they'd found a deserted shack near
Piney Creek and made it into a fort. Millard pretended to
be in the cavalry and she was a pioneer woman. Once
they'd built a fire and made biscuits that were doughy in
the middle and had black edges. Gretchen didn't think she
would have liked being a pioneer woman, especially after
Millard told her how the Indians sometimes swooped
down and scalped everybody they caught. He said the
movies never showed how the pioneers took the land
away from the Indians. In fourth grade, Gretchen learned
about the Trail of Tears and the Five Civilized Tribes who
were moved to Indian Territory, pushed out of land the
white man wanted. Lots of the kids were part Cherokee.
Gretchen thought Gloria Walkingstick had the most beautiful dark brown eyes she'd ever seen.

The path curled around a stand of cottonwoods and
dipped toward the creek. A soft light glowed in the open
doorway of the shack.

Gretchen ran. "Millard?"

"Hey, Gretchen." He sounded like Millard. Almost.
But his voice was kind of choked and happy and sad all
at once. "You came."

She skidded to a stop in the doorway. Millard waited
just inside. He was thinner, and his eyes were tired. His
cream shirt had a stain on it—she'd never seen Millard
that he wasn't neat as a pin—and his Levi's looked grimy.
The dirt floor of the shack had been swept, and there was

a sleeping bag rolled up in a corner. A wooden crate held some bottles and cans.

They stared at each other, then both talked at once.

"Why did you run away?"

"You didn't tell anybody about the fort?"

And then were both silent.

Gretchen hated the emptiness of the fort. Maybe it had been fun when they were kids, but was this where Millard was staying? All by himself? With scraps to eat? And no books. Millard read books all the time.

Millard pointed at a log outside the door. "We can sit there."

They sat down, and the moon painted the trees and ground with cream.

"Millard, your mama is so sad." She stared at his round face and wished the light were brighter. His features were indistinct, and his hair looked dark, not red.

"But not my dad." His voice was bitter.

"Was he mad because you said nobody came that day?" Gretchen had been over it and over it in her mind, and she didn't understand. Why would that make Mr. Thompson so mad?

"I fell asleep. Once I kind of heard something and I almost woke up, but I was so tired. Later I thought about it, and I know somebody was there and it was somebody I knew. But I can't remember what it was that made me think so."

"You mean somebody came and you didn't see them? Were you afraid to tell your dad you were asleep? How come you were so tired?" Gretchen remembered Millard slumped against the counter and the way he'd trembled awake.

"Somebody came while I was asleep and stole a whole

bottle of morphine tablets. That's a strong medicine. It's the kind people steal and sell for money."

Money. Gretchen heard Mrs. Thompson's voice, ". . . not until we found the money . . ."

Gretchen moved uneasily on the log, felt the ridge of bark against her legs. "You had some money."

"Yeah. I did. Money I worked for—"

She grabbed his arm. "Why didn't you tell your dad, explain that you were asleep, that you'd earned money?" She frowned. "How did you earn money, Millard?" He worked at the store all day in the summers and every day after school in the winter.

"The Blue Light." His voice was defiant. "It's—"

"I know." Actually, she didn't know much about it, just enough to cross to the other side of the road when she biked past the dance hall on her way out to Aunt Lela's farm to pick up eggs or honey or fresh vegetables. "Oh, golly." No wonder Millard didn't tell his father. Mr. Thompson was a deacon at the First Baptist Church, and he was real strong against dancing and alcohol. Everybody knew bootleg whiskey was easy to get at the Blue Light.

"They needed somebody in the band. Everybody's been drafted, and I can play the saxophone. I worked every night until midnight and then we'd clean up and I didn't get home until two and then I had to get up early . . ."

Gretchen was sure Millard played the saxophone real well. He played a lot of instruments, but he had to play the tuba in the band because he was big and strong enough to carry it.

She stared at the shadowed face. "Your dad thought you sold that stuff to somebody?"

"Yes." The single word bristled with anger and hurt.

Gretchen snapped off a piece of bark from the log, twisted it in her fingers. "You played in the band and you were tired. You fell asleep, and somebody stole that medicine. But Millard, if you'd told your folks, they might've been mad, but—"

"If I told them," and his voice was drained, "it would have meant I couldn't go to the Blue Light anymore. And I almost had enough money. I almost did! I ran away, but I was going to go home that night and get my money—I hid it in my sock drawer—but when I got close to the house, I heard Dad yelling at Mom, and he was saying I was worse than a thief, I was bad and I wasn't any son of his, not anymore."

"Millard, you should have told them. How could they know you didn't take money if you didn't tell them!"

"I shouldn't have had to tell them."

She understood. How could his dad have believed him to be a thief? But the stuff was gone, and there was money in Millard's sock drawer. "A lot of money?"

Millard was always quick. "Twenty-three dollars."

"Millard!" That was enough money to buy a new coat and shoes and a couple of dresses.

"I had to earn it all again." He jumped up, hurried into the shack. He came back with a wad of money in his hand. "I've got enough. It's for Julie."

Gretchen stared at the money. "But Julie's rich." Julie's father owned the bank and they lived in the biggest house in town and Mr. Kraft drove a black Cadillac, one of the last ones made before the factories turned to making tanks.

Millard thrust the money toward her. "I used to watch Julie at band practice and she—" He broke off, shook his head. "She's so beautiful." There was awe in his voice. He sounded the way Gretchen felt the day she and Millard came up over a rise and saw a valley blanketed by monarchs, and it was so beautiful her heart almost stopped. "When Julie comes into the room, it's like a sunrise or the smell of wheat after the rain. So clean and good."

Gretchen knew about love, the way she felt when her mother called and told her how brave she was to help Grandmother, the look in Grandmother's eyes when Gretchen won the spelling bee, the long-ago memory of her father tucking her into bed and singing a lullaby. But this was something different.

"Julie loves Buzzy Lewis." Millard spoke in his precise way, reporting a fact. "Her folks won't let her marry him. He's going overseas pretty soon. If Julie had enough money, she could take the bus to Georgia."

The cicadas rasped so loud it almost sounded like the clack of train wheels.

"Gretchen," his voice broke, "please."

Gretchen loved the library, the musty smell of books, the shine of the hardwood floors, the big casement windows that were cranked wide in the summer, and the welcoming smile of Mrs. Parker, who helped Gretchen find all kinds of wonderful books, like *The Man in the Iron Mask* and *Treasure Island*. After the clatter and bustle of the café, Gretchen loved the peace of the library, the silence broken only by the snap of shoes on the floor and the rustle of paper and the whirr of ceiling fans. She went to the desk with her books: *Lad, a Dog, My Friend Flicka*, and *The Count of Monte Cristo*.

As she walked toward the fiction stacks, she searched the reading room, darted glances down the long rows. Julie Kraft stood on a step stool in the second row, shelving books. Sun slanted through a west window, turning her hair to gold.

Gretchen turned into the aisle, hurried up to Julie. Gretchen touched the envelope in her pocket.

Julie looked down. "Hi, Gretchen. Can I help you find something?" Her voice was kind of husky like June Allyson's. She looked directly into Gretchen's eyes, really looked, making Gretchen feel taller and older and special. Julie's light blue eyes had a dark blue edge. Her face was thinner than Gretchen remembered from school. Her pink cotton sundress didn't have a single wrinkle.

Gretchen looked around, then bent forward and whispered, "I have something for you from Millard."

"Millard!" Julie clapped a hand over her mouth. She glanced toward the reading room, but no one came. "Oh." Now her husky voice was low. "I'm so glad. Is he back?"

"No." The word felt as hard as a cherry pit in Gretchen's mouth. She pulled out the envelope. "He wants you to have this. He says it's enough money so that you can go to Buzzy."

Julie's face moved from shock to wonder to despair. It was like watching fireworks, the beginning flicker in the sky, the shower of sparks, the blinding brilliance, and then the fading clusters and light dimming to darkness. She stared at the envelope, her lovely eyes darkening. "They say Millard sold drugs."

"He didn't." No snake ever hissed harder. "No, he didn't, Julie. He's been playing in the band at the Blue Light. Somebody else stole the drugs. Millard had money, and he couldn't tell his dad how he got it because it was for you. He ran away and he worked more and now he has enough again."

"For me?" Julie pressed her hands together. "Millard

did that?" Not fireworks this time, but the soft glow of moonrise.

"He wants you to be happy." More than he wanted to come home. More than he wanted to be in his room with its bunk beds and posters of the periodic elements and constellations and world map. More than he wanted to work behind the fountain and jerk sodas as good as his brother had.

Julie sat down on the step stool, buried her face in her hands. Her shoulders shook.

Gretchen reached out, touched Julie's arm. "He wouldn't want you to cry."

Julie lifted her face. Tears rolled down her cheeks. "I want to go so bad. I want to be with Buzzy. But I can't take the money. Please, tell Millard I can't take his money."

"It's not from drugs." Gretchen would have stamped her foot, but Mrs. Parker might hear.

Julie used her fingers to wipe away the tears. "I believe you. I told everyone that Millard wouldn't do that. And he could play in anybody's band. But," she sniffed, "it isn't right to take Millard's money."

"Because you aren't related?" If Millard was Julie's brother that would make it all right. Or even if maybe Millard was a girl. Or did Julie turn the money down because it wasn't right to ask other people for money? Not unless it was the bank. . . . "You could borrow the money."

"Borrow—" Julie tasted the word like new food.

Millard wanted Julie to be happy. If he were here . . . Gretchen held out the envelope. "You can borrow it. And when you get there and get married—" when people were married, their husbands paid their bills—"you can send the money back to Millard."

*   *   *

Millard pulled the Coke bottles out of a tub with ice in it. "Want a Coke, Gretchen?"

"Sure." It was funny to drink anything after midnight.

He used the bottle opener, snapped off the caps. "How did Julie look?" He kept his tone casual except for the way he said her name, as if the syllables clung to his tongue.

"Pretty. She had on a pink dress. She almost didn't take the money—"

His head jerked toward her.

"—but finally she said she would borrow it. Millard, I've never seen anybody so happy."

He sat down on the log and looked at the water of the creek. "I wonder when she'll get to Georgia."

Gretchen knew he wasn't really asking.

He picked up a rock, tossed it into the water. "Will you come tell me if you hear?"

Gretchen frowned. "Millard, aren't you going to come home now?"

He drank some Coke. "I can't go back. I still don't know who took the morphine. My dad wouldn't believe me now, especially since I ran away."

"You can't stay out here." In the moonlight, the shack looked almost pretty, but the door was half off its hinges, and the windows were broken. "It will get cold. And you don't have any clothes. Or anything."

"I got a sleeping bag. Mrs. Hopper loaned it to me. She's real nice. She owns the Blue Light. But I'm not staying much longer. I've almost got enough money to go—" He broke off. "Don't worry, Gretchen. A lot of guys join up early. Sometimes recruiters don't even ask to see a birth certificate. I'll find one that needs to meet a quota."

Gretchen brought the pitcher of iced tea to booth three. It was like church; people always sat in the same places.

Mr. Douglas clapped his hands, good humored but exasperated. "Wake up, girl; we asked for coffee."

"I'm sorry." She hurried to the serving stand, used a hot pad to pick up the heavy pot. She better start minding her p's and q's. Even grandmother'd asked this morning if she had her head in the clouds. The heat had finally broken with a gully washer the night before and thunder that sounded like barrels bouncing down cellar steps. She couldn't stop thinking about the shack and how cold and miserable Millard must be. She would have been scared. And if he got wet in the night, how could he get any dry clothes? And school was starting next week. If only Millard could come home. . . .

She moved back and forth between the kitchen and the tables, bringing chicken-fried steaks and grilled cheeses and fried eggplant. They would sure be out of meat tomorrow and have to fix macaroni and cheese and maybe a big pot of navy beans.

If she could figure out who took the medicine, Millard could come home. He'd been too sleepy to wake up, but there was something that made him think he knew who'd come in. There must have been a sound or a smell he recognized. Somebody who came in often. Oh, maybe someone who got medicine a lot. Yes, it would have to be—

"We have bread pudding or Jell-O today."

—someone who'd gotten that medicine before. Otherwise, how would they know where the medicine was kept?

She looked across the room at the counter. Every day Dr. Jamison took the third stool from the left. He ordered chili and coffee in the winter, bean soup and iced tea in the summer. If the person who stole the medicine was a regular customer at Thompson's Drugs, they would come with a prescription from Dr. Jamison.

Gretchen rode her bike to the back door of the Jamison house. She wore her swimsuit under her clothes and had a towel rolled up in the basket. She'd told Grandmother she was going out to Shady Grove Lake. The doctor and his wife lived next door to the Krafts. She leaned her bike against an elm tree and ran up the back steps and knocked hard before she got too scared to try.

Mrs. Jamison, drying her hands on a dish towel, came out onto the screened-in porch. "Why, Gretchen." Her blue eyes clouded. "Is your grandmother sick?"

"No, ma'am. Please. Could I see Dr. Jamison for a minute?"

Her round face creased. "We're just about to sit down to dinner—"

"Matty, who's here?" His voice was tired. He stepped out onto the porch. Dr. Jamison looked like one of the Smith Brothers on the cough-drop box. His white hair was untidy, his mustache drooped, and long sideburns ran down his jaws. He hooked his thumbs behind his suspenders.

Gretchen said fast, "Dr. Jamison, I have to talk to you. Please. About some medicine."

Dr. Jamison's bristly eyebrows drew down.

"William—"

He waved his hand at his wife. "It's all right, Matty.

Bring us out some lemonade." He held open the screen door, gestured toward the rocking chairs.

Gretchen perched on the edge of the smaller rocker. He lowered himself onto the big black one, looked at her soberly. "You need medicine, Gretchen?"

"No, sir." She started at the beginning, the day she'd gone to the drugstore for a cherry fausfade. She spoke loud enough for him to hear over the drone of big planes in the sky. Millard had told her the big army planes flew in formation.

Mrs. Jamison brought a tray with two big, cold glasses of lemonade. She placed it on the wicker stand and turned back to the kitchen.

Dr. Jamison listened without comment, sipping the lemonade.

". . . so you see, it had to be someone who came to the store all the time. Because Millard almost knew who it was. Maybe it was the sound of the footsteps. Or a smell." She closed her eyes. Sometimes Grandmother smelled like licorice, the candy she loved. Mom wore a perfume, Evening in Paris, and whenever Gretchen smelled it, she thought of Mom. She opened her eyes, looked at him hopefully. "Anyway, I thought you might know who would steal that kind of medicine."

For an instant, there was a startled look in the doctor's light brown eyes.

Gretchen plowed ahead. "If you know who it could be, maybe you could talk to them and tell them how bad it was for Millard and if they'd just tell Mr. Thompson . . ."

"Do you know where Millard is?" Dr. Jamison's face was what Grandmother called a brown study.

Gretchen's hands held tight to the arms of the rocker. "I think I could find him," she said carefully. But she wasn't going to tell anyone about their fort, no matter what.

Dr. Jamison pushed up from the rocker, paced to the end of the porch. He stood with his back to her for a minute or more. Finally, he turned, took a deep breath. "I'll see what I can do, girl."

Gretchen hugged her secret to herself. Dr. Jamison knew who to talk to. She was sure of that. There had been that look in his eyes when she told him what happened. She hugged her secret and her hope. The next morning her grandmother smiled at her. "You haf a happy step today. I haf been vorried about you. Maybe it is that you are glad school is soon to start?"

Grandmother had arranged for Callie Perkins's mother to work in the café until Gretchen arrived after school. Mrs. Perkins was starting this morning so she could see how everything was done. They were standing behind the counter, Gretchen opening the cupboard with sugar and salt, when she looked through the front window and saw Dr. Jamison's dusty black car. Thoughts exploded in her mind like marbles hit by a lucky agate. Dr. Jamison didn't come downtown this early. Somebody else was in the car. He'd promised to do his best. "I've got to run an errand," she told the thin woman beside her. "I'll be back in a minute." She left Mrs. Perkins looking mournfully at the contents of the cupboard. Grandmother wouldn't be out in front—she was busy cooking. Mrs. Perkins could take care of things for a little while.

Gretchen darted out the front and saw Dr. Jamison holding open the front door to Thompson's. And she heard the tap of Mrs. Whittle's cane as she limped inside. Gretchen ran past the store, darted down the side street to the alley in back. Just as she'd thought, the back door was open. It was still too hot to close the doors, and some air crept past the screen doors.

"Bert, Emma wants to talk to you for a minute. I'll wait out in the front."

"Hello, Emma." The druggist's voice was kind.

"Bert—"

Gretchen edged near enough the screen door to peek inside. Mrs. Whittle's fair hair, streaked with gray, drooped around her face. She didn't have on any makeup, and her big blue eyes looked dull as a mud-splashed car.

"I got to tell you the truth. Millard didn't take that morphine. I did. He was asleep that day when I came in. I was coming back to get a prescription for my throat. William said I couldn't have any more morphine, but I can't sleep, Bert. Not since Billy—" Her face screwed up like a broken doll and her voice washed away in a gulping sob.

Gretchen ran faster than a bull bucking a rider. She ran all the way even though it was still pretty hot, close to ninety-five. But she didn't care if she got hot and it hurt to breathe. Millard could come home. Millard could come *home*. She was so glad, but she pushed away the memory of those sobs. She burst out into the clearing near the creek and the shack. "Millard!" She didn't have to be quiet or . . .

Cottonwood leaves rustled in the ever-present wind. Cicadas still rasped, though their glory days were past. Birds chittered. The shack door was ajar. Even from the edge of the clearing, Gretchen saw the dusty floor, the slant of sun through the broken window, the emptiness.

"Oh, Millard." But no one heard except the birds.

*   *   *

Gretchen knew she had to hurry. What if Mrs. Perkins told Grandmother she'd left? Sweat slid down her back. Her pedal pushers stuck to her legs. But still she hesitated in the shadow of a huge old sycamore, looking across the road at the Blue Light. The long, low wooden building looked shabby, its paint dulled to a mustard brown, the tar-paper roof patched and uneven. The dusty parking lot was empty except for an old pickup truck.

Millard said Mrs. Hopper was nice. But Grandmother's friends looked the other way when Mrs. Hopper rattled into town to buy groceries. And she might not know where Millard had gone.

A side door banged open. A big woman with flaming red hair—but not a nice red like Millard's—stood on the low steps and flung soapy water from a pail.

Gretchen took one step, two, broke into a run as the woman turned to open the door. "Ma'am. Ma'am!" Gretchen skidded to a stop, near the wet patch with little soap bubbles.

Mrs. Hopper's skin was a tired white, but her mouth was bright as red neon. Huge eyes with thick black lashes cut a glance as sharp as a knife. "This is no place for kids." She pulled open the door.

"Please, Mrs. Hopper."

The woman's big dark eyes were as still as a pond at midnight.

"I'm a friend of Millard's. He said you were nice to him. He said you loaned him a sleeping bag. If you know where he is, please write him that he can come home, that his dad knows somebody else stole the medicine."

Mrs. Hopper pushed back a thick swath of dyed hair.

"People come and go," she said brusquely. She yanked open the door and stepped into dimness. The door banged shut behind her.

Every parking place downtown was taken on Saturdays. Despite the shortages and the coupon books, everybody came to town to shop, and the Victory Café was full from early until late. The roar of conversation was loud as bees buzzing around a hive. The jukebox blared "Chattanooga Choo Choo." The counter was full and so were the booths and tables. Gretchen and Mrs. Perkins worked fast. Gretchen was hurrying to the stand for a fresh pot of coffee when Mr. Thompson called out, "Gretchen."

She knew before she turned that he wasn't going to ask for ketchup or another ashtray, though the one on that table was full and she needed to change it. His voice was proud, like the principal reading the honor roll.

When she reached the table, Mr. Thompson held out a silver picture frame. She took it and stared at Millard in a sailor uniform with a little round white hat. He was her Millard, and yet he was different, thinner, and the look in his eyes . . .

". . . guess we have to accept it when our kids grow up. Stubborn young idiot wouldn't tell me what he was up to." Mr. Thompson's voice puffed like dough in hot grease. "Of course he was wrong to work at night. But he said he played in a band until he got enough money to go out to San Diego. He went through boot camp there and . . ."

The words rippled in her mind like Aunt Lela's pond on a March day, the wind kicking up little waves. You couldn't see through the surface of the muddy red brown water. You couldn't see the tadpoles and minnows and crawdads. Or even the water moccasins slipping by.

Gretchen held the frame and looked at an old young face that she'd once known so well. Words slipped past on the surface of her mind:

". . . mighty proud of him but his mama . . ."

". . . Julie will be home soon because Buzzy's shipped out. I guess I underestimated that boy since he saved enough money to send for Julie and marry her. . . ."

She handed back the frame. "I'll get some more coffee."

As she walked away, Mr. Thompson said, "Funny, I thought Gretchen would be interested. But I guess she and Millard are too far apart in age . . ."

She walked away with her secret that darted like a tadpole beneath the surface of the pond, like Dr. Jamison's secret and Mrs. Whittle's secret and Mr. Thompson's secret and Julie's secret and Mrs. Hopper's secret and Millard's secret. She picked up the coffeepot and moved slowly around the room, refilling the cups and looking at familiar faces and wondering about the secrets inside that nobody knew about.

THE FIRST ONE TO BLINK

Gar Anthony Haywood

Gar Anthony Haywood is the Shamus and Anthony Award–winning author of eight mystery novels—six featuring African-American private investigator Aaron Gunner, and two recounting the adventures of Joe and Dottie Loudermilk, Airstream-owning crime solvers extraordinaire. His first Gunner mystery, Fear of the Dark, won the Private Eye Writers of America's Shamus Award for Best First Novel of 1989, while the New York Times called his first Loudermilk mystery, 1994's Going Nowhere Fast, "a dizzying and hilarious escape." Haywood's sixth Aaron Gunner novel, All the Lucky Ones Are Dead, was published by Penguin Putnam in January 2000. The author's first Aaron Gunner short story, "And Pray Nobody Sees You," appeared in the Doubleday anthology Spooks, Spies, and Private Eyes, and won both the PWA's Shamus and the World Mystery Convention's Anthony Awards for Best Short Story of 1995. A Joe and Dottie Loudermilk short story, "A Mother Always Knows," appeared in Funny Bones, an E. P. Dutton anthology of humorous crime stories published in the spring of 1997. Haywood, who has written for both the Los Angeles Times and the New York Times, has been on the writing staff of the Fox Television program New York Undercover, and has coauthored two Movies of the Week for the ABC Television Network. He is a former president of the Mystery Writers of America's Southern California chapter.

*Haywood presently lives with his wife and three daughters
in the Silver Lake area of Los Angeles.*

Emory Tennyson, her late husband's attorney of some
thirty-one years, approached Celia at the postfuneral
gathering. A gaunt, soft-spoken gentleman with a head of
snow-white hair and the bowed posture of a palm tree, he
caught her alone in a corner of the dining room, away
from the other mourners, and said, "I feel the need to
apologize."

Celia smiled at him politely, appearing not to have understood. "Apologize? For what?"

"For not having said and done more to defend you.
The way Philip treated you was a travesty. You were the
best thing that ever happened to him, only he was too
damn paranoid to notice."

"Emory, please. This isn't really—"

"I know. This isn't the time or place. You're right, of
course. Still, I felt compelled to say something. To ask
your forgiveness for allowing the damn fool to bully you
the way he did."

Celia reached out to take the old man's hand. "You're
very kind," she said, still smiling. "But no apologies are
necessary. You were Philip's lawyer, Emory, not his father. It wasn't your job to lecture him on how to best treat
his wife."

"No, but—"

"Besides. He wasn't so bad, really. In fact, all in all,
I'd say he was wonderful."

She was being generous, of course, but not particularly
untruthful. For the most part, Philip January *had* been a

wonderful husband to Celia for the seven years they'd been together. Seventeen years her senior, Philip had been strikingly handsome, sexually proficient, and what some people would simply describe as "filthy rich." A wildly successful producer of direct-to-video action films, he had been worth in excess of fourteen million dollars when the untimely heart attack that took his life had befallen him, and it was not an exaggeration to say he had tried very hard to spend every dime of his sizable fortune attempting to keep Celia happy.

And yet, despite these obvious compensations, life as Mrs. Philip January, as Philip's attorney had so observantly noticed, had not been entirely pleasant. Far from it. For Philip had been an insanely jealous man. The kind who could see signs of unfaithfulness and betrayal in anything his wife might choose to do. Never mind that she had never given him any reason whatsoever to doubt her; trust had always been something Philip had little use for, in business or at home.

So for seven years, he leaned on Celia like a cop trying to break a suspect. Never actually accusing her of anything but always remaining firmly convinced that one day her answers to his questions would confirm his darkest fears about her. At least once, he had even hired a private investigator to follow her around. She wasn't supposed to have noticed, but she did. Philip simply couldn't help himself; expecting the worst from people, while making constant preparations for the moment they would invariably fail him, was just his way. Waiting or hoping for him to change would have only been a waste of Celia's time.

Another woman, subjected to such relentless scrutiny and mistrust, might have lost her mind or walked away. But not Celia. Celia had the patience of Job. She had learned a long time ago that anything worth having always came with a price, and marriage to a man like Philip January was no exception. So she had simply dug in her heels and endured. With little complaint, she had played all the roles Philip needed her to play—wife, friend, secretary, lover—and let him fear what he would. She knew all his spying and probing would prove fruitless in the end; it was only a matter of time before he faced the fact and put his uneasy mind to rest.

Only he never got the chance. A cardiac arrest took him first, and now, all his suspicions were moot. Having taken his last breath without ever having had Celia prove herself unworthy of him, he could do nothing to compensate her for the hell he'd put her through but speak from the grave through his last will and testament to bequeath her everything that he owned.

To Emory Tennyson, the dear soul, this was no doubt the just conclusion to a good woman's needless suffering, and that was at least partly true. But it was also something else. It was also the fruits of labor Celia had been counting on reaping all along.

She just hadn't thought it would take her seven years to do so.

Two days after Philip's funeral, Celia went into the office for a few hours to take care of some minor business and dropped several pieces of outgoing mail into the collection slot down in the building's lobby on her way out. This last would not have been particularly noteworthy except that it was the first time in years Celia could remember depositing mail for delivery in such a casual fashion.

It felt good.

For the greatest complication of waiting for Philip January to die had not been his lack of faith in Celia but his infernal insistence that things be done, at all times, in his own peculiar way. If they had only shared a home together, this character trait might not have proven so problematic, but part of Celia's duties as Philip's wife was managing his personal affairs at the office, and it was here that his anal retentiveness most drove her to distraction. Everything had to be done exactly as Philip dictated; any deviation from his guidelines was unacceptable. It was maddening and almost always wholly unnecessary, but it was how the man functioned, and Celia had to either conform to his methods or go home. Something she could not afford to do as long as she wanted to be thought of as the perfect, all-purpose wife.

So Celia bit her lip and went along with the program, day after day after day, working on a precise timetable to perform the most insignificant tasks as if she were a nuclear power-plant technician rather than just the personal secretary of some C-movie Hollywood schlock meister. And after a while, she even found herself doing it all automatically, without conscious effort.

It disturbed her, seeing the changes life with Philip gradually brought about in her, but she never came close to being spooked enough to leave. Because she hadn't married Philip just to end up with a hefty divorce settlement; that was chump change. Celia was after the works, the kind of money a woman could live on for the rest of her life without ever having to cast so much as a sideways glance at the bottom line. And that kind of money only came in two forms: lottery winnings and inheritances. Her numbers never came up in the lottery, so she had to settle for the next best thing: marriage to a wealthy man she really didn't love.

It took a little time, but Celia eventually found the ideal pigeon. Her girlfriend Donna was a receptionist for a well-known cardiologist out in Beverly Hills, and one night she called Celia at home—almost unable to speak, she was so excited. "I think I've found your man," she said.

"Tell me."

"His name's Philip January. Can you believe that? January. He's a movie producer. Not a famous one or anything, but successful. *Very* successful. Rolls-Royce Corniche convertible–grade successful, girl."

"Go on."

"It gets better. He's sixty-one years old, but he's a looker, and he's unattached. A widower with no kids. *No kids.* So when it comes time to cut up the pie . . ."

"More pie for me. I get it."

"You haven't heard the best part yet. The poor man isn't long for this world. He's got a bad case of PS."

"PS.?"

"Pulmonary stenosis. Means he's got an obstruction of the pulmonary valve in his heart that reduces the flow of blood to his lungs. He's about to undergo surgery for it, and ordinarily, he'd be okay afterward, but in this case, the long-term prognosis isn't good."

"No?"

"No. Mr. January follows his doctor's orders like I resist the temptation to eat cheesecake. Which is to say, not at all. He won't slow down, and he won't take care of himself. His work is all he knows, and they say he goes at it like a dog tearing meat off a bone. So . . ."

"He could make some lucky girl a widow in a few short years."

"Or maybe even sooner than that," Donna said. "Who knows?"

If Celia had known then that she would have to wait more than five years for Philip's bad heart to finally give out, what happened next might never have occurred. But she was an optimist, looking for a quick score and not a protracted one, so she and Donna formed a plan that placed Celia in the hallway outside the Beverly Hills cardiologist's office door on the afternoon of Philip's next appointment. It was an old gag, manufacturing a meeting with a man by "accidentally" colliding with him, but it still worked better than some. Donna called Celia on her cell phone from inside the office, alerting Celia to Philip's exit, and Celia bumped into him expertly seconds later, an armful of file folders scattering across the floor at their feet, begging to be picked up. Philip couldn't believe his good fortune. He took the bait, and half of Celia's line with it.

They were dating only a week later, and for Celia, with more enthusiasm than expected. This wasn't going to be the joyless, ungratifying, mercenary exercise she thought it might prove to be. It turned out that Philip January had a lot more going for him than money; he was charming and generous and a better lover than most men half his age. In fact, were it not for his almost crippling paranoia, which became more and more obvious to Celia as their time together wore on, he might have been a perfect partner. No one Celia could ever love unconditionally, of course—she was reserving that honor for someone much younger and more deserving of her—but a man she could spend considerable time with without feeling dead inside all the while.

Hence, accepting Philip's eventual marriage proposal required little or no thought at all. She figured she was locking herself into a few passionless years of aggravation at most, countered by a luxurious lifestyle she would never have the opportunity to know otherwise.

It was wishful thinking. Both the time she would have to invest and the frustrations she would have to endure ended up being far greater than she had bargained for. Because Philip stopped trusting her completely before the ink had fully dried on their marriage certificate. He had shown himself to be a man burdened by some insecurity during their courtship, but it wasn't until after they were married that Celia learned just how deep his insecurities really ran.

What she gradually came to discover was that her husband dealt with everyone—friends, family, business associates—as if they were thieves laying in wait to cut his throat. His behavior went beyond mere mistrust; it was utter paranoia. He was an orphan who had never known his real parents, and his abandonment at their hands had left him forever convinced that no one who promised him anything could ever be taken at their word. So he ran his business and lived his private life forever on the defensive, in constant preparation for disappointment. It was like a game to him, waiting to see who would betray his faith next.

For Celia, his every order was a test of her commitment. Failure to comply was nothing if not an outright admission of indifference toward him. For if she loved him, truly loved him, she would do his bidding gladly, no matter how pointless and/or inane his bidding struck her. It was a mind-set that kept Celia jumping through hoops like a dog in a circus, always watching the clock to make sure she performed no trick before—or after—its appointed time:

Order new stationary when there are exactly sixteen sheets left in the box.

Never wait more than three and a half rings for someone to pick up the phone.

Hand-carry all outgoing mail to the post office personally.

Always leave important voice mail messages in duplicate.

Use yellow Post-it notes for messages related to money, and white for everything else.

It was insane. Insipid and nonsensical, childish and ridiculous—but none of it was more than Celia could put up with if she had to. And she had to. Because she had never quit on anything in her life, and she wasn't going to start now. Philip wanted her to disappoint him; he wanted her to either leave him or cheat on him, one or the other, just so he could stop worrying about her doing both. But Celia wasn't going to accommodate him. She would neither move from Philip's side nor sleep with another man until her husband was either dead or too tired to question her anymore.

So around and around the two went for seven years. Circling each other like combatants in a cockfight, each waiting to see who would be the first one to blink.

Philip, by way of a fatal heart attack, blinked first.

"Hi. I'm looking for Phil January?"

He was a slender, good-looking redhead Celia had never seen before. She'd been working at the office late this afternoon, two weeks now after Philip's death, and the stranger had rapped on the door, stuck his head inside the room before she could get up to see who it was.

"Philip isn't here, Mr. . . ."

"Ridley. Tom Ridley." He stepped all the way inside, closed the door behind him. He had a very disarming smile. "Do you expect him back soon, or . . . ?"

"No. I'm afraid not." Celia offered him her hand. She knew the name but couldn't quite place it. "I'm Celia January, Mr. Ridley. Philip's wife. Perhaps there's something I could help you with?"

He shook her hand, said, "Well, I don't know. You ever hear of a script called *The Concrete Shadow*?"

"*The Concrete Shadow*?" Celia shook her head, fought the urge to curl up her nose. "I don't think so."

"Your husband was reading it. I submitted it to him over six months ago, he was supposed to give me a call this week to discuss it."

"Oh. I see."

He was a writer. Just the latest in a long line of same to whom Philip had made promises he'd never really intended to keep. Now Celia knew why his name had struck her as familiar; she'd probably seen it in Philip's calendar book somewhere. She looked around at the endless stacks of screenplays littering the room and said, "If I knew where to look . . ."

"Hey. Don't worry about it. Just tell Mr. January I came by, huh?" He turned to leave.

"My husband's dead, Mr. Ridley. He passed away two weeks ago."

Ridley stopped, faced her again. Looking genuinely saddened to hear. "Wow. I'm sorry."

"Yes. We all are."

An uncomfortable silence wedged itself between them. Finally, Ridley said, "I don't really know what to say. Except . . ." He shrugged, smiled with some embarrassment. "In that case, if you don't mind, maybe we should look around for my script before I go. Seeing as how—"

"Philip won't be buying it. Sure. Pull up a chair, Mr. Ridley. I'll take a look."

The redhead sat down in front of Philip's desk as Celia started to move from one stack of scripts to another, leafing through each to check all the title pages. *Jesus,* she thought to herself, The Concrete Shadow. It sounded like just the kind of dreck Philip was always in the market for.

"What's your script about?" Celia asked, feeling obligated to feign interest. "If you don't mind my asking?"

"The script? Oh, it's about a hit man. And this old guy who hires him to kill his wife."

"Oh?"

"Yeah, I know. Sounds like something you've seen or heard a million times before, right?"

"Well . . ."

"That's where my hook comes in. Producers are always looking for a hook. The old guy doesn't actually hire the hit man to do his wife outright, see. He only hires him to do it on a contingency basis."

"A contingency basis? I don't—"

"What I mean is, he pays the hit man a large retainer up front, then sends him a hundred dollars every month afterward just to keep him on standby. The deal is, he only wants his wife done under two circumstances: If he gives the go-ahead himself, or if the last monthly check the hit man receives is more than two days late."

Celia frowned, moved on to the next stack of scripts. Yes, this was definitely the kind of exploitative crap Philip might have wanted to produce.

"Two days late?" she asked.

"Yeah. Because the old guy's checks always arrived on the first or the second of the month, one or the other, just like clockwork. So if one ever arrived a couple of days after that, and it turned out to be the last check the old guy would ever live to send, well . . . Obviously, that would be some kind of sign that something was not quite right." Ridley paused, then added, "Wouldn't it?"

And Celia's hands stopped flipping through the script pages in front of her, a small ball of black fear rapidly hardening in the pit of her stomach. For the first time in several minutes, she turned around to face Ridley again . . .

. . . and saw the gun now resting in his lap, aimed ever so leisurely in her direction. Everything about it terrified her, of course, but the large, cylindrical silencer mounted to its muzzle scared her most of all.

"Wait. Please . . ." she said.

The man who called himself Ridley stood up from his chair, said, "Sorry, Mrs. January. I don't know what the hell it means, either. But orders are orders, right?"

He put the first bullet in Celia's heart, the next one in her throat as she was falling. In the mere seconds she had left to live, she watched him move to stand over her, wipe his fingerprints off everything he had touched, then leave.

A sideways view of the badly stained office carpeting was the last image of the world Celia's mind recorded, along with a single, melancholy thought: That day she'd been here shortly after Philip's funeral, she should have taken the outgoing mail to the post office rather than drop it in that goddamn mail slot downstairs. It was the last time she would have ever had to prove to Philip that she loved him enough to always do things his way.

And she blew it.

THE TUNNEL

M. D. Lake

M. D. Lake is the pen name of Allen Simpson, professor of Scandinavian literature at the University of Minnesota until he took early retirement to write full time. He has published ten mysteries featuring a campus cop named Peggy O'Neill, in which professors, students, administrators, and the occasional unfortunate outsider do one another in. Two of his short stories, "Kim's Game" (in Malice Domestic II, *published by Pocket Books) and "Tea for Two" (in* Funny Bones, *published by Signet), have won Agathas, and "Tea for Two" was also reprinted in* The Year's 25 Finest Crime and Mystery Stories, *edited by Ed Gorman and Martin H. Greenberg (Carroll and Graf, 1998).*

*Lake's work has been translated into French, Russian, and (he's been told, but has no proof, monetary or otherwise) Bulgarian. Among the nicest things said about his work are: "Lake blends the mundane and the terrifying with consummate skill" (*Drood Review of Mystery*), "O, how I love Peggy O'Neill!" (Barbara Paul), and "Peggy is the most likeable character I've met in a long time" (Joan Hess).*

Lake lives in Minnesota.

It wasn't true what they thought, that he loved fire, but it was true he'd started one in the woods behind the house and, before that, he'd almost burned the house down. But those were accidents, and lots of kids have accidents with fire. It doesn't mean they're crazy.

Back in June, right after he and his mom moved here, he'd strung some old blankets on a clothesline in the basement to make a clubhouse for himself. That's where he went when he wanted to read the scary books his mom didn't approve of and make up stories that someday he'd write down.

He'd been down there one night after dinner when his mother was out shopping. The phone rang, and he ran upstairs to answer it, hoping it was his dad. It was, and they'd talked a long time, and then he went upstairs to his room to do his homework, forgetting about the burning candles in the basement. One of them fell over somehow, and a blanket caught on fire, but luckily his mother came home just then. She put out the fire before it did any damage, but she called the fire department anyway, since the house was so old.

His mother gave him a severe talking to after the firemen left, and she'd made him promise never to play with fire again. After that, he read with the help of a flashlight, but it wasn't the same, and a few months later, while poking around in the basement, he'd found the tunnel entrance in the coal room, and the skeletons, and then he no longer needed the clubhouse. He'd taken candles into the tunnel, knowing his mother would never catch him and knowing that even if he was careless, nothing in there would burn except maybe the skeletons in their moldy, old-fashioned clothes. He read in there by candlelight and made up stories in his head. It was the perfect place for the kind of stories he liked.

The second fire was in November. He'd been sitting on a rock on the hill behind his house one chilly afternoon after school, burning his name into old leaves with the magnifying glass his dad had given him for his birthday and waiting for his mother to get home from work. Below he could see his house, an old Victorian with lots of gingerbread on it, and Big Mom's house next door, almost identical to his. Big Mom, his great-grandmother, owned both houses and let him and his mom live in the one in exchange for taking care of her—doing her shopping and laundry, cleaning her house, and other things like that. If they didn't live next door to her, she'd have to move into an old people's home. The two houses stood all alone, surrounded by what had once been farmland. Big Mom owned all that, too.

He remembered the first time he'd met her, right after he and his mom moved here. He'd still been angry about his parents' divorce and having to leave his dad and his friends behind, and it must have shown, for as he passed within reach of Big Mom in her rocking chair, one of her hands shot out and her crooked old fingers clamped onto his arm and dug in, like claws.

"You don't look happy," she'd said with a kind of twisted grin. She was missing some of her front teeth, and long hairs grew on her face. He didn't say anything, just waited for her to let him go.

The claws dug in more deeply, causing him to wince. "So why don't you run away? That's what your great-grandfather did. You look like Lewis, too. You have his eyes and mouth. A lady-killer's eyes and lips."

"I can't run away," he'd answered, meeting her faded gray eyes with his own bright blue ones. "They'd just make me come back."

She'd nodded at that. "That's right; you can't run away. Nobody can!"

When they were back in their own house, he'd asked

his mother what had happened to Lewis, her grandfather.

"He left Big Mom," she'd replied tersely, not wanting to discuss it.

"Has she always been mean?"

His mother smiled and shook her head. "She's not mean, just old and crotchety. She was wonderful to Dorothy and me after our parents died." Her parents had been killed in a car accident when she was a child. Dorothy was her sister.

Later, after he'd found the two skeletons in the tunnel, he brought up the subject again.

"Did your granddad run away alone?"

She gave him a startled look. "Why do you ask that?"

"Just wondered."

"He ran away with another woman," she said, then noisily began filling a pot with water for the spaghetti they were having for dinner.

Sometimes, when he'd gone over to help Big Mom with something, she'd offer him cookies and milk. He could see that she was trying to make friends with him but didn't know how to do it. . . .

The wind came up suddenly, blowing smoke at him from leaves he'd burned his name into earlier. He spun around and saw fire spreading among the dry leaves and underbrush. He jumped up and stomped it out, running back and forth, sparks flying around his tennis shoes. Only when he was sure he'd gotten it all did he go down the hill to his house.

He was watching television when he heard the sirens, and with a sick premonition he ran outside and saw smoke coming from the woods. The firemen put the fire out quickly, but it left an ugly burned patch on the hill.

At dinner that night, his mother noticed that he wasn't eating much and asked him if he was all right. He told her he was fine—and then the doorbell rang. People didn't usually call this time of night, so he knew what it had to be. He heard his mother talking to someone in the front hall, and then there he was—a tall man in a fireman's uniform, with thick, dark hair; a long, leathery face; and cold eyes.

"Sam," his mother said, her eyes worried, "this is the fire marshal. Were you playing with fire on the hill today?"

"No," he answered. Burning your name into leaves with a magnifying glass wasn't playing with fire!

The fire marshal held out his big hand. In the palm was a leaf with "Sam" burned into it and Sam's magnifying glass, the leather case badly scorched.

"Oh, Sam!"

"I tried to put it out!" he cried, fighting tears. "It looked like it was all out!"

"Didn't you start a fire in the basement a couple of months ago, son?" the fire marshal asked.

"I didn't *start* one," Sam replied. "It was an accident."

The marshal talked to him about what could have happened if the fire on the hill had gotten out of control, how it could have burned up over the hill and destroyed houses on the other side, in the new development that had crept almost to the top of the hill.

His mother made him go to his room without finishing his supper, and he could hear her and the marshal talking for a long time and wondered what they were talking about that took so long.

The next night, his Aunt Dorothy and Uncle Blaine came over after dinner and he had to sit there and listen as they discussed the fire and the accident with the candles. Aunt Dorothy didn't say much, just made sympathetic noises, then glanced at her husband to see if that was appropriate. She checked with Blaine before going to the bathroom, he'd heard Big Mom say more than once. Big Mom made no secret of the fact that she didn't like him.

"I think the boy should see a therapist," Blaine said, gazing steadily at Sam through his rimless glasses. "This is a perilous time to be a boy in our society—especially a boy who spends so much time alone." It sounded to Sam as though Uncle Blaine was hinting that any day now, he'd get a gun and go into his school and shoot it up.

Blaine turned to Sam's mother and added, "And it's not healthy for Sam to live this far out in the country, either, with so few opportunities to make friends."

Sam had to agree with that, even though he knew Uncle Blaine didn't really care about him; he just wanted his mom to move into town, which would force Big Mom to move to an old people's home. Then they could sell her land to a developer and they'd all make a ton of money.

His mother shook her head and said, "I can't let Big Mom go into a home, Blaine—not until she's ready. And you know that, mentally, she's as sharp as any of us." She looked over at Sam, smiled, and said, "But I'll try to figure out a way for Sam to spend more time with his friends at school."

She hadn't done that yet when, one Saturday afternoon a few weeks later, she went down into the basement to do the laundry. Sam was watching TV in the living room and snow was falling outside. He heard the sound of the laundry basket hitting the floor and then his mother's feet on the basement steps, rushing upstairs. He looked over at her as she burst into the room. Her face was white with anger and there were tears in her eyes.

"How could you?" she shouted. "How could you?"

"What?"

"You know what! Those candles—in your clubhouse!"

"What candles? I don't know what you're talking about!"

She rushed at him and slapped him hard across the face, something she'd never done before. "Don't lie to me. Please, Sam—don't lie to me!"

"I'm not lying!" he yelled, his head ringing from the slap, tears in his eyes. "What candles?"

She turned away from him and threw herself on the couch. The television droned on, Tom Sawyer and Jim on a raft, in bright colors. "Oh God, oh God!" she moaned, burying her face in a pillow. "What am I going to do?"

Sam ran down into the basement. Three candles were stuck in pop bottles on one of the boxes in his clubhouse. Streams of wax had melted down the sides of the bottles. Confused and scared, he went back up to the living room.

"Mom, I didn't put them there. Honest I didn't!"

"I don't believe a word you say," she said and started crying again. He went over to try to comfort her but stopped himself before he did and just stood there helplessly.

"Somebody else must've put them there," he tried again, "while I was at school and you were at work."

She gave him a pitying look. "Who, Sam?" she asked. "Who would do a thing like that?"

He thought wildly. Who had a key to their house? Aunt Dorothy, of course—and Uncle Blaine!

"Uncle Blaine!" he said, almost shouting the name. "Uncle Blaine, to make us move into town so Big Mom'll have to go to an old people's home!"

"Oh, Sam," his mother said, and started crying again. "Blaine's right—you're going to have to see a therapist. What else can I do?"

He hardly slept at all that night. He lay in bed won-

dering if he really had put those candles in the basement—
even lit them and read by them. That would mean he
really was crazy, a kind of Dr. Jekyll and Mr. Hyde. But
it wasn't true! And if it wasn't true, then somebody else
must've put them there. It had to be Uncle Blaine, but
how could he convince his mother of that? How could he
convince anybody?

On Monday, his mother told him Blaine had found a
therapist who specialized in children and came highly rec-
ommended. She'd made an appointment for Sam to see
her on Wednesday.

He fell into an uneasy sleep that night, and then suddenly he was awake and screaming: The house was on
fire, the downstairs a sea of flame that rose greedily from
giant cracks in the floor and poured from the walls. Black
smoke filled the stairwell and boiled down the hall.

Sitting up in bed, sweating, he realized it had only been
a dream, a nightmare, and the noise he'd heard must have
been the sound of the blizzard outside—except he could
still smell the smoke! He jumped out of bed and ran to
the door, threw it open, and with a cry fell back from the
wall of flame that seemed to be waiting for him in the
hall. He slammed the door shut and shouted, "Mom!
Mom!" as loud as he could, but of course she couldn't
hear him through the closed door and the noise of the fire.

He ran to the window and shoved it up, but the storm
window was frozen in place, so he grabbed his bedside
lamp and used it to smash the pane. Snow and cold blew
into the room. He went back to his bed, found his shoes,
and put them on as tongues of flame began licking their
way into the room beneath the door. He pulled on his
winter jacket and crawled through the broken window
onto the roof, where he lost his footing and slid out into
the darkness.

He landed in the snow, struggled to his feet, and looked up at his mother's bedroom window, blazing with light.

"Mom!" he hollered, and again, "Mom!" He picked up snow and made a hard ball of it, threw it at the window, but it didn't reach—and then the window exploded, fragments of glass raining down around him with the falling snow as fire erupted into the night and began eating its way up the wall.

Terrified, sobbing, the boy thrashed his way over to Big Mom's house, but as he crossed the area between the two houses, he saw something in the snow that puzzled him: snowshoe tracks, almost erased by the falling snow and blowing wind, going away from the house up the hill.

At Big Mom's house, he pounded on the side door, but had to give up when the cold started to become unbearable. Panicking, he turned back to his own house, with the fire blazing in its windows now. He was going to have to try to make it to the next closest houses, around the hill—but maybe he could warm up first, in the heat of his own burning house.

As he approached, he looked down and, through a gap in the snow, saw the window in the coal room in his basement. The room was dark; the fire hadn't reached it yet. *The tunnel!* he thought. If he could get into the tunnel, maybe he'd be safe.

He fell onto his knees and cleared snow away from the window with his freezing hands, then pulled off his jacket and used it to protect his arm as he smashed in the windowpane. He threw the coat over the frame and, teeth chattering uncontrollably, backed his way through the opening and dropped to the coal room's dirt floor. He pulled his coat in after him and put it on, then ran to the door and pushed it cautiously open.

The fire—which seemed to have started on the other

side of the basement, where his clubhouse had been—had been sucked up the wooden basement steps to the upper floors of the house but hadn't reached this side of the basement yet. He slammed the door shut, then turned back into the room. There was no light in there, but he knew how to find what he wanted anyway.

The coal room ran along the side of the house. The walls were of brick that had been painted white some time in the distant past, but the paint was peeling, and the mortar between the bricks was rotten and falling out. An ancient bedspring leaned up against one wall, and cardboard boxes, empty and mildewed, rotted on the floor, along with pieces of wood and empty bottles and cans. At the end of the room, against the short wall facing Big Mom's house, stood an old bookcase, its shelves holding rusting cans of paint, paint thinner, and pesticides. Sam groped his way over to it and dragged one corner of it away from the wall. He squeezed in behind it and began removing bricks from the wall, making an opening into the tunnel he'd found when he'd explored the basement in August. When it was large enough, he crawled through, reached back out, and pulled the bookcase into place over the hole.

He sat a few minutes, shivering, his back against the tunnel's wall, then groped in the darkness for his candles, lit one, and set it on the old wooden box he'd dragged in to use as a table. It cast its warm glow on the brick walls and, a few feet farther in, on the two skeletons in their long winter coats, lying side by side on the dirt floor.

Sam wrapped himself in an old blanket he kept there on account of the chill, propped himself up against the wall, and, thinking of his mother, cried for a long time. His exhausted mind tried to figure out what he should do next—but after a while, he couldn't hold a thought for more than a few moments before he started to fall asleep.

He'd come in here to escape the fire and the storm. He would come out when they put out the fire . . . if he survived.

He jerked awake at the realization that he'd be blamed for the fire! He stared into the candle flame a long time, thinking about that, and then—in spite of trying not to— he cried himself to sleep.

When he woke up, he thought it must be the middle of the night and he'd been having a nightmare, but then he felt the cold earth beneath him and the hard wall behind his back and head, and he knew it wasn't a nightmare; it was more horrible than any nightmare—it was real.

He groped for a new candle and lit it. Slowly, he went over in his mind the events of the night before—or whenever it had been, for he had no idea how long he'd slept or what time it was now.

He crawled back to the tunnel opening and listened for a minute or two, straining to hear anything, then shoved the bookcase away from the wall and peered out. Dull winter light seeped through the snow that clogged the broken window he'd climbed through, showing him that the fire hadn't reached the coal room. He crawled out, went over and put his ear to the door, listening for sounds in the basement. There were none, so he tried to push the door open, but it moved only about a foot before being stopped by some obstacle. He peered through the opening and saw that the whole house seemed to have collapsed into the basement in a chaos of ice, snow, and water. Looking up, he could see the wintery gray light of day through what was left of an upstairs wall. The paint on the coal room door was blistered, the wood charred in places and still warm to his hands. He started to push the door wider, meaning to squeeze through, when he heard voices coming from somewhere above him.

". . . must be out in the snow somewhere."

"Maybe for the best. Killing your mother'd be hard to live with."

". . . say he was troubled—might've even started it on purpose."

". . . supposed to see a therapist, according to his uncle."

"What about the old lady next door? His grandmother?"

"Great-grandmother. Didn't hear a thing."

They talked some more, mostly about how fast the house had burned, how the stairwell from the basement, where the fire had started, had acted as a kind of flue that had sent the fire racing through the upper stories of the house.

"They found a smoke detector—with no batteries in it."

"You suppose the kid could've . . ." The voices drifted away.

Sam pulled the door shut, went back into the tunnel, sat down, and began crying again, thinking of his mother. And when he couldn't cry anymore—and had to pee, badly—he walked farther into the tunnel, peed, and came back and sat down to try to figure out what to do next.

Uncle Blaine was responsible for the fire, he was sure of that, but he'd never be able to prove it. After all, he was a liar and Uncle Blaine was a lawyer and a deacon in his church. If he told people Uncle Blaine had done it, they'd think he was an even bigger liar—or crazier—and he'd be in even more trouble than he already was, if that was possible.

Should he try to make his way to his dad? What good would that do? His dad wouldn't believe him, either. No, he was going to have to figure out some way to run away and start a new life somewhere else. But how?

His eyes fell on the two grinning skulls and an idea came to him: Big Mom! She'd *have to* help him because he knew her secret—at least, he was pretty sure he did. But then he had another thought: If he was right, Big Mom was a murderer. He'd have to be careful around her, watch what he ate in case she tried to poison him—which reminded him that he was hungry.

He went down the tunnel to Big Mom's end, carrying a candle to light the way. The mortar holding the bricks in place there wasn't as rotted as it was at his end, but it still looked crumbly. He went back to the other end, listened at the coal room door to make sure nobody was in his basement, then pushed his way into it and made his way quickly through the snow, ice, and charred wood to the tool room. He found a large screwdriver and a hammer, took them back into the tunnel, and used them to dig out the mortar between the bricks in Big Mom's wall. The first few bricks took a while, but once he got them out, the rest almost fell out, and after a couple of minutes he had a hole large enough to crawl through into Big Mom's coal room. He pushed the door to her basement open a crack, slipped through, tiptoed over to the stairs. He listened a while, but when he couldn't hear anything, he climbed to the first floor as quietly as he could.

She was waiting for him, leaning heavily on her walker, one hand holding a trembling pistol aimed at his stomach, her brows angry over her hooded old eyes.

"I figured all that hammering had to be you," she said. "They still down there—in the tunnel?"

"Wh-who?"

"Don't lie to *me!*" she snapped, the pistol shaking even more. "You know who I mean."

"Yes," he said. He couldn't take his eyes off the pistol.

"Huh." She seemed to stare through him at something else. "Sometimes I think it was only a dream, a nightmare." Her eyes focused on the boy again. "Maybe you'll have dreams like that someday—about your mother."

"I didn't kill Mom!" he almost shouted, and tried to say something else but couldn't.

"Oh?" Big Mom's voice was hard, disbelieving. "It's just a coincidence, when the firebug's house burns down?"

"I didn't do it!" he sobbed. "I didn't!"

"Who did, then?"

He started to say something, a name, but nothing came out—it was all so hopeless—and then the doorball rang. Big Mom saw the desperate look on his face. "You ready to turn yourself in?"

He shook his head violently.

She looked hard at him a moment before saying, "Then get back down there!"

He ran downstairs but stopped at the bottom. He'd never get the bricks back in the wall the way they were, so if whoever was at the door came down into the basement and looked in the coal room, they'd find the opening he'd made.

After a while he heard Big Mom's voice—and then Uncle Blaine's.

". . . extremely troubled, acting out in the most terrifying way. His mother, with my encouragement, was taking him to a therapist tomorrow."

"A therapist!" Big Mom exclaimed.

"That's almost certainly what drove him over the edge. I'd urged her to get him to a therapist weeks ago, but she wouldn't listen."

When Big Mom didn't say anything to that, Blaine

added, "He's a pyromaniac, Big Mom, and if he's alive, he needs help. The sooner he gets it, the better."

Sam couldn't hear what Big Mom answered to that because they walked out of the kitchen.

After what seemed an eternity, she called down to him that he could come back upstairs. He went up, holding his breath, half-expecting to find Uncle Blaine waiting for him, but Big Mom was alone.

"You should've seen his eyes," she muttered. "Roaming all over the place. He probably suspects I'm hiding you. He thinks you're insane. Are you?"

"No!"

"Huh!" She regarded him skeptically a moment, then used her walker to get over to the kitchen table. "I don't trust him," she muttered. "Never have. I put the chain on the door, so he can't come sneaking back in here without warning. You say you didn't start that fire. If you didn't, who did?"

"*He* did! Uncle Blaine." Big Mom looked at him as though he were crazy, as he knew she would.

He told her about how his mom had found the candles in the basement on Saturday, in his clubhouse. "I'm not crazy, Big Mom; I wouldn't've put them there! It had to've been him! He's got a key to the house, and he knew I'd been caught playing with fire before and lied about it. And I heard some people talking—over there." He nodded in the direction of his house. "They said one of the smoke detectors didn't have batteries in it. But they all did! Mom was careful about stuff like that, on account of the house was so old. She made me put new batteries in a couple of months ago, and we tested them, and they worked fine. Uncle Blaine could've easily got in while Mom was at work and I was at school."

Big Mom considered that for a moment or two, then said, "That man drools over my land. He's been trying to get me to sell it for a long time—even offered to let me move in with him and Dorothy, that's how eager he is. The land's worth a fortune, you know. I was ready to sell, with him leaning so hard on me, but then your parents got divorced and you and your mom moved here. If it wasn't for the two of you, I'd be in a home now and where we're sitting would be one of a hundred identical-looking houses marching up that hill." She looked him in the eye and said, "Swear to me you didn't light those candles, Sam!"

"I swear, Big Mom," he answered, staring back at her without blinking.

"Well, it doesn't matter, either way," she said after a moment. "Nobody else is gonna believe you. You don't have any proof."

Then he remembered the tracks of the snowshoes he'd seen the night before. "They couldn't've been more than fifteen, twenty minutes old," he said, "on account of the snow."

"Blaine likes to snowshoe, says it's the only exercise he gets in the winter. But those tracks'll be gone now."

They sat there a minute or two in silence, then Big Mom shot Sam a glance and asked him when he'd found the tunnel.

"A couple of months ago. I read in there and make up stories."

"You weren't scared?"

He shrugged. "Sort of, at first. That's what I liked about it."

"But you never told anybody about—about them?"

He shook his head. "I didn't think Mom would want to know. And I figured they'd probably put you in prison or something, and Mom wouldn't be happy about that, either."

She stared at him a long time without saying anything, her eyes glistening, her chin quivering slightly. Then she cleared her throat. "You're probably hungry. You know where I keep the bread and cold cuts."

As he made himself a sandwich, he glanced over at her and asked, "Why'd you do it, Big Mom?"

She knew what he meant. "Because he was leaving me for another woman." She thought a moment, then went on: "I married Lewis when I was nineteen. My parents didn't like it, said he was too old for me. Lewis was only a bank clerk then, but he was ambitious. After the honeymoon—Niagara Falls, that's where everybody went in those days—we moved into the house next door. This was my parents' house and yours had been my grandparents'. Granddad dug the tunnel himself. He was a frugal man, you see, and wanted to save on the cost of delivering the coal. So he had it dumped into his coal room through the window and my father hauled his share over here in a wheelbarrow.

"After we'd been married about ten years, Lewis started an affair with one of the girls who worked for him in the bank. He was assistant manager by then, but he wasn't happy. He thought he was good for more than just working in a bank, and he didn't like it when I got pregnant with Mary Louise, either. That just made him feel like the walls were closing in on him even more. So he took a mistress, the way some men do when they feel trapped in the lives they've made for themselves. And then they got the notion to run away together, him and Muriel—that was her name—and take some of the bank's money with them."

She gazed at Sam—through Sam—for a minute with

her pale, hooded eyes. "I'd known something was wrong for a long time, but it wasn't until a few weeks before they disappeared that I learned about Muriel. All I could think of to do was try to be an even better wife than I'd been, but it didn't do any good. Probably just made it worse.

"One night—the night they disappeared—he came home from work early and told me he was going out of town for a few days on bank business. He'd done that before, of course, but not on such short notice, so I figured something was going on. I waited till he was in the bathroom cleaning up, then opened his suitcase and found the money—it was over sixty thousand dollars, a small fortune back then—and two train tickets in his overcoat pocket. That's when I decided to kill him."

"Why?" Sam asked. "Why didn't you just call the police?"

She ran a hand through her thin hair, shook her head. "I don't know anymore! At the time, I guess I just thought about how much I'd loved him once, about how I'd gone against my parents' wishes to marry him, and about how they'd accepted him finally as one of the family. They'd even given us the house—your house—when they learned I was pregnant with Mary Louise. But none of that meant anything to Lewis. He was going to throw it all away for a pretty red-headed girl named Muriel McIntyre, and leave me and our baby with nothing but the shame." Her voice throbbed with the old anger recollected.

"So I waited until he came out of the bathroom, pink and clean-shaven, smelling of bay rum, and as he dressed, I told him I knew about Muriel and the money and the train tickets. I told him I wanted a share of the money— and I wanted to give Muriel a piece of my mind before they left, too. I told him I'd call the police if he didn't get Muriel over to our house pronto.

"He was scared out of his wits, of course. Maybe, if he'd had more guts, he would've tried to kill me, but I was ready for that, too. I grew up on the farm; I knew all about guns, and I've always kept a pistol in the house in case of burglars. Even now we're pretty isolated out here, but it was worse back then. If Lewis had been as smart as he thought he was, he might've noticed how I didn't mind killing chickens—and a turkey once, too, for Thanksgiving.

"So he called Muriel. Oh, I could hear her squawking on the phone. She didn't like it, but she came—she had no other choice if she didn't want to go to jail. I sat them down at the kitchen table and shot them dead, both of 'em."

She paused a moment, stared at something only she could see but Sam could imagine. He wondered if the old kitchen table in his house, at which he'd eaten so many meals, was the same one. It was probably burned up now, anyway.

"I drove her car to a roadside tavern," she went on, "where I knew they used to meet after work sometimes, parked it in an out-of-the-way spot, and walked home. It was snowing, just like now, and I was wearing one of Lewis's coats and hats. I was eight months pregnant, so I must've looked like a fat, prosperous banker, if anybody'd noticed me. Then I dumped the bodies in the tunnel and hid the door behind a bookcase. Nobody knew about the tunnel—it hadn't been used in years, not since we got gas heating—so even if the police had suspected me and searched the house, why would they move a bookcase to look at a wall? A couple of years later, figuring that when Mary Louise was old enough to start exploring the house she'd wonder about the doors, I removed 'em, bricked up the openings, and painted 'em over."

"And the police never suspected you?"

She shook her head. "Why should they? Oh, they and the FBI made up all kinds of theories to fit the few facts they had, but I didn't figure in any of 'em. There was a war on, too, you know. The FBI was busy looking for spies and saboteurs, not small-town embezzlers, and most of the local cops were overseas, fightin' in the war."

"What'd you do with the money?"

"Burned it—every last cent. I didn't kill them for money! I got a job in a factory—lots of women were working in factories then, with the war on and all—and my parents took care of Mary Louise while I worked. When they died, I moved over to this house and rented out yours, and I've been here ever since."

They sat together in silence when she'd finished, their eyes not meeting, Sam busy making another sandwich.

"They won't do much to you, y'know," Big Mom said at last, "unless they decide you're crazy. You'll end up living with your dad. That's what you want anyway, isn't it?"

He shook his head. "Not anymore. Dad's not gonna want me."

"But you'll get a lot of points when you tell what's in the tunnel."

"I won't tell."

She smiled at that, then shrugged. "Well, they'll find 'em anyway, when they raze the house, and then they'll put me in the looney bin. Maybe we can be in the same one," she added. "You know any good card games?"

Sam gaped at her, but when she laughed, he suddenly laughed, too, though he didn't know why, and all the rest of his life he would remember that moment of laughter they had together. But then he started crying again, for his mother, for himself, and for Big Mom, too. After a few minutes, Big Mom tossed him a paper napkin.

"I could help you hide 'em better," he said between hiccups as he wiped his eyes, "if you'll help me get away."

She shook her head. "You can't get away, Sam. There's no place a boy your age can hide."

"I could live in the tunnel. Maybe sneak out at night and buy food and stuff for us."

Her eyes glistened with tears. "Then you'd be just like me—a prisoner in this house."

"What do you mean?"

"I mean I've wanted to run away for a long, long time, but those two down there—they're what's kept me here. The minute I sell the house, they'll tear it down and turn the whole damned area into a big development, just like the one on the other side of the hill. And when they tear down the house, they're gonna find 'em. I knew it would happen sooner or later, I just didn't want it to happen till after I'm gone."

They heard a scraping noise in the basement—the coal room door!—and a moment later, heavy footsteps on the stairs. Sam jumped to his feet but sank back into his chair when he realized he had no place to hide now and no-where to run. Big Mom reached across the table and took his hand, and a moment later, Blaine appeared in the kitchen.

"I had a feeling you might be here," he said. "I mentioned my suspicions to Dorothy when I got home, and she told me she'd heard stories when she was a child about a tunnel. So I came back and looked for it over there. You've got quite a lot to answer for, young man. From the looks of it, you've spent a lot of time with those two corpses in the tunnel. I wonder what the therapist will make of that—and the fact that you burned down your house, killing your mother, to avoid seeing the therapist in the first place."

Sam jumped up, started to shout, "You—!" but before he could say any more, Big Mom told him to sit back down and shut up. She struggled to her feet, leaning heavily on the walker. "Sam didn't kill his mother, Blaine. You know that as well as I do."

Blaine shrugged. "Whether it was intentional or not, I'll leave that to the experts—and to God. But the fact is, Sam burned down his house and managed to get out of it alive—and leave his mother behind."

"He didn't burn down that house," Big Mom said. "You did."

Blaine gaped at her. "*I* did? What kind of senile nonsense is that?"

"I couldn't sleep last night," she said, her eyes boring into his, "thinking of all the trouble I've been putting Sam and his mother to by asking them to take care of me. I knew I couldn't go on living in this house much longer, even with their help. I finally got up and went to the window—the window that looks out on the back of the house next door and the hill, and I saw something."

"What—what did you see?"

"A man on snowshoes."

"You couldn't have seen that. It was snowing too hard."

She went on quietly, as though he hadn't spoken: "He turned and looked back, and I saw his snow-crusted glasses. I thought it was you, Blaine, and wondered why you were out there."

"You're lying!"

She shrugged. "I suppose I could have been mistaken.

We'll have to ask Dorothy if you were home all last night."

"I wasn't! I went for a walk—a long walk. I do every night."

"In a blizzard?"

"Nobody's going to believe a word you say!"

"And then," she continued, "last Friday, I think it was, while Sam and his mother were at school and work, I happened to glance out the kitchen window—that one there—and saw you coming out of their house. What were you doing there, Blaine? Putting candles in the basement and disabling the fire alarms?"

"You're lying," he said again. "I'll have you declared incompetent. And don't forget—*you're* a killer, too!"

Those last words hung in the air for all of them to hear.

Big Mom's lips smiled. "Can you do that? Maybe, if the police know what they're looking for, maybe they can find a few snowshoe tracks frozen in the snow on the hill. What're the three things cops look for in a murder case, at least on TV? Opportunity, means—and motive? Dorothy's told me about the business losses you've had lately. She's very concerned about that."

"Goddamn you!" Blaine said, almost whispering. "Sam's going to kill you and then himself, and what's in the tunnel will explain everything!"

One of Big Mom's hands groped in her bathrobe for her pistol as Blaine lunged at her.

"No!" Sam screamed, and started around the table, but before he could get there, the gun went off. As Big Mom fell back into her chair, Blaine turned and pointed the gun at Sam.

There was a blur of motion at the basement door, and then the fire marshal was in the room. He grabbed Blaine's hand and twisted it back until he dropped the pistol, and when Blaine took a swing at him with his other hand, the marshal punched him in the face, knocking him to the ground.

"Big Mom!" Sam cried, kneeling beside her. The marshal was on the phone, the pistol in his hand pointing at Blaine on the floor, whimpering, holding his broken wrist.

Sam and the marshal stayed in the hospital with Big Mom that night. The marshal told Sam how he'd seen the broken window in the coal room and noticed the glass on the floor inside that told him somebody had come through it. Then he'd seen the bookcase that Blaine had pulled out from the wall, and, of course, he found the tunnel.

Around midnight, the marshal shook Sam awake, said Big Mom wanted to see him, and let him walk into the room alone. She was lying on her back, tubes in her nose and coming from the back of one hand.

She watched him come, and when he stood next to her, she moved one of her hands until it touched his. He took it.

"Her hair," she whispered. "What's it look like now?"

Sam knew what she was talking about. He thought back to the tunnel and the candle glowing on the skeletons that had lain there so many years.

"It's still red," he answered.

She didn't say anything for a long time. Then she said, so quietly Sam could barely make out the words, "It never had a chance to turn gray, and she never had a chance to grow, maybe to regret what she'd done. I had to be sorry for both of us—for everything."

Sam said, "Mom loved you because you were so good to her when she was little. And you tricked Uncle Blaine into admitting he set the fire. If you hadn't, what would've happened to me?"

Big Mom didn't say anything to that, but the ghost of a smile seemed to tremble on her lips as her eyes closed. Sam held her hand until she no longer needed it, then went on holding it a while longer, for himself.

TILL 3:45

Margaret Maron

Born and raised in eastern North Carolina, Margaret Maron lived "off" for several years before returning to her family's home place. In addition to a collection of short stories, she's also the author of sixteen mystery novels featuring Lieutenant Sigrid Harald, NYPD, and District Court Judge Deborah Knott of Colleton County, North Carolina. Her works have been translated into seven languages and are on the reading lists of various courses in contemporary Southern literature. They have also been nominated for every major award in the American mystery field. In 1993, her North Carolina–based Bootlegger's Daughter *won the Edgar Allan Poe Award and the Anthony Award for Best Mystery Novel of the Year, the Agatha Award for Best Traditional Novel, and the Macavity Award for Best Novel—an unprecedented sweep for a single novel. She has served as past president of Sisters in Crime, president of the American Crime Writers League, and as a director on the national board of Mystery Writers of America.*

From nine in the morning until three every afternoon, Mara Wolfe was a diligent worker, moving papers from her in basket to her outgoing with care and efficiency. She was patient on the telephone, even-tempered with her coworkers, and did not grumble when yet another

task was added to her workload . . . until the hands of the
little clock on her desk edged past three. That's when her
concentration began to falter, and callers were cut short
or put on hold as soon as her other line lit up to signal a
second incoming call.

3:10. 3:15.

Mara had timed her daughter's walk through lower
Manhattan. Fourth grade let out at 3 P.M. Allowing for
red lights at every corner, the walk from the schoolyard
gate to the door of their small apartment over a used book
store was precisely fourteen and a half minutes.

Add five minutes for giggling with her friends at the
corner, then another thirty seconds for checking that no
one loitered in their building's communal vestibule before
Gwen pulled out the brass latchkey she wore on a ribbon
around her neck.

Allow four more minutes in case she had to scurry to
the bathroom—"Sometimes I can't wait," Gwen had said
rebelliously—and that made 3:24 the absolute earliest
Mara could reasonably expect her daughter to call.

The telephone rang, and Mara scooped it to her ear.

Business. Aware of her supervisor's considering
glance, Mara managed to keep a smile in her voice as she
answered the client's question.

The light on her second line remained dark.

3:27, 3:30, and her imagination began to picture all the
grim things that could happen in this city to a wiry little
ten-year-old with short brown curls, a chipped front tooth,
and a trusting nature.

After her ex-husband ran to another state to avoid paying child support, Mara couldn't afford their heavily
mortgaged West Side condo, and she'd moved downtown

to be near her only living relative. As long as Aunt May could keep Gwen after school, everything was manageable, an adventure even; but after her aunt moved to Florida, reliable day care strained their slender budget to its limits, and Gwen hated it.

"They're all babies," she grumbled. "Nobody else in my class goes to day care. I'm big enough to take care of myself."

As was bound to happen sooner or later, Gwen woke up sneezing and sniffling on the same winter morning Mara was scheduled for a business meeting she simply couldn't afford to miss. There was no other choice. She left Gwen tucked into bed with telephone, tissues, and orange juice on the nightstand; the television on her dresser; a half-brave, half-excited expression on her face; and Mr. Ed, their big, horse-faced tomcat, snuggled at her feet.

Old Mrs. Bersisky in the next apartment grudgingly gave permission for Gwen to call her in an emergency ("A real emergency, mind you, and not just because she's bored"), and the bookstore owner downstairs said, sure, he'd keep an ear out for any unusual crashes overhead.

In the three years Mara and Gwen had lived there, the shop directly beneath them had changed hands several times. In fact, Mr. Ed was a legacy of the first tenant, a frail and kindly old gentleman whose musty stock of organic herbs and spices seemed to attract a surprisingly large clientele right up to the day an undercover narcotics agent arrested him for selling peyote and other more exotic hallucinogens.

Organic Herbs had been succeeded by Citizens for a Caring Congress, Mason's Used Furniture, and the Purl 2 Co-op.

Mara still regretted that last. Used furniture had meant

a strong smell of paint thinner and hot glue wafting up the stairs, and she had been terrified of the fire hazard, but the co-op brought a stream of friendly knitters who placed their sweaters and scarves on consignment at ridiculously low prices.

Unfortunately, Mara and Mrs. Bersisky seemed to be their only customers, and the business melted away entirely in last June's heat wave.

The latest venture had opened in November. Rechristened the Murder for Money Bookstore, it stocked nothing but used murder mysteries, detective and spy stories, and thrillers, and it seemed to draw as varied a clientele as had the old herb and spice shop.

Mara didn't approve of the store. Or its proprietor. Dayton McGuire was a tall, loose-knit man who appeared to be five or six years older than she. He wore glasses, and his shaggy brown head even showed a few responsible gray hairs, but Mara was not convinced. His eyes were vague and preoccupied behind those glasses, and he had a very casual attitude toward business. He took anybody's personal check without asking for three IDs, kept his bills and receipts wadded together in an old shoebox beside the cash register, and never answered the telephone if someone else was nearer.

Mr. Ed seemed to like him, though. Something about used books must have excited old memories of herbs and spices because when Mara or Gwen unlocked the door, the big yellow cat would often sneak between their feet, shoot down the stairs, and lurk at the bottom until someone opened the door to the vestibule where Murder for Money's door was usually ajar.

"Hey, no problem," Dayton McGuire had said when Mara retrieved their pet with profuse apologies the first time.

The second time they missed the cat, Mara and Gwen found him purring atop a stack of Mike Hammer mysteries. "Come on down, Mr. Ed," Gwen coaxed.

The third time, Mr. McGuire said, "I think his real name's Edward Macavity."

Gwen giggled at the silly sounding name, but Mara was suspicious. "Macavity?"

"T. S. Eliot," their new neighbor grinned. "One of his poems was about Macavity the Mystery Cat. Or, in Mr. Ed's case, the mystery lover."

"I doubt it." Mara stood on tiptoes to reach their truant animal, unaware that Dayton McGuire was regarding her long, slender legs with an appreciation usually reserved for a first edition of an early Rex Stout.

"You don't approve of murder mysteries?" he asked mildly.

"Not really." She held Mr. Ed in a firm grip. "They seem a waste of time, although I suppose there are people who enjoy that sort of thing."

McGuire nodded in solemn agreement, and his eyes behind those wire-rimmed glasses were very blue. "Yeah, mystery readers are a lazy bunch of slackers: presidents, scientists, philosophers."

Really, his eyes were the most astonishing blue, thought Mara. Then, as his words penetrated, she realized that those same blue eyes were also mocking her. She flushed to the roots of her honey-blond hair and left with as much dignity as she could muster while clutching a squirming cat.

Except for Gwen's bad cold a few days later, Mara might never have spoken to him again, but she couldn't leave her daughter alone upstairs without covering as many contingencies as possible, even though Dayton McGuire struck her as flip and irresponsible when she finally got him on the phone after the store opened.

As it was, that whole day proved the most anxious in Mara's life. She telephoned as soon as she got to the office and again whenever she had a free moment until Gwen complained at lunchtime, "Mom, you woke me up *again!*"

When she got home, Mara found that Gwen had passed the afternoon very amusingly. "Day brought me an Encyclopedia Brown book, and I figured out nearly all the answers."

"Mr. McGuire," Mara corrected automatically.

"He said for me to," Gwen argued. "He said if I could call a cat mister, I ought to call misters by their first names."

It would have been churlish not to go down and thank him for his kindness, but Mr. McGuire brushed off Mara's thanks.

"Part of my strategy," he said. "Hook 'em while they're young, and they're customers for life."

Gwen rapidly progressed from Encyclopedia Brown to Nancy Drew, the Hardy Boys, and Wendelin Van Draanen's street-smart Sammy Keyes; and when her cold cleared up, she dug in her heels about returning to the after-school center. As far as she was concerned, she'd proved she could take care of herself.

Mara felt guilty about letting her daughter become a latchkey kid, but there was no denying that her salary would go farther without day-care fees. Gwen promised that she'd come straight home after school and call as soon as she was safely in, that she would stay inside and keep the door locked, and that she would not play with matches nor turn on the stove.

During the icy, slushy months of February and March, Gwen had kept her promises. She fed Mr. Ed, tidied her

room, did her homework, worked on her Girl Scout
badges, and then watched television or read steadily
through the books Mr. McGuire lent her. With the coming
of spring, though, the novelty of looking after herself
started to wear thin, and of late she'd begun to dawdle
with her friends on the way home from school.

It was not enough to call outright disobedience, just
enough to keep Mara on edge as she watched the hands
on her desk clock move past 3:35.

Gwen shifted the weight of her pink nylon book bag
to her other shoulder as she climbed the steep stairs
and wondered if old Mrs. Bersisky would come out of the
other apartment today to ask if the mail had come. Mrs.
Bersisky rarely had a smile on her thin lips, was quick to
find fault, and had made it quite clear that she was nobody's surrogate grandmother.

"And I won't put up with childish racket," she'd said
when Gwen and her mother first moved in. "No running
on the stairs. No banging doors. You hear?"

Gwen was scared of the crotchety, arthritic woman,
and she rather thought her mother was, too. But Mom
expected her to be polite to all adults. Even cranky ones.
"It's probably because she never had any children of her
own," she'd said.

Fortunately, Mrs. Bersisky wasn't there today as Gwen
unlocked the apartment door.

For the past four days, the old woman had been leaning
on her walking stick and standing in the doorway of her
own apartment when the child came home, and Gwen had
been surprised by her smile of sudden friendliness.

The first day, she'd thrust a small key into Gwen's
hand and croaked in what was probably meant to sound

like a friendly chirrup, "Now don't dawdle, little girl. I'm expecting an important letter."

Startled, Gwen had dropped her book bag on the landing and headed back downstairs with the key to the mailbox next to hers and Mom's. The postman usually came around the time she was getting home, and she'd offered several times to fetch Mrs. Bersisky's mail, only to be refused.

"I may have arthritis, but I can still climb stairs." She had eyed Gwen's Scout uniform sharply that last day. "And I'm not your good deed, miss!"

Which had made Gwen flush because that really was the only reason she'd kept offering.

But if Mrs. Bersisky wanted to be nice now, that was fine with Gwen, and she had emptied the box quickly without trying to read the envelopes. All junk mail though, she was pretty sure.

"Thank you, little girl," Mrs. Bersisky had simpered, "and here's your dime for saving me all those steps."

Before Gwen could say that she didn't want to be paid, Mrs. Bersisky had shut the door in her face.

The same thing happened the next day and the next: Mrs. Bersisky in her open doorway, the key, a couple of circulars addressed to occupant, the dime, the closed door—all as if they'd been doing this for months.

Yesterday was different again, though. No sign of Mrs. Bersisky. But just as Gwen was taking the key out of the lock, the woman's door opened and Mr. Ed, who had been winding around Gwen's ankles, scampered across the landing and into Mrs. Bersisky's apartment.

Appalled, Gwen had dropped her book bag and darted after him, apologizing frantically.

Inside, the apartment was both brighter and less cluttered than she'd imagined except for a row of potted plants in the sunny front window. No sign of her cat, though. She turned and almost jumped out of her skin. Immediately behind the door stood a tall, dark-haired young woman who held the cat in her arms as she scratched under his chin.

"He's a real lover, isn't he?" she asked with a friendly smile.

"Not usually," Gwen said, confused. She didn't know Mrs. Bersisky ever had company and, while Mr. Ed liked to be petted, he didn't usually let strangers actually pick him up.

"So you're the nice little girl who gets Granny's mail for her every day." The woman smiled. "She's been telling me all about you. Why don't I hold on to Mr. Ed while you go check her box?"

"Okay," said Gwen.

The box held a magazine, a circular, and a long, thin envelope with the name of a bank on it. Through the window of the envelope Gwen saw Mrs. Bersisky's name printed on a pale green background. The young woman took the envelope from her with a happy smile. "Here's the first one, Granny!"

Mrs. Bersisky's shoulders seemed to slump as she handed Gwen a dime.

Today, Gwen was so distracted by Mrs. Bersisky's unexpected absence after four days of being there that she forgot to call her mother and began to fix herself a snack. A new Nancy Drew book lay on the table, and as Gwen spread peanut butter on some crackers, half her mind was on the plot, the other half on why Mrs. Bersisky's granddaughter had stood behind the door yesterday while the older woman handed over the mailbox key. Had she been there every day?

But if Mrs. Bersisky never had any children, how could she have a granddaughter?

Absentmindedly, Gwen let Mr. Ed lick a smear of peanut butter from her fingers.

And that was another thing. How did she know their cat's name?

Maybe, thought Gwen, she used to live in the neighborhood. There *was* something familiar about her.

And then Gwen remembered. Someone else used to work in the store downstairs when they first moved here three years ago.

"I was just a little kid then," she told Mr. Ed, "but I remember that old man who used to own you. And there was a grown-up girl. Purple hair. She had a ring through her lip, one through her nose, another one through her eyebrow, and even one in her belly button. Her hair's black now and she doesn't have any rings except in her ears, but it's the same person, isn't it, Mr. Ed? That's why you let her pick you up, isn't it?"

Mom said the old man had gone to jail for selling drugs. Did the girl go to jail, too?

"I bet she's not really Mrs. B's granddaughter," Gwen told her cat.

Mr. Ed no longer listened. Instead, he'd gone over to sniff at the apartment door. As Gwen followed, she heard a noise outside on the landing and pressed her eye to the peephole.

Across the landing, Mrs. B.'s granddaughter, if that's who she was, pulled the door to and headed for the stairs with something in her hand. The mailbox key!

Gwen quietly eased the door open and slipped across to Mrs. Bersisky's door, Mr. Ed at her heels. As she suspected, it wasn't latched, and she pushed it open and let the cat run inside again, half expecting to get yelled at.

Instead, she was shocked to see her elderly neighbor seated upright in a heavy wooden chair, her arms bound behind her with a pair of pantyhose, and a gag in her mouth.

The old woman's eyes rolled frantically as she tried to speak.

"Is she coming right back?" Gwen whispered fearfully.

Mrs. Bersisky nodded emphatically just as the vestibule door banged at the foot of the stairs.

With no time to get away, Gwen dived behind the couch under the front windows and lay on her stomach so she could see past the fringe that didn't quite brush the floor.

A moment later, the young woman came through the door, waving two long, narrow envelopes over her head. "Payday, Granny! Just like I thought."

Checks, thought Gwen, remembering the envelopes Aunt May and Uncle Pete used to get every month.

The young woman ripped these two open and her eyes widened as she read the figures. "Why, Granny, what big dividends you have!"

To Gwen's dismay, Mr. Ed chose that precise moment to come wandering out of the bedroom and rub against the woman's ankle.

"What're you doing here, Ed?" Her eyes narrowed suspiciously as she looked around the living room. "I pulled the door shut, so how did you—? The little girl!" She gave Mrs. Bersisky's white hair a vicious tug. "Is she in here, old lady? You don't tell me, I'm gonna—"

Mrs. Bersisky closed her eyes stubbornly.

The woman picked up Mrs. Bersisky's stout walking stick and headed for the bedroom.

As soon as she'd passed the couch, Gwen eeled out and hurried toward the door, but before she'd taken three steps, the walking stick caught her on the shoulder so hard that it knocked the breath out of her, and she felt herself falling.

3 :44. 3:45.
Gwen had never been this late.

Ignoring her supervisor, Mara dialed her apartment. After ten rings, she broke the connection and looked up the number of the Murder for Money Bookstore. Her fingers were unsteady as she dialed because she was half angry that Gwen might be carelessly breaking the rules and more than half terrified that something serious had happened.

The bookstore telephone rang and rang and rang. It was maddening the way Dayton McGuire could ignore the phone if he were shelving books or talking to a customer about the differences between Dashiell Hammett and Ross Macdonald.

"If it bothers you, answer it and take the message," he'd said more than once when she'd practically shrieked at him that his phone was ringing.

Her other line lit up, and Mara eagerly switched over. Instead of Gwen, it was a long-winded client who seemed to take forever to state his needs. By the time both lines were free, it was almost four o'clock. She called her apartment again. No answer.

She tried Mrs. Bersisky's number. Busy.

Whimpering with pain, Gwen rolled away as the woman grabbed for her. Gwen rushed back to the front windows. "Help!" she cried, trying to tug one open. "Help!"

The young woman gave a bitter laugh. "Scream your head off, kid. This is New York. Nobody comes when you yell for help in this town."

Remembering all the things she'd read, Gwen knew she was right. She tugged harder at the window. It wouldn't budge, and one of Mrs. Bersisky's potted plants crashed to the floor.

"Get away from that window!" snarled the woman, flourishing the walking stick. As she swung at Gwen again, she caught the telephone instead and sent it flying.

The telephone! Gwen felt like kicking herself. Instead of hiding like a jerk, why didn't she dial 911 as soon as she saw Mrs. B. tied up? *Stupid, stupid, stupid!* She snatched up another of Mrs. B.'s potted plants.

The woman laughed. "Put it down, kid, and I won't hurt you. I'll just tie you up while Granny and me go cash these checks at the bank. Soon as I get the money, I'll let her go. Promise."

As Gwen hesitated, the woman moved closer. The child was trapped between the couch and windows, and she screamed again as the woman lifted the heavy cane to smash over her head.

4:05, and Mara held the receiver to her ear, grimly determined to let it ring a hundred times if that's what it took to make Dayton McGuire answer his phone. She wished there were some way she could turn up the volume and make it ring even louder at his end.

Eventually someone picked up, and a lackadaisical male voice said, "Hello?"

"Mr. McGuire?" (He had never invited *her* to call him Day, and they remained Mr. McGuire and Mrs. Wolfe.)

"No."

"Is he there?"

"No."

"Well, who's minding the shop?"

"I am, I guess," the voice admitted. "They left in such a hurry—"

"Who did?" she asked impatiently.

"Him and that little girl from upstairs. When the ambulance was taking too long, Professor Martin said he could drive them to the hospital in his car, but Day would have to go along and—"

Mara's heart seemed to stop in midbeat. "Which hospital? What happened? Is she hurt?"

"She was breathing again when they got her in the car. I don't know what hospital. Look, I gotta go. You call back when Day's here, okay?" And ignoring Mara's pleas for information, he hung up.

Her supervisor came over. "Is something wrong?" she asked, concerned by Mara's suddenly bloodless face.

"I don't *know!*" Mara cried, reaching for her purse. "They've taken Gwen to a hospital, and I don't know which one. Or why. Please, I have to go!"

"Of course you do." The woman pulled a twenty-dollar bill from her pocket. "Take a cab. It'll be quicker. And call me as soon as you learn anything."

"Oh, thank you!" Mara exclaimed, and dashed from the office.

"She was breathing again," the man had said.

Did that mean Gwen had *stopped* breathing? Why? A fall? An electrical shock? Had she choked on something? Had someone hurt her?

A thousand images of her daughter's thin little face rigid with pain or limp with death rushed through Mara's mind as the cab slipped in and out of traffic lanes, strained at red lights, and squeezed the yellows. Her thoughts were an anguished blur, but one thing she knew: If the worst had happened, she'd never *ever* forgive herself.

Day McGuire thought she was too uptight with Gwen, set too many rules, kept her too closely penned after school.

"Why don't you let her play downstairs?" he'd asked when Mara stopped in to pay him for that last batch of Nancy Drews on Friday. "She ought to be out in the fresh spring air, not cooped up reading every afternoon."

"Don't you read the newspaper?" Mara had asked. "Don't you even read your own books? Here you are surrounded by thousands of books on murder and mayhem, and you ask why I don't let a little ten-year-old girl play on the sidewalk?"

"I could keep an eye out."

"Oh, sure," she'd said sarcastically. "Right up to the moment someone asked you how many cases Lord Peter What's-his-name solved."

As the cab swung onto her street, Mara strained forward on the edge of her seat until she spotted her building. Everything looked normal in the afternoon sunshine, even prosaic. There were no milling crowds beneath the tree outside the bookstore, no police questioning witnesses, no yellow tape, no television cameras.

She gratefully doubled the cabbie's tip because he'd brought her home so quickly and hurried across the sidewalk.

The bookstore was unlocked but completely deserted. Mara raced upstairs to the apartment. Gwen's book bag was by the door and the makings of a snack cluttered the table, but no sign of her daughter. And no sign of Mr. Ed, either. She darted across the landing to ring and pound on Mrs. Bersisky's door, but no one responded.

A terror so thick she could almost touch it settled onto

Mara's heart as she hurried back to her own apartment and called the nearest hospital. She willed her voice to steadiness while asking about a ten-year-old, Gwen Wolfe, who might have been brought in within the last hour or so.

They switched her to the emergency room, and the harried nurse who answered assured her that no little girl had been treated there that afternoon. No one remembered a Dayton McGuire or a Professor Martin, either.

It was the same at the second nearest hospital and at two others farther away.

The police! she thought, and phoned the local precinct. The desk officer was kind, but he knew nothing about any young girl at that address.

Frustrated, Mara tried to call Mrs. Bersisky again and found the line still busy. Once more she pounded on the woman's door and even put her ear against the cool panel to listen. No sounds.

There were two more apartments upstairs. Mara knew both couples worked all day, yet she could not quit without trying them, too.

Nothing.

She was halfway down the stairs when her own telephone rang, but by the time she could rush back, the ringing had stopped. Too late to wish she'd squeezed their budget for an answering machine.

Blocked at every turn, Mara wanted to put her head down and howl for the first time since her divorce. Until 3:45 this afternoon, she had felt that she and Gwen were living an adventure of sorts. Not that everything was perfect, but at least she was in control, making her own choices. Now, just thinking of all the possible horrors left her helpless and hopeless.

Wrapped in a numb fatalism, she went downstairs to

the bookstore, where she found Mr. Ed asleep on a carton of books. Whatever happened to Gwen had probably happened over an hour ago, and there was nothing she could do to change it. Day McGuire and one of his customers had taken Gwen somewhere for help. Sooner or later, he would have to come back, and then she would know. Until then, she had no choice but to wait.

There had been two people browsing through back shelves when she'd entered the store, and several more soon arrived, but none knew where the store's owner had gone. She took their money, gave them receipts, and began straightening out some of McGuire's clutter behind the sales counter.

She was sorting through a sheaf of canceled checks when the bell over the door tinkled again. She looked up automatically, and the sales counter seemed to sway and tilt as Day McGuire held the door open for Gwen, who bounced in, looked surprised, and exclaimed, "Mom! Where have you been? We've been calling *everywhere!*"

The next thing Mara knew, she was lying on the floor behind the sales counter, and McGuire's warm, deep voice was reassuring Gwen, "She just blacked out for a minute. See? She's already coming around."

He lifted Mara's head. "Okay now?"

Mara felt the room steady and pushed herself into a sitting position. Gwen was kneeling beside her, and Mara put her arms around the child, held her tight, and began to cry.

Gwen squirmed with embarrassment. "Don't cry, Mom. Everything's okay."

"I thought you were hurt," said Mara. "Someone said you'd stopped breathing."

"Not me," said Gwen. "Mrs. Bersisky. After her phony granddaughter—"

"Phony who?"

"Used to sell drugs out of this store," McGuire explained. "She's running from a parole violation and decided to steal Mrs. Bersisky's annuity checks to finance her getaway. Gwen put a stop to that."

Gwen quickly described the events that led up to this afternoon. "Mrs. B. told her I always got the mail for her, and that I'd be suspicious if she quit letting me. She was hoping to slip me a note or something, but she never got a chance."

When Gwen told about getting hit by the walking stick, Mara felt a rage she'd never experienced before.

"Oh, honey." She gently stroked Gwen's bruised arm. "How did you get away?"

"She said nobody would come if I yelled for help," Gwen said proudly, "so I threw a flowerpot through the front window and yelled *'Fire!'* as loud as I could."

"Almost beaned my best-paying customer," Day McGuire grinned, "but it sure got our attention. We went charging upstairs with a fire extinguisher."

"The woman ran away, but while they were chasing her, Mrs. Bersisky quit breathing, so I gave her CPR just like we learned in Scouts."

"Probably saved her life," said McGuire. "Gwen did CPR till Mrs. Bersisky started breathing again, then got an aspirin down her and we took her to the hospital. The doctor thinks she had a mild heart attack, but thanks to your daughter here, she'll probably be all right."

"I just tried to think what Sammy Keyes would do," Gwen said. Then, remembering her previous grievance, she scowled at Mara. "But where were *you?*"

"That's right," said McGuire. "Gwen did all the responsible things, but what about you? We tried to get you at your office, but your boss said you'd gone charging out a half-hour earlier, so we called you at home and first the line stayed busy and then you wouldn't answer. No message where you were going, no thought of how worried Gwen would be."

There was nothing vague or preoccupied about the bookseller's manner now, and he sounded almost angry as he hauled Mara to her feet. "This is the last place I'd have thought to find you."

Something about the tone of his voice made Mara swallow the sarcastic retort she normally would have made.

8:46. All the excitement had been talked out, and things were almost back to normal. Mr. Ed was asleep on the windowsill. Gwen had finished her homework, had taken her bath, and was helping Mara make sugar cookies for tomorrow's Scout meeting when Mr. McGuire knocked at their door with a stack of used books in his arms.

"Sherlock Holmes for you," he told Gwen, "Dorothy L. Sayers for your mother. Along with a proposal."

Mara was startled, but his next words dispelled whatever she might have thought he meant.

"I need somebody to keep my shelves in alphabetical order, so I thought I'd hire Gwen if that's okay with you? An hour and a half a day, five days a week, for, let's say, a dollar an hour?"

Gwen's eyes were shining as she quickly calculated her weekly take. "Can I, Mom? Please?"

"That's very generous of you, Mr. McGuire," Mara began, when the oven timer rang and the smell of well-done sugar cookies sent them to the kitchen.

"Call me Day," he said, trailing along after them, and

as he reached for a hot cookie, Mara automatically poured him a glass of milk, too.

"I thought we could trade," he said. "You do my book-keeping, and I'll watch Gwen. You've already made a good start on straightening out my system."

"That shoebox is a system?" Mara asked dryly. Her smile agreed to his plan though, and Gwen was ecstatic. Nevertheless, Mara couldn't quite quash a small twinge of disappointment when the tall man stood to leave. She should have known he was only being neighborly.

As she held the door for him, he said, "Read the books I gave you in order. There'll be a test at the end of *Gaudy Night*."

Mara was puzzled.

"That's the one where Lord Peter proposed to Harriet Vane," he explained diffidently.

His sudden shyness made Mara's heart begin to beat absurdly fast. "Did she accept?"

"Why don't we talk about it over dinner this week-end?" he asked, and something more than neighborliness gleamed behind the laughter in his eyes.

A NIGHT AT THE LOVE NEST RESORT

Robert J. Randisi and Christine Matthews

Individually, the authors have published extensively in several genres. Together, they have written Murder Is the Deal of the Day *(St. Martin's Press, 1999), the first in a series featuring married amateur detectives Gil and Claire Hunt. The second Gil and Claire novel will be published in 2001. This is their eighth collaborative short story.*

At first her moaning aroused him. He'd tried turning the volume of the TV up but kept hitting the mute button whenever they got loud enough for him to make out some of the words.

Stephen had made reservations at the Love Nest Resort right after Christmas. Victoria had thrown one of her tantrums when the holidays fell flat. It was all his fault, she told him many times. He lacked imagination. He didn't care enough about her to make things special. She wasn't going to put up with his laziness much longer.

He knew she was right. The purple sweater hadn't

looked all that good in the store, but he figured it was just the lighting. And when the sales clerk tried convincing him the velvet slacks were a perfect match, he wondered if she was color-blind. But his feet hurt and he wanted to get out of the crowded, noisy mall, so he'd handed over his Visa card, never giving the gifts another thought. When Victoria locked herself in the bathroom, he mumbled his apology through the door, swearing that he hadn't noticed both items were three sizes too large for his wife.

But Stephen Yager was a man who believed that if a person tried hard enough to change, it would happen. And so it came to pass that on December twenty-seventh, while waiting his turn in the dentist's chair, he'd spotted an ad for a honeymoon resort on the back page of *Bride Beautiful* magazine. Like a beacon, he'd been shown the way. Tearing carefully along the dotted lines, he stuffed the thin paper quickly into the pocket of the leather jacket Victoria had given him three Christmases before. How he loved that jacket. It had been one of the most extravagant presents anyone had ever given him. As he rubbed his fingers along the supple hide of his sleeve, he thought how very surprised she'd be on Valentine's Day.

He'd hoped for snow. What could be more romantic than a nice long drive in the country? He imagined big, soft snowflakes gliding down from the blue sky, drifting into heaps of billowy fluff. But the winter had been mild, temperatures had stayed in the forties and fifties. He had also imagined Victoria beside him in the luxurious car he'd rented. But that didn't happen, either.

*   *   *

H e felt more than stupid while he registered. Large hearts made of dozens of white and red carnations flanked either side of the long, marble desk. The clerk wore a small red heart pinned to the lapel of his black jacket; behind him a gold Cupid was etched in the large mirror covering the entire wall. And he'd felt embarrassed when the clerk asked, "Will the wife be joining you later, sir?"

Stephen wondered if this grinning idiot standing in front of him had been trained to speak in such a condescending manner.

"Yes, she will."

"Good, good. We'll be sure to escort her to your front door the minute she arrives. Each suite has been decorated to enhance your romantic experience. Due to the wide variety of accommodations, it can get confusing. If you'll follow Raymond, he'll take you over."

Raymond wore a quilted ski jacket with matching pants. He got into a golf cart and pointed toward a group of modern buildings on the west side of the property. When they came to a parking lot, Raymond signaled again, and Stephen parked.

Raymond got out and grabbed Stephen's suitcase. "This way, sir."

The room was plush, large, and very red.

"This is your fireplace." Raymond flipped a switch, and the artificial logs burst into flame. "You have your dimmer switch over here, the other switches behind the bed control the curtains and your stereo."

Stephen only heard part of what the man was saying. He knew he wouldn't be needing any of the amenities. His eyes kept being drawn back to the large heart-shaped bed, which took up half the room. It was covered in a red velvet spread edged in gold tassels and scattered with white and lavender heart-shaped pillows.

"The bathroom is behind this door."

Stephen followed Raymond into the pink marble room. Twin heart-shaped sinks were separated by a pink vanity. A heart-shaped, sunken tub with a chandelier hanging over it was the centerpiece of the room. A shower was tucked into an alcove on the wall opposite the sinks. And discreetly hidden in a corner was the toilet. The walls in both rooms were smothered with red carpeting; the ceiling was covered with a similar plush in a light shade of mauve.

"Will there be anything else, sir?"

"No, that's plenty for me to deal with now. Thanks." Stephen slipped the man a five-dollar bill.

"Breakfast is served between six and ten in the main dining room. We have a fully equipped gym and . . ."

"Thanks, I'll find everything tomorrow." Stephen walked the man to the door.

When he was finally alone, Stephen slumped onto the bed and stared at the phone. It took almost fifteen minutes before he talked himself out of calling to apologize. He got up and began to unpack. It took another fifteen minutes for him to stop wondering why he'd even come to a honeymoon resort alone.

The food was paid for. Every meal for the next three days was taken care of. All he had to do was show up and eat. He had needed to get away for some time. Work was stressing him out. And then there was his wife. She'd been so unreasonable lately. It was almost as if she was trying to get him to leave. No, it had to be his imagination. Victoria would never cheat on him. Looking around the room, Stephen decided maybe the weekend was just what he needed—to unwind, relax—especially now. He just hadn't expected everything to be so . . . cute.

Nor did he expect to be able to hear the couple in the next room so clearly.

He turned off the TV and moved closer to the wall. After all, the only woman he'd ever heard in the throes of passion, live and in person, was his wife. He'd often wondered what sounds other women made. Real women, not actresses in porn movies.

Victoria was a loud lover. It usually took her a long time to climax, but when she did, he was often tempted to put a pillow over her face so the neighbors wouldn't hear the cries.

He mashed his ear tight against the wall, wondering if he'd be able to make out the squeaking of bedsprings. If the walls in this place were thin, maybe the beds were cheap.

Remembering all the sitcoms he had watched, Stephen was trying to decide if a water glass held to his ear would amplify the action on the other side of his wall when the volume picked up on its own. What he was able to make out didn't sound like lovemaking. The couple now seemed to be having an argument.

". . . never satisfied?" the man was shouting. "You make too damn much noise for someone who's never satisfied!"

"I have to fake it!" she screamed. "It's the only way I know how to make you feel like a real man!"

"Keep it up, Valerie. You're askin' for it!"

"Ooh, what a big man you are, Alec," she taunted, showing no signs of fear. "Whatcha gonna do? Smack the poor little woman?"

"Little?" the man laughed. "Have you taken a good look at your ass lately?"

"You bastard!"

It sounded like a chair was knocked over. Stephen imagined the couple struggling, and then there was the sound of a slap. Another followed and then a cry from the woman. Stephen assumed she had slapped the man, and he had retaliated—with a closed fist.

"Don't you dare hit me again!" the woman cried out.

"You deserve it," the man growled. "You're a selfish, vicious, ungrateful bitch!"

"Get away from me!" the woman screamed. Since there was no sound of a blow, Stephen assumed the man must have grabbed her, maybe by the hair. More struggling and then something or someone crashed into the spot where Stephen's ear rested against the wall. Startled, Stephen jumped back, landing on his butt in the middle of the room.

As he sat there, he wondered if he should do something. But what? Call the front desk? The police? Maybe all it would take was for him to go next door, introduce himself, let them know their conversation could be heard by a perfect stranger. The word *perfect* made him cringe. In a perfect world they'd smile, apologize for disturbing him, maybe even invite him in for a drink.

Who was he kidding? People like that didn't care who heard them. They were the Jerry Springer people. They thrived on suffering, enjoyed complaining about all the raw deals they've gotten to anyone who looks in their general direction, let alone actually listen for more than five minutes.

Maybe they weren't fighting at all. Stephen had just read an article about rough sex. It went into titillating detail, explaining how some couples took turns tying each other up, whipping exposed flesh, becoming aroused when they caused pain.

"Whatever rattles your chains," he said out loud. Then,

even louder, toward the direction of the wall, he shouted, "but I don't have to hear it!"

How could people want to be brutalized during love-making? He'd never understood the whole S and M thing. Was that what he'd find if he went down the hall to complain? Would a man wearing leather jockey shorts answer the door?

He returned to his place by the wall and pressed his ear against the carpeting, amazed that sound traveled so well through the pile.

The only sounds he heard were moans. Maybe the fighting was over. Maybe he should stop listening. He suddenly felt ashamed of himself.

Stephen stretched out on the bed and turned the TV back on. He hardly paid attention to it, though. He thought about his sex life with Victoria, which had become something of a bore. Would a little violence spice it up? How, he wondered, would his wife react if he slapped her during sex? Maybe spanked her a little? Would that turn her on?

Lately he had no idea what turned her on. She had become as indifferent as the remote he held in his hand. Tossing the control across the room, he turned over to lie on his back. Glancing toward the phone, he felt a sharp twinge of guilt. Should he be a man and call? Ask forgiveness? No. Why should he beg? It was her fault he was here in this honeymoon hell alone.

The voices started up again. At first they were hardly intelligible, just murmurings. But it didn't take very long before shouting began. She called him an asshole, he was calling her a tramp.

The woman yelled then, it was more like a scream, and Stephen wondered how he could possibly be the only other innocent guest hearing this. Wasn't there someone in the room on the other side? Then came a shriek for help.

He suddenly leaped off the bed and rushed to the door. His hand was on the doorknob before he knew what his own body had planned. Reflex was all that was guiding him.

His shoes didn't even whisper in the thick carpeting covering the hallway. Within a few seconds, he was standing in front of room 231. When he reached out, his hand brushed the knob. A small spark jumped from the metal to his finger. The shock caused not only his hand but his whole body to recoil.

Staring at the gold numerals snuggled inside the red enamel heart, Stephen looked around for someone to help him decide what to do next. He listened a minute longer, and when the silence made his ears buzz, he turned and walked back to his room.

"Okay, they settled down," he told himself. "Maybe the fighting makes them tired."

Realizing he was getting hungry, Stephen searched the room for a menu.

The steak was overdone, the potatoes were cold, and the tomatoes arranged on his salad were cut in the shape of little hearts. But at least the people next door had seemed to calm down for the night.

Rolling the dinner cart into a corner, Stephen unpacked until he couldn't avoid the bathroom any longer. When he flipped on the lights, the room shimmered with crystal and pinkness. He washed his hands and decided he'd take his shower in the morning.

It must have been the time of night, the time when Victoria and he liked to watch old reruns and have a snack. He suddenly missed her very much. The thought of being at the Love Nest Resort without her made him curl up in the middle of the bed and rock himself, trying to console his broken heart. Whimpering followed loud sobs, but neither were coming from him.

"Shut up! Shut your mouth or I'll shut it for you!"

Stephen lifted his head to make out what the woman named Valerie would say next.

"Fucker!"

While he was trying to decide if he should take up his post by the wall again, what he could only assume was furniture started crashing against the walls and on the floor of room 231. In spite of the thunderous fury, however, the voices next door still managed to drown out the commotion.

"Don't you run away from me! Get back here!"

"Stay away from me, Al! I'll call the cops, I swear it! You'll go back to prison."

"Put the goddamn phone down!"

Stephen could hear the phone jack being ripped from the wall.

"You threatenin' me, bitch? Don't you ever... ever..."

She seemed to be dodging him. "Or what? What's the big man gonna do?"

A lamp or something made of glass crashed against the wall.

Stephen wondered why Valerie antagonized Al? Why didn't she play it smart? Tell him whatever he wanted to hear until she could get out?

"Frank told me all about you. I shoulda listened!"

"How many times I gotta tell you I didn't sleep with your brother? Listen to me!"

"No more, baby! I'm through listenin'."

"That hurts. Al, you're hurtin' me! Get your hands off me!"

Her screams started off angry; they pierced the air, and Stephen paced, feeling cowardly. At least he could call the front desk or security. He went to the phone.

The change in her tone throughout the next set of screaming made him hesitate. Now she was almost laughing.

"You're pathetic, know that? I shoulda listened to *my* brother when he said you were scum."

Al was silent. Had Valerie gotten the upper hand somehow?

"How do you like it, huh? How does that feel?"

Al still made no comment.

Stephen stood frozen, listening, holding his breath.

Then Valerie's screams changed into something Stephen had heard only one time before when a car hit a German shepherd caught in the middle of a busy highway. She yelped. He knew without any proof that she was hurt. He ran to the wall and listened.

"They're gonna have to scrape your guts off the floor when I'm finished."

"I'm sorry, Al. It's just that you get me so mad. You know how I get." She sounded like a sorry six-year-old.

"It don't matter. I gotta teach you a lesson now. You can't talk to me that way. No one can."

"Please . . . no, Al . . . please . . . no, no, oh God, no . . ."

Then came the quiet again.

If the very worst thing had happened, if Al had murdered Valerie, there'd be some sort of sound in there. Wouldn't he want to wash the blood off his hands? Why wasn't there any noise? Running water? Scrambling to clean up the murder scene?

Nothing.

He ran to the wall and pressed his ear to it but heard nothing. He grabbed a clean drinking glass from the desk, where it stood next to an ice bucket, and pressed that to the wall. He held his ear to the glass, but there was still no sound.

Just . . . deadly silence.

His mind raced in two directions at the same time—or in the same direction on two different tracks. Should he call the police and report what had happened in the next room? Then make his own phone call?

First he had to do something for that poor woman next door. He was now convinced that what he'd been hearing all night had nothing to do with sex or passion but simply was an ongoing fight that had escalated into deadly violence.

He was convinced the woman now lay dead or dying, and he had to do something. He could at least call the front desk. A place like this must surely have security.

But there was always the chance he was wrong. Maybe they had gotten tired of fighting and just gone to sleep. He had to make sure.

He went to his patio door, unlocked it, and slid it open. He thought about taking something as a weapon but reasoned that he was just going to take a look around. An innocent stroll for some fresh air.

There were flowerpots on the ledge separating the adjoining patios, so he had to be careful not to knock any over. He was wearing jeans and shoes, but just a T-shirt on top; his skin immediately responded to the cold with goose bumps. When he finally got onto his neighbors' patio, he moved slowly toward the glass doors and tried looking inside. They had the curtains closed, but there was a small gap right in the middle, enough for one eye. He peered in anxiously. He was able to see a small portion of the bed, some of the floor, but not much more. He moved, trying for a better angle, and then he spotted something. A foot. It was obviously a woman's bare foot, and it was on the bed. But it wasn't moving.

He watched and waited. The foot did not move. Had the man killed her and laid her out on top of the giant red heart? If so, where was he? In the bathroom, watching the blood turn pink as it swirled around the sink and ran down the drain? He wouldn't even need soap as the blood would still be wet, and water would have washed it away easily.

Abruptly, Stephen hurried back to his room, almost knocking a stone vase from the ledge. He ran inside, his body welcoming the heat even if his mind didn't notice it. He quickly went into the bathroom, calculating that it backed up to theirs. He listened but did not hear water running. Had Alec finished cleaning up his bloody mess?

He hurried back to his bed and sat down, looming over the phone. He was about to pick it up when he suddenly heard voices coming from the other room. Two voices!

Dashing to his spot by the wall, he pressed his ear against the soft carpeting and held his breath.

". . . know I love you," the woman was saying.

"And I love you, too."

"I'm sorry, baby," she cooed. "Sometimes I just get so afraid you'll leave me, and then I get mad at myself for being so awful to you."

"I know, so do I. I didn't mean what I said—I never do."

"Neither do I."

"Now, come over here, sexy. I wanna get my money's worth outta this big love mattress."

She laughed.

Stephen couldn't believe what he was hearing. Love talk? Making up? After all the shit she put him through they could just forget all the hatred so easily? Was it really possible that two people could be so vicious to each other and then just . . . make up? What if the man had killed his wife? What if he had grabbed her around the neck and squeezed her throat? His thumbs would press on her trachea. Hard.

It grew quiet in the other room, and he moved away from the wall. Suddenly he felt lonely . . . and guilty.

Stephen walked over to the phone. It was a plastic reproduction of an antique he'd seen in pictures of ladies' boudoirs. It fit the decor of the room perfectly, but there were no directions printed around the dials, and Stephen could not find a directory among the papers scattered across the desk.

He picked up the phone and dialed the operator.

Eric Giles loved working at the Love Nest Resort. Arranging honeymoon weekends or anniversary vacations made him feel sort of like Cupid. It appealed to the romantic in him. There was no question about it, when he found that special someone, he was going to come here and stay in one of the love nests.

His phone rang, breaking into his reverie. "Front desk."

"Yes, I—I was trying to get an outside line."

"Mr. Yager?" Eric shook his head slowly back and forth at the thought of the poor man who had checked in all by himself earlier that evening.

"That's right."

"We're still keeping our eyes peeled for Mrs. Yager, sir. She hasn't shown up yet. But you can rest easier knowing I'll personally escort her to your room whenever she arrives."

"I—I'm afraid she won't be coming after all."

"Oh ... my ... I'm so sorry to hear that, sir. Nothing serious I hope? Is there anything we can do for you?"

"I just need an outside line, please."

"Simply press nine, sir."

"Thank you." Stephen hung up before the cheerful clerk could ask any more questions.

If he didn't do it now, he never would.

Stephen punched the nine on his phone. After listening to the dial tone for a few seconds, he placed his call.

"This is the nine-one-one operator, do you have an emergency?"

"Yes ... yes, I do. I'm over at the Love Nest Resort," Stephen began.

"And what is the nature of your emergency?"

"Well ... I ..."

"Sir? Are you all right?" The operator sounded impatient. Stephen felt badly about taking up her time with his family problems.

"I'm really sorry about this, but I wanted to report a murder. I hope I called the right number."

"A murder, sir?"

"Yes, you see, I murdered my wife yesterday."

Tea for Two

Nancy Pickard

Nancy Pickard's newest heroine is true crime writer Marie Light-foot, who was introduced in The Whole Truth. *Pickard is the author of the ten-book Jenny Cain mystery series and three books in the Eugenia Potter culinary mystery series. Her novels and short stories have won the Anthony, Agatha, Macavity, and Shamus Awards, and she is a double Edgar Award nominee. She is a member of PEN and is a former president and founding member of Sisters of Crime. She lives in Prairie Village, Kansas, with one son, three computers, two cats, and two miniature longhaired dachshunds.*

"What's the matter, John?"

"I'll be damned. That's so weird. There's a woman sitting on a barstool over there. Don't look! I thought she was young, but then she turned around, and I saw she's definitely not."

"She's old?"

"Seventy, if she's a day. But she's got blond hair and she's thin, and she's got on a sweater and a belt over it and a long skirt, kind of like you've got on. You look lovely, by the way, Heather."

"Thank you, John."

"You make me smile when you do that, the way you

say it, so perky, like you're going to curtsy. You really do look adorable."

"How would you know?"

"What? How would I know?"

"When you're looking over there and not over here."

"Sorry. I can't get over the shock. I was so sure she was young. I didn't even question it. It's not just her clothes and her hair, either. There's something about her posture, the way she's bent over her drink and her cigarette—"

"No wonder she looks old."

"Now, now. Don't be mean. No, she looks old because she *is* old. But before she turned around, I was positive . . . Have you ever seen somebody driving in a convertible, like a Mercedes, and when you see their face it's a shock because it's all wrinkled, and you thought it was going to be smooth? That's how this felt. I expected a beautiful young woman to turn around, and it was her grandmother."

"Is she, like, an old lady trying to look young? That's so pathetic."

"No . . . I know what it is. She looks like somebody out of an F. Scott Fitzgerald story, you know what I mean?"

"No . . ."

"You don't? You've read Fitzgerald, haven't you?"

"I guess, maybe in high school."

"God, sometimes I forget how young you are. Fitzgerald was a major influence on me. *Poor Little Rich Girl. The Great Gatsby.*"

"Oh, right, with Robert Redford. . . . What's funny?"

"Nothing. I'm sorry. Do you remember Daisy . . . in the movie?"

"I don't think so."

"She was the one that Jay Gatsby—Robert Redford—
fell in love with. From the back, that's who this woman
makes me think of. Daisy Buchanan. If Daisy had lived
long enough to get old. Not a flapper, but somebody rich
and thin and elegant. Like an elderly socialite, that's it.
Or a very old ingénue."

"What's an ingénue?"

"A starlet. A young, beautiful actress."

"Like Neve Campbell."

"Who?"

"You don't know who Neve Campbell is?"

"What do you want to bet she's drinking Manhattans?
Oh, shh, she got off her barstool, she's coming this way.
You don't think she could hear us, do you?"

"No way. Anybody that old has got to be deaf. Don't
laugh!"

"You're wicked."

"Duh. That's why you love me more than your wife."

"Heather, shh!"

"Oh, who's going to hear me?"

"Somebody might. She might. Here she comes. Try to
look at her when she goes by; you'll see what I mean.
Pretend we're talking about something else."

"Like what? Like how you didn't call me all weekend?
We could talk about that, John. Let's talk about that,
okay? Oh, dammit, I swore I wasn't going to cry when I
saw you. But I was so lonely all weekend, you don't
know, you're home with your family, and I'm all by myself watching reruns of *Friends*. I waited and waited for
you to call! I don't hear anything from you since last
week, and then suddenly you call and want me to drop
everything and come over here to see you. If you think
I'm going to have a nice cozy little lunch with you, and
then—"

"I'm sorry, Heather."

"You don't look sorry, you look like the only thing you care about is if somebody hears us."

"That's not true. I'm really sorry."

"Well, then *look* at me when you say it!"

"Did you see what I mean?"

"About her? My God, John, will you forget about her? And anyway, her hair's not blond, it's gray."

"Okay, but under the bar lights it looked—"

"Do you want to order now? Since you're not paying any attention to me anyway? If we can get the waiter. This time of the afternoon there's nobody here, and I think they all go hide in the kitchen. The smoked salmon Caesar salad is good. I'm having it. And iced tea, I can never get enough iced tea."

"Sue? How are you? It's Claire, I'm at the Dennis Grill—"

"My God, John, is that her talking? Can she talk any louder? What's she doing?"

"She's talking on the pay phone. What a voice."

"It sounds like when they file my nails."

". . . not so good. I'm almost out of my prescriptions. What are you doing this afternoon? Can you come down and meet me for tea?"

"Tea? You suppose that's another name for Manhattans?"

"Is she annoying, or what? I can't even think with her talking so loud."

"She'll be off in a minute, Heather."

"I see. All right, I'll talk to you later."

"She hung up. Guess they couldn't meet her for, uh, tea."

"Thank God! Oh, hi, Randy. John, this is my friend Randy. He waits on me all the time, don't you Randy?

This is my boyfriend I was telling you about. John. Don't even tell me your specials. If you *say* them, I'll gain ten pounds. I'll just have the salmon Caesar salad and a very tall glass of iced tea, and I'd really appreciate it if you could keep it filled. You know how I am, I'm an iced tea addict. Thanks."

"Hello, Randy. And I'd like to order—"

"Hi! Is this Sara? Sara, this is Claire Eberhardt. Not too well; I kept waking up all night and coughing. What? I woke up every hour and coughed and coughed until I just felt awful. But you don't want to hear about that. I didn't call to complain about my health. Is Jim Grayson in the sanctuary or in his office? He's not? He went home this early?"

"Hell, I can't even remember what I wanted to order now. Oh, yeah. Crab cakes. Cole slaw. French fries. Beer, whatever you've got on draft. Oh, and keep it refilled, will you, Randy? I'm addicted, too, like Heather with her iced tea."

"Very funny, John."

"I'm kidding. It was a joke. I'm no alcoholic, Heather."

"No, no message. Okay. Thanks. Bye."

"Guess ol' Reverend Jim didn't want to talk to her. I wouldn't, either, if I had to listen to that voice for very long."

"You think she was calling her minister, John?"

"Well, she asked if he was in the sanctuary or his office."

"And they say people my age are rude? Who does a person have to think she is to bust everybody's eardrums like that? If I stare at her, do you think she'll take the hint?"

"Don't stare, Heather. Set a good example for the elderly. Heather, you told that waiter I'm your boyfriend. Do you think that was a good idea?"

"Well, why not? Men flirt with me, you know."

"They'd have to be crazy not to, but what does that have to do with it?"

"Hi, Annabelle, it's Claire. I'm at the Dennis Grill. You want to come down and have tea with me? Oh. What? No, I'm not feeling so good. Annabelle, didn't you say one time you like that blue quilt I've got on my guest bed? Would you like to have it? I mean it. Okay, it's yours. I've written it down. 'Annabelle gets the blue quilt.' I'm not kidding. That's all right, if you have to run. Goodbye."

"I have to tell them something to get them to back off, John. If I didn't tell Randy about you, he would have kept asking me out. It's not like he knows who you are, not really. All he knows is I've got a boyfriend and his name is John. That's all."

"And now he knows that's me."

"Well, so what? He's not going to remember you. I don't mean to hurt your feelings, but somebody his age is not going to remember somebody your age."

"Even if he saw my picture in the paper sometime?"

"Why would he do that? Is your picture going to be in the paper?"

"No, but it could be. I might get an award sometime, or get tenure."

"Yeah, like I'm sure they'll put that in the paper."

"Hi, Mary, this is Claire. Just called to say hi. Bye."

"She must have got somebody's answering machine that time. Does she think this is her private office? Is she planning on calling everybody she ever knew?"

"Is she finished yet, Heather?"

"God, no, she's dialing again."

"Irving? Hi, it's Claire. Do you know if we're having choir practice tonight? We're not? I never heard that. When did they announce that?"

"She *sings?* With that voice?"

"Shh, Heather, she'll hear you."

"John, she's ruining our conversation. She doesn't care if we hear her. Why should I care if she hears us?"

"I wish I had known it was canceled, Irving. Well, I would have made it to last week's practice if I had known there wasn't going to be one this week."

"Heather, we have to talk. Oh, Heather! Don't cry, please don't cry. How do you know what I'm going to say before I say it? All right. You're right. But, Heather, you knew this was going to happen someday. I'm a married man, you're my student, you knew that from day one. And you said you could live with it. You said you wouldn't get serious, you agreed this was just for fun. And it has been a lot of fun, hasn't it? I know it has been for me—"

"How great for you—"

"Come on now, Heather. You know I'm very fond of you. I think the world of you, you know that. But it's just gotten to be too difficult. I think some of my colleagues are beginning to suspect something, and that wouldn't be good for your reputation on campus. You wouldn't want people talking about us behind your back, would you? And my wife—Where are you going?"

"To the bathroom! Do I have to raise my hand to get permission to go to the bathroom?"

"Hello. My name is Claire Eberhardt, and I would like to cancel my credit card. The balance should be all paid off. Yes, I will, I have it right here . . ."

"Thanks, Randy, that looks good. Heather just went to the ladies' room; I don't know what's taking her so long.

You know I'm not really her boyfriend, don't you? I
shouldn't even say this, but I don't want her hurt by
having you think badly of her. I'm her . . . minister. Old
friend of her family. I'm trying to counsel her about some
problems she has with telling the truth. It's a shame, isn't
it, such a pretty girl? Say, what's with the old lady on the
telephone? She's talking so loud, we can't even hear ourselves talk. Is there any way you can get her to shut up?"

"The expiration date is oh-two, oh-two, oh-two."

"Yeah, I guess you can't very well tell an old lady to
get off the damn phone. Maybe she'll stop soon. I hope.
Oh, hi, Heather. Randy has brought our food. I don't think
we'll be needing anything else for a while, Randy; thank
you."

"What's the matter with him? He looked at me like I
was going to bite him. I'm not hungry anymore."

"Heather, are you all right?"

"How do you think I am? God, who's she calling
now?"

"You wouldn't believe it. Since you've been gone, she
has called a credit card company and canceled her credit
card, and the gas company, and the electric company, and
the telephone company, and it sounds like she's on with
the water company now."

"Why's she calling all of them?"

"She's getting everything shut off. She must be moving."

"She can't call from home?"

"No, I guess she has to ruin our lunch."

"My lunch is already ruined."

"Heather, please. I said I'm sorry."

"Yeah, and that makes everything just fine."

*"Frankie? This is Claire calling. I was hoping I could
catch you at home and you'd come down to the Dennis*

Grill this afternoon and have tea with me. Sorry I missed you. Bye."

"Your waiter friend Randy says she's a regular."

"Like me. All the lonely females, where do we all come from? See, I know some things, too, John. I'm not entirely stupid—"

"Heather."

"I know that was a—what do you call it—paraphrase of a Beatles' song, even if I wasn't born yet. Or, maybe that wasn't good enough, since it wasn't the Great Fucking Gatsby, or Ernest Hemingway, or whatever."

"Come on, Heather. What are you so upset about? It'll take you all of a week to replace me. What? What did I say? Heather! You're a free spirit, isn't that what you always say, you're a free spirit, just a fun-loving girl. Right? So why the long face?"

"Hi, it's Claire. Could you pick me up here at the Dennis Grill and give me a ride home? I walked. Oh. If you can't take me all the way home, could you drop me off at the Pawnee Bridge?"

"I really hate you at this minute."

"I know, but you're young, you'll get over it."

"Really, really hate you, increasingly, by the minute."

"What's the matter now, Heather?"

"Do you think we ought to offer her a ride?"

"Didn't she say the Pawnee Bridge? That's over the northbound interstate, and I'm going south from here. She's got a big enough personal directory, she'll find somebody to drive her."

"I could give her a ride in that direction."

"And listen to that voice all the way? What did you think was going to happen with us, Heather?"

"This. I thought exactly this was going to happen."

"Well, then?"

"But I hoped it would be something else."

"You didn't, really."

"I did, really. She's awfully old to walk all that way. I can't believe she'd really walk over that bridge. It's dangerous, all that traffic. People jump off that bridge all the time, you know, and kill themselves. Maybe I'll do that. I'll drive her home, and then I'll go back and jump off the bridge."

"Heather, don't talk like that."

"I wouldn't. You're not worth it."

"That's my girl. God, you're adorable. How about one last—"

"Damn you!"

"What? What did I say now?"

"Heather, come back here, you didn't touch your salad—Oh, hi, Randy. I don't know what's wrong with her. She was going to give that old lady a ride, and she's run out without doing it. I think I'm going to have to talk to her family about getting her medication changed. Do you take checks? At least the old woman's off the phone. Back on her barstool, I see. What's she drinking? Vodka. I would have guessed Manhattans or whiskey sours. How many has she slugged down? No kidding. Don't you think somebody ought to cut her off? At this rate, she won't be long for this world."

APRIL IN PARIS

Peter Robinson

Peter Robinson was born in Yorkshire, England. He is the author of the Inspector Banks series, which includes the Edgar Award–nominated Wednesday's Child. *The tenth in the series,* In a Dry Season, *was selected as one of the* New York Times Book Review's *"notable mysteries" of 1999 and won the Anthony for best novel. The most recent is called* Cold Is the Grave. *Robinson's short stories have been published widely and nominated for both the Agatha and Anthony Awards, and "The Two Ladies of Rose Cottage" won the Macavity Award in 1998. His stories have been collected in* Not Safe After Dark and Other Stories, *published by Crippen & Landru in 1998. He lives in Toronto with his wife, Sheila Halladay.*

The girl sitting outside the café reminds me of April. She has the same long, hennaed hair, which she winds around her index finger in the same abstracted way. She is waiting for someone, clearly—a lover, perhaps—and as she waits she smokes, holding her cigarette in the same way, taking the same short, hurried puffs as April used to do. With her free hand, she alternates between taking sips of milky pastis and tapping her cigarette packet on the table. She is smoking Marlborough, as everyone in Paris seems to do these days. Back then, it was all Gitanes, Gauloise, and Disque Bleu.

Still, it wasn't smoking that killed April; it was love.

*   *   *

It is late September, and though the weather is mild, it is still too cold outside for an old man like me, with blood as thin and as lacking in nutrients as workhouse gruel. Instead, I sit inside the little café on the Boulevard St. Germain over a *pichet* of red wine, just watching the people come and go. The young people. I have spent most of my life surrounded by the young, and though I grow inexorably older every year, they always seem to stay young. *Immortal youth.* Like Tithonus, I am "a white-haired shadow roaming like a dream." But unlike Tennyson's luckless narrator, who gained eternal life but not eternal youth, I am not immortal.

Six months, perhaps less, the doctors say. Something is growing inside me; my cells are mutating. As yet, I feel little pain, though my appetite has diminished, and I often suffer from extreme weariness.

Dying, I find, lends an edge to living, gives a clarity and a special, golden hue to the quotidian scenes parading before me: a swarthy man with a briefcase, glancing at his watch, speeding up, late for an important appointment; a woman chastising her little girl at the corner, wagging her finger, the girl crying and stamping her foot; a distracted priest stumbling briefly as he walks up the steps to the church across the boulevard.

Dying accentuates the beauty of the young, sets their energy in relief, enhances the smooth glow of their unwrinkled skin. But dying does not make me bitter. I am resigned to my fate; I have come to the end of my three-score and ten; I have seen enough. If you wish to travel, my doctors told me, do it now, while you're still strong enough. So here I am, revisiting the scene of my one and only great amour.

April. She always pronounced it *Ap-reel.* When I think of her, I still hear Thelonious Monk playing "April in Paris," hesitant at first, feeling his way into the song, reluctant to define the theme, then worrying away at it, and once finding it, altering it so much that the music becomes his own, only to be abandoned finally.

Of course, April didn't give a tinker's for Thelonious Monk. She listened to him dutifully, as they all did, for they were the heirs of Kerouac, Ginsberg, and Burroughs, to whom Monk, Bird, Trane, Miles, and Mingus were gods, sacred and cool. But April's generation had its own gods—The Doors, Cream, Jimi Hendrix, Bob Dylan—gods of words and images as well as of music, and it was they who provided the sound track to which I lived during my year as a visiting lecturer in American literature at the Sorbonne in 1968.

This café hasn't changed much. A lick of paint, perhaps, if that. It probably hasn't changed much since Hemingway and Fitzgerald used to hang out around here. Even the waiters are probably the same. It was here I first met April, of course (why else would I come here?), one fine evening toward the end of March that year, when I was still young enough to bear the slight chill of a clear spring evening.

That April was beautiful almost goes without saying. I remember her high cheekbones, smooth, olive complexion, dark, watchful eyes, and rich, moist lips, downturned at the edges, often making her look sulky or petulant when she was far from it. I remember also how she used to move with grace and confidence when she remembered, but how the gaucheness of late adolescence turned her movements into a country girl's gait when she was at her most un-self-conscious. She was tall, slim, and long-legged, and her breasts were small, round, and high. The breasts of a Cranach nude.

We met, as I say, one late March evening in 1968 at this café, the Café de la Lune, where I was then sitting with the usual group: Henri, Nadine, Brad, Brigitte, Alain, and Paul. This was only days after Daniel Cohn-Bendit and seven other students had occupied the dean's office at Nanterre to protest the recent arrest of six members of the National Vietnam Committee, an event that was to have cataclysmic effects on us all not long afterward. Much of the time in those days we spoke of revolution, but that evening we were discussing, I remember quite clearly, F. Scott Fitzgerald's *Tender Is the Night*, when in she walked, wearing a woolly jumper and close-fitting, bell-bottomed jeans with flowers embroidered around the bells. She was carrying a bulky leather shoulder bag, looking radiant and slightly lost, glancing around for someone she knew.

It turned out that she knew Brad, an American backpacker who had attached himself to our group. People like Brad had a sort of fringe, outlaw attraction for the students. They seemed, with their freedom to roam and their contempt for rules and authority, to embody the very principles that the students themselves, with their heavy workloads, exams, and future careers, could only imagine or live vicariously. There were always one or two Brads around. Some dealt in drugs to make a living; Brad, though he spoke a good revolution, lived on a generous allowance wired regularly by his wealthy Boston parents via Western Union.

April went up to Brad and kissed him on both cheeks, a formal French gesture he seemed to accept with thinly veiled amusement. In his turn, Brad introduced her to the rest of us. That done, we resumed our discussion over another bottle of wine, the tang of Gauloise and café noir infusing the chill night air, and April surprised me by demonstrating that she not only had read *Tender Is the Night*, but had thought about it, too, even though she was a student of history, not of literature.

"Don't you think those poor young girls are terribly *used?*" she said. "I mean, Nicole is Dick's *patient*. He should be healing her, not sleeping with her. And the way Rosemary is manipulated by her mother . . . I'd go so far as to say that the mother seems to be *pimping* for her. Those films she made"—and here April gave her characteristic shrug, no more than a little shiver rippling across her shoulders—"they were no doubt made to appeal to older men." She didn't look at me as she said this, but my cheeks burned nonetheless.

"Have you read *Day of the Locust?*" Henri, one of the other students, chimed in. "If you want to know about how Hollywood warps people, that's your place to start. There's a mother in there who makes Rosemary's look like a saint."

"Huxley?" asked Nadine, not our brightest.

"No," said April. "That was *After Many a Summer. Day of the Locust* was Nathanael West, I think. Yes?"

Here, she looked directly at me, the professor, for the first time, turned on me the full blaze of her beauty. She knew she was right, of course, but she still deferred to me out of politeness.

"That's right," I said, smiling, feeling my heart lurch and my soul tingle inside its chains of flesh. "Nathanael West wrote *Day of the Locust*."

And from that moment on, I was smitten.

*　　*　　*

I told myself not to be a fool, that April was far too young for me, and that a beautiful woman like her couldn't possibly be interested in a portly, forty-year-old lecturer, even if he did wear faded denim jeans, had a goatee, and grew what wisps of hair remained a little longer than some of his colleagues thought acceptable. But after that first meeting, I found myself thinking about April a lot. In fact, I couldn't get her out of my mind. It wasn't mere lust—though Lord knows it was that, too—but I loved the sound of her voice, loved the way she twisted strands of hair around her finger as she spoke, the way she smoked her cigarette, loved the passion of her arguments, the sparkle of her laughter, the subtle jasmine of her perfume.

Love.

That night, she had left the café after about an hour, arm in arm with Brad—young, handsome, rich, footloose and fancy-free Brad—and I had lain awake tormented by images of their passionate lovemaking. I had never felt like that before, never felt so consumed by desire for someone and so wracked by pain at the thought of someone else having her. It was as if an alien organism had invaded my body, my very soul, and wrought such changes there that I could hardly cope with the more mundane matters, such as teaching and writing, eating and sleeping.

The second time I met her it was raining. I was walking along the *quai* across from Notre Dame, staring distractedly at the rain pitting the river's steely surface, thinking of her, when she suddenly ducked under my umbrella and took my arm.

I must have gasped out loud.

"Professor Dodgson," she said. Not a question. She *knew* who I was. "Sorry I startled you."

But that wasn't why I gasped, I wanted to tell her. It was the sudden apparition of this beautiful creature I had been dreaming about for days. I looked at her. The driving rain had soaked her hair and face. Like Dick in *Tender Is the Night*, I wanted to drink the rain that ran from her cheeks. "How did you recognize me under this?" I asked her.

She gave that little shrug that was no more than a ripple and smiled up at me. "Easy. You're carrying the same old briefcase you had last week. It's got your initials on it."

"How sharp of you," I said. "You should become a detective."

"Oh, I could never become a fascist pig." She said this with a completely straight face. People said things like that back then.

"Just a joke," I said. "Where are you going?"

"Nowhere special."

"Coffee?"

She looked at me again, chewing on her lower lip for a moment as she weighed up my invitation. "All right," she said finally. "I know a place." And her gentle pressure on my arm caused me to change direction and enter the narrow alleys that spread like veins throughout the Latin Quarter. "Your French is very good," she said as we walked. "Where did you learn?"

"School, mostly. Then university. I seem to have a facility for it. We used to come here when I was a child, too, before the war. Brittany. My father fought in the first war, you see, and he developed this love for France. I think the fighting gave him a sort of stake in things."

"Do you, too, have this stake in France?"

"I don't know."

She found the café she was looking for on the Rue St. Severin, and we ducked inside. "Can you feel what's happening?" she asked me, once we were warm and dry, sitting at the zinc counter with hot, strong coffees before us. She lit a Gauloise and touched my arm. "Isn't it exciting?"

I couldn't believe what I was hearing. *She* thought something was happening between us. I could hardly disguise my joy. But I was also so tongue-tied that I couldn't think of anything wise or witty to say. I probably sat there, my mouth opening and closing like a guppy's before saying, "Yes. *Yes,* it is exciting."

"There'll be a revolution before spring's over, you mark my words. We'll be rid of de Gaulle and ready to start building a new France."

Ah, yes. *The revolution.* I should have known. It was the topic on everyone's mind at the time. Except mine, that is. I tried not to show my disappointment. Not that I wasn't interested—you couldn't be in Paris in the spring of 1968 and *not* be interested in the revolution one way or another—but I had been distracted from politics by my thoughts of April. Besides, as radical as I might have appeared to some people, I was still a foreign national, and I had to do my best to keep a low political profile, difficult as it was. One false step and I'd not only be out of a job but out of the country, and far away from April, forever. And I had answered her question honestly; I didn't know whether I had a stake in France or not.

"What does Brad think?" I asked.

"Brad?" She seemed surprised by my question. "Brad is an anarchist."

"And you?"

She twisted her hair around her finger. "I'm not sure. I know I want change. I think I'm an anarchist, too, though I'm not sure I'd want to be completely without any sort of government at all. But we want the same things. Peace. A new, more equal society. He is an American, but they have had many demonstrations there, too, you know. Vietnam."

"Ah, yes. I remember some of them."

We passed a while talking about my experiences in California, which seemed to fascinate April, though I must admit I was far more interested in tracing the contours of her face and drinking in the beauty of her eyes and skin than I was in discussing the war in Vietnam.

In the end she looked at her watch and said she had to go to a lecture but would probably see me later at the café. I said I hoped so and watched her walk away.

You will have gathered that I loved April to distraction, but did she love me? I think not. She liked me well enough. I amused her, entertained her, and she was perhaps even flattered by my attentions; but ultimately, brash youth wins out over suave age. It was Brad she loved. Brad, whose status in my mind quickly changed from that of a mildly entertaining, reasonably intelligent hanger-on to the bane of my existence.

He always seemed to be around, and I could never get April to myself. Whether this was deliberate—whether he was aware of my interest and made jealous by it—I do not know. All I know is that I had very few chances to be alone with her. When we were together, usually at a café or walking in the street, we talked—talked of what was happening in France, of the future of the university, of literature, of the anarchists, Maoists, Trotskyites, and Communists, talked about all these, but not, alas, of love.

Perhaps this was my fault. I never pushed myself on her, never tried to make advances, never tried to touch her, even though my cells ached to reach out and mingle with hers, and even though the most casual physical contact, a touch on the arm, for example, set me aflame with desire. After our first few meetings, she would greet me with kisses on each cheek, the way she greeted all her friends, and my cheeks would burn for hours afterward. One day she left a silk scarf at the café, and I took it home and held it to my face like a lovesick schoolboy, inhaling April's perfume as I tried to sleep that night.

But I did not dare make a pass; I feared her rejection and her laughter far more than anything else. While we do not have the capacity to choose our feelings in the first place, we certainly have the ability to choose not to act on them, and that was what I was trying to do, admittedly more for my own sake than for hers.

When I did see April alone again, it was late in the morning of the third of May, and I was still in bed. I had been up late the night before trying to concentrate on a Faulkner paper I had to present at a conference in Brussels that weekend, and as I had no actual classes on Fridays, I had slept in.

The soft but insistent tapping at my door woke me from a dream about my father in the trenches (why is it we never seem to dream at night about those we dream about all day?), and I rubbed the sleep out of my eyes.

I must explain that at the time, like the poor French workers, I wasn't paid very much; consequently, I lived in a small pension in a cobbled alley off the Boulevard St. Michel, between the university and the Luxembourg Gardens. As I could easily walk from the pension to my office at the Sorbonne, usually ate at the university or at a cheap local bistro, and spent most of my social hours in the various bars and cafés of the Latin Quarter, I didn't really need much more than a place to lay my head at night.

I stretched, threw on my dressing gown, and opened the door. I'm sure you can imagine my shock on finding April standing there. *Alone.* She had been to the room only once previously, along with Brad and a couple of others for a nightcap of cognac after a Nina Simone concert, but she clearly remembered where I lived.

"Oh, I'm sorry, Richard—" She had started calling me by my first name, at my insistence, though of course she pronounced it in the French manner, and it sounded absolutely delightful to me every time she spoke it. "I didn't know . . ."

"Come in," I said, standing back. She paused a moment in the doorway, smiled shyly, then entered. I lay back on the bed, mostly because there was hardly enough room for two of us to sit together.

"Shall I make coffee?" she asked.

"There's only instant."

She made a typical April moue at the idea of instant coffee, as any true French person would, but I directed her to the tiny kitchenette behind the curtain, and she busied herself with the kettle, calling out over her shoulder as she filled it and turned on the gas.

"There's trouble at the university," she said. "That's what I came to tell you. It's happening at last. Everything's boiling over."

I remembered that there was supposed to be a meeting about the Nanterre Eight, who were about to face disciplinary charges the following Monday, and I assumed that was what she meant.

"What's happening?" I asked, still not quite awake.

April came back into the bedroom and sat demurely

on the edge of my only chair, trying not to look at me lying on the bed. "The revolution," she said. "There's already a big crowd there. Students and lecturers together. They're talking about calling the police. Closing down the university."

This woke me up a little more. "They're what?"

"It's true," April went on. "Somebody told me that the university authorities said they'd call in the police if the crowds didn't disperse. But they're not dispersing; they're getting bigger." She lit a Gauloise and looked around for an ashtray. I passed her one I'd stolen from the Café de la Lune. She smiled when she saw it and took those short little puffs at her cigarette, hardly giving herself time to inhale and enjoy the tobacco before blowing it out and puffing again. "Brad's already there," she added.

"Then he'd better be careful," I said, getting out of bed. "He's neither a student nor a French citizen."

"But don't you see? This is everybody's struggle!"

"Try telling that to the police."

"You can be so cynical sometimes."

"I'm sorry, April," I said, not wanting to offend her. "I'm just concerned for him, that's all." Of course I was lying. Nothing would have pleased me better than to see Brad beaten to a pulp by the police or, better still, deported, but I could hardly tell April that. The kettle boiled and she gave me a smile of forgiveness and went to make the coffee. She only made one cup—for me—and as I sipped it, she talked on about what had happened that morning and how she could feel change in the air. Her animation and passion excited me, and I had to arrange my position carefully to avoid showing any obvious evidence of my arousal.

Even in the silences, she seemed inclined to linger, and in the end I had to ask her to leave while I got dressed, as there was nowhere for her to retain her modesty, and the thought of her standing so close to me, facing the wall, as I took off my dressing gown was too excruciating for me to bear. She pouted and left, saying she'd wait for me outside. When I rejoined her, we walked to the Sorbonne together, and I saw that she was right about the crowds. There was defiance in the air.

We found Brad standing with a group of anarchists, and April went over to take his arm. I spoke with him briefly for a while, alarmed at some of the things he told me. I found some colleagues from the literature department, and they said the police had been sent for. By four o'clock in the afternoon, the university was surrounded by the Campagnies Républicaines de Sécurité—the CRS, riot police—and a number of students and lecturers had been arrested. Before long, even more students arrived and started fighting with the CRS to free those who had been arrested. Nobody was backing down this time.

The revolution had begun.

I took the train to Brussels on Saturday morning and didn't come back until late on Tuesday, and though I had heard news of events in Paris, I was stunned at what awaited me on my return. The city was a war zone. The university was closed, and nobody knew when, or in what form, it would reopen. Even the familiar smell of the city—its coffee, cheese, and something-slightly-overripe aroma—had changed, and it now smelled of fire, burnt plastic, and rubber. I could taste ashes in my mouth.

I wandered the Latin Quarter in a dream, remnants of the previous day's tear gas stinging my eyes, barricades improvised from torn-up paving stones all over the place. Everywhere I went I saw the CRS, looking like invaders from space in their gleaming black helmets, with chin straps and visors, thick black uniforms, jackboots, and heavy truncheons. They turned up out of nowhere in coaches with windows covered in wire mesh, clambered out, and blocked off whole streets, apparently at random. Everywhere they could, people gathered and talked politics. The mood was swinging; you could taste it in the air along with the gas and ashes. This wasn't just another student demonstration, another Communist or anarchist protest; this was civil war. Even the bourgeoisie were appalled at the violence of the police attacks. There were reports of pregnant women being beaten, of young men being tortured, their genitals shredded.

This was the aftermath of what later came to be known as Bloody Monday, when the Nanterre Eight had appeared at the Sorbonne, triumphantly singing the "Internationale," and sparked off riots.

I had missed April terribly while I was in Brussels, and now I was worried that she might have been hurt or arrested. I immediately tried to seek her out, but it wasn't easy. She wasn't at her student residence nor at Brad's hotel. I tried the Café de la Lune and various other watering holes in the area, but to no avail. Eventually, I ran into someone I knew, who was able to tell me that he thought she was helping one of the student groups produce posters, but he didn't know where. I gave up and went back to my room, unable to sleep, expecting her gentle rap on the door at any moment. It never came.

I saw her again on Thursday, putting up posters on the Rue St. Jacques.

"I was worried about you," I told her.

She smiled and touched my arm. For a moment I let myself believe that my concern actually mattered to her. I could understand her dedication to what was happening;

after all, she was young, and it was her country. I knew that all normal social activities were on hold, that the politics of revolution had little time or space for the personal, for such bourgeois indulgences as love, but still I selfishly wanted her, wanted to be with her.

My chance came on the weekend, when the shit really hit the fan.

A ll week, negotiations had been going back and forth between the government and the students. The university stayed closed, and the students threatened to "liberate" it. De Gaulle huffed and puffed. The Latin Quarter remained an occupied zone. On Friday, the workers threw in their lot with the students and called for a general strike the following Monday. The whole country was on its knees in a way it hadn't been since the German occupation.

Thus far, I had been avoiding the demonstrations, not out of cowardice or lack of commitment, but because I was a British subject, not a French one. By the weekend, that no longer mattered. It had become a world struggle: us against them. We were fighting for a new world order. I was in. I had a stake. Besides, the university was closed, so I didn't even have a job to protect anymore. And perhaps, somewhere deep down, I hoped that heroic deeds on the barricades might win the heart of a fair lady.

So confusing was everything, so long-running and spread-out the battle, that I can't remember now whether it was Friday or Saturday. Odd that, the most important night of my life, and I can't remember what night it was. No matter.

It all started with a march toward the Panthéon, red and black flags everywhere, the "Internationale" bolstering our courage. I had found April and Brad earlier, along with Henri, Alain, and Brigitte, in the university quadrangle looking at the improvised bookstalls, and we went to the march together. April had her arm linked through mine on one side, and Alain's on the other.

It was about half-past nine when things started to happen. I'm not sure what came first, the sharp explosions of the gas grenades or the flash of a Molotov cocktail, but all of a sudden, pandemonium broke out, and there was no longer an organized march, only a number of battle fronts.

In the melee, April and I split off, losing Brad and the rest, and we found ourselves among those defending the front on the Boulevard St. Michel. Unfortunate drivers, caught in the chaos, pressed down hard on their accelerators, honked their horns and drove through red lights to get away, knocking pedestrians aside as they went. The explosions were all around us now, and a blazing CRS van silhouetted figures throwing petrol bombs and pulling up paving stones for the barricades. The restaurants and cafés were all closing hurriedly, waiters ushering clients out into the street and putting up the shutters.

The CRS advanced on us, firing gas grenades continuously. One landed at my feet, and I kicked it back at them. I saw one student fall to them, about ten burly police kicking him as he lay and beating him mercilessly with their truncheons. There was nothing we could do. Clouds of gas drifted from the canisters, obscuring our view. We could see distant flames, hear the explosions and the cries, see vague shadows bending to pick up stones to throw at the darkness. The CRS charged. Some of us had come armed with Molotov cocktails and stones, but neither April nor I had any weapons, any means to defend ourselves, so we ran.

We were both scared. This was the worst the fighting had been so far. The demonstrators weren't just taking what the CRS dished out, they were fighting back, and that made the police even more vicious. They would show no quarter, neither with a woman nor a foreign national. We could hardly see for the tears streaming from our eyes as we tried to get away from the advancing CRS, who seemed to have every side street blocked off.

"Come on," I said, taking April's hand in mine. "This way."

We jumped the fence and edged through the pitch-dark Luxembourg Gardens, looking for an unguarded exit. When we found one, we dashed out and across to the street opposite. A group of CRS saw us and turned. Fortunately, the street was too narrow and the buildings were too high for the gas guns. The police fired high in the air and most of the canisters fell harmlessly onto the roofs above us. Nobody gave chase.

Hand in hand, we made our way through the dark back streets to my pension, which, though close to the fighting, seemed so far unscathed. We ran up to my tiny room and locked the door behind us. Our eyes were streaming, and both of us felt a little dizzy and sick from the tear gas, but we also felt elated from the night's battle. We could still hear the distant explosions and see flashes and flames, like Guy Fawkes Night back in England. Adrenaline buzzed in our veins.

Just as I can't say exactly what night it was, I can't say exactly who made the first move. All I remember is that suddenly the room seemed too small for the two of us, our bodies were pressed together and I was tasting those moist, pink lips for the first time, savoring her small, furtive tongue in my mouth. My legs were like jelly.

"You know when I came here the other morning and

you were in bed?" April said as she unbuttoned my shirt.

"Yes," I said, tugging at her jeans.

She slipped my shirt off my shoulders. "I wanted to get into bed with you."

I unhooked her bra. "Why didn't you?"

"I didn't think you wanted me."

We managed to get mostly undressed before falling onto the bed. I kissed her breasts and ran my hands down her naked thighs. I thought I would explode with ecstasy when she touched me. Then she was under me, and I buried myself in her, heard her sharp gasp of pleasure.

At last, April was mine.

I lived on the memory of April's body, naked beside me, the two of us joined in love, while the country went insane. I didn't see her for three days, and even then we were part of a group; we couldn't talk intimately. That was what things were like then; there was little place for the individual. Everything was chaos. Normal life was on hold, perhaps never to be resumed again.

The university was closed, the campus hardly recognizable. The pillars in the square were plastered with posters of Marx, Lenin, Trotsky, and Che Guevara. There was a general strike. Everything ground to a halt: Metro, buses, coal production, railways. Everywhere I walked I saw burned-out vans and cars, gutted news kiosks, piles of paving stones, groups of truncheon-swinging CRS. People eating in the cafés had tears streaming down their faces from the remnants of tear gas in the morning-after air.

And every morning was a morning after.

I spotted Brad alone in a side street one night not long after dark, and as I had been wanting to talk to him about

April, I thought I might never get a better opportunity.
He was on his way to a meeting, he said, but could spare
a few minutes. We took the steps down to the Seine by
the side of the Pont St. Michel, where we were less likely
to get hassled by the CRS. It was dark and quiet by the
river, though we could hear the crack of gas guns and
explosions of Molotovs not so far away.

"Have you talked to April recently?" I asked him.

"Yes," he said. "Why?"

"I was wondering if . . . you know . . . she'd told you . . . ?"

"Told me what?"

"Well . . ." I swallowed. "About us."

He stopped for a moment, then looked at me and
laughed. "Oh, yes," he said. "Yes, she did, as a matter of
fact."

I was puzzled by his attitude. "Well?" I said. "Is that
all you have to say?"

"What do you want me to say?"

"Aren't you angry?"

"Why should I be angry? It didn't mean anything."

I felt an icy fear grip me. "What do you mean, *it didn't
mean anything?*"

"You know. It was just a quickie, a bit of a laugh. She
said she got excited by the street fighting and you happened to be the nearest man. It's not the first time, you
know. I don't expect April to be faithful or any of that
bourgeois crap. She's her own woman."

"What did you say?"

"I said it didn't mean anything. You don't think she
could be serious about someone like you, do you? Come
off it, Richard, with your tatty jeans and your little goatee
beard. You think you're a real hip intellectual, but you're
nothing but a joke. That's all you were to her. A quickie.

A laugh. A joke. She came straight to me afterward for a real—"

The blow came from deep inside me, and my fist caught him on the side of his jaw. I heard a sharp crack, distinct from the sound of a distant gas gun, and he keeled over into the Seine. We were under a bridge, and it was very dark. I stopped, listened, and looked around, but I could see no one, hear only the sounds of battle in the distance. Quickly, my blood turning to ice, I climbed the nearest stairs and reentered the fray.

I had never imagined that love could turn to hatred so quickly. Though I had fantasized about getting rid of Brad many times, I had never really intended to harm him, and certainly not in the way, or for the reason, that I did. I had never thought of myself as someone capable of killing another human being.

They pulled his body out of the Seine two days later, and the anarchists claimed that he had been singled out and murdered by the CRS. Most of the students were inclined to believe this, and another bloody riot ensued.

As for me, I'd had it. Had it with April, had it with the revolution, and had it with Paris. If I could have, I would have left for London immediately, but the cross-channel ferries weren't operating, and Skyways had no vacancies for some days. What few tourists remained trapped in Paris were queuing for buses to Brussels, Amsterdam, or Geneva, anywhere as long as they got out of France.

Mostly, I felt numb in the aftermath of killing Brad, though this was perhaps more to do with what he had told me about April than about the act itself, which had been an accident, and for which I didn't blame myself.

April. How could she deceive me so? How could she be so cold, so cruel, so callous? I meant nothing to her, just the nearest man to scratch her itch.

A quickie. A joke.

I saw her only once more, near the Luxembourg Gardens, the same gardens we jumped into that marvelous night a million years ago, and as she made to come toward me, I took off into a side street. I didn't want to talk to her again, didn't even want to see her. And it wasn't only April. I stayed away from all of them: Henri, Alain, Brigitte, Nadine, the lot of them. To me they had all become inextricably linked with April's humiliation of me, and I couldn't bear to be with them.

One day, Henri managed to get me aside and told me that April had committed suicide. He seemed angry rather than sad. I stared at him in disbelief. When he started to say something more, I cut him off and fled. I don't think anyone knew that I had killed Brad, but clearly April lamented his loss so much she no longer felt her life worth living. *He wasn't worth it,* I wanted to say, remembering the things he had told me under the bridge that night. If anyone was the killer, it was Brad, not me. He had killed my love for April, and now he had killed April.

I refused to allow myself to feel anything for her.

The people at Skyways said I might have some luck if I came out to the airport and waited for a vacancy on standby, which I did. Before I left, I glanced around my room one last time and saw nothing I wanted to take with me, not even April's silk scarf, which I had kept. So, in the clothes I was wearing, with the five hundred francs that was all the Bank of France allowed me to withdraw, I left the country and never went back.

*   *   *

Until now.

I think it must be the memory of tear gas that makes my eyes water so. I wipe them with the back of my hand, and the waiter comes to ask me if I am all right. I tell him I am and order another *pichet*. I have nowhere else to go except the grave; I might as well stay here and drink myself to death. What is the point of another miserable six months on earth anyway?

The girl who reminds me of April crushes out her cigarette and twists a strand of hair. Her lover is late. I dream of consoling her, but what have I to offer?

"Professor Dodgson? Richard? Is that you?"

I look up slowly at the couple standing over me. The man is gray-haired, distinguished-looking, and there is something about him. . . . His wife, or companion, is rather stout with gray eyes and short salt-and-pepper hair. Both are well-dressed, healthy-looking, the epitome of the Parisian bourgeoisie.

"Yes," I say. "I'm afraid you have me at a disadvantage."

"Henri Boulanger," he says. "I was once your student. My wife, Brigitte, was also a student."

"Henri? Brigitte?" I stand to shake his hand. "Is it really you?"

He smiles. "Yes. I wasn't sure about you at first. You haven't changed all that much in the face, the eyes, but you . . . perhaps you have lost weight?"

"I'm ill, Henri. Dying, in fact. But please sit down. Be my guests. Let's share some wine. Waiter."

Henri looks at Brigitte, who nods, and they sit. She seems a little embarrassed, uncomfortable, though I can't for the life of me imagine why. Perhaps it is because I told them I am dying. No doubt many people would feel uncomfortable sitting at a café drinking wine with death.

"Funnily enough," I tell them, "I was just thinking about you. What are you doing here?"

Henri beams. "Now *I'm* the professor," he says with great pride. "I teach literature at the Sorbonne."

"Good for you, Henri. I always believed you'd go far."

"It's a pity you couldn't have stayed around."

"They were difficult times, Henri. Interesting, as the Chinese say."

"Still . . . It was a sad business about that girl. What was her name?"

"April?" I say, and I feel an echo of my old love as I say her name. *Ap-reel.*

"April. Yes. That was around the time you went away."

"My time here was over," I tell him. "I had no job, the country was in a state of civil war. It wasn't my future."

Henri frowns. "Yes, I know. Nobody blames you for getting out . . . it's not that . . ."

"Blames me for what, Henri?"

He glances at Brigitte, who looks deep into her glass of wine. "You remember," he says. "The suicide? I told you about it."

"I remember. She killed herself over an American boy the CRS beat to death."

"Brad? But that wasn't . . . I mean . . ." He stares at me, wide-eyed. "You mean you don't *know?*"

"Don't know what?"

"I tried to tell you at the time, but you turned away."

"Tell me what?"

Brigitte looks up slowly from her wine and speaks. "Why did you desert her? Why did you turn your back on her?"

"What do you mean?"

"You rejected her. You broke her heart. The silly girl

was in love with you, and you spurned her. *That's* why she killed herself."

"That's ridiculous. She killed herself because of the American."

Brigitte shakes her head. "No. Believe me, it was you. She told me. She could talk only about you in the days before . . ."

"But . . . Brad?"

"Brad was jealous. Don't you understand? She was never more than a casual girlfriend to him. He wanted more, but she fell for you."

I shake my head slowly. I can't believe this. Can't *allow* myself to believe this. The world starts to become indistinct, all shadows and echoes. I can't breathe. My skin tingles with pins and needles. I feel a touch on my shoulder.

"Are you all right? Richard? Are you all right?"

It is Henri. I hear him call for a brandy, and someone places a cool glass in my hand. I sip. It burns and seems to dispel the mist a little. Brigitte rests her hand on my arm and leans forward. "You mean you really didn't know?"

I shake my head.

"Henri tried to tell you."

"Brad," I whisper. "Brad told me she just used me, that she thought I was a joke. I believed him."

Henry and Brigitte look at one another, then back at me, concern and pity in their eyes. A little more than that in Henri's, too: suspicion. Maybe everybody wasn't convinced that the CRS had killed Brad after all.

"He was jealous," Brigitte repeats. "He lied."

Suddenly, I start to laugh, which horrifies them. But I can't help myself. People turn and look at us. Henri and Brigitte are embarrassed. When the laughter subsides, I am left feeling hollow. I sip more brandy. Henri has placed his cigarettes on the table. Gauloise, I notice.

"May I?" I ask, reaching for the packet, even though I haven't smoked in twenty years.

He nods.

I light a Gauloise. Cough a little. What does it matter if I get lung cancer now? I'm already as good as dead. After a few puffs, the cigarette even starts to taste good, brings back, as tastes and smells do so well, even more memories of the cafés and nights of 1968. I begin to wonder whatever happened to that silk scarf I left in the drawer at my pension. I wish I could smell her jasmine scent again.

Outside, the girl's lover arrives. He is young and handsome and he waves his arms as he apologizes for being late. She is sulky at first, but she brightens and kisses him. He runs his hand down her smooth, olive cheek, and I can smell tear gas again.

THE PEOPLE'S WAY

Eve K. Sandstrom

Eve K. Sandstrom is the author of seven published mysteries, all of them set in fictionalized versions of her native state, Oklahoma. She holds a degree in journalism from the University of Oklahoma and worked as a reporter, editor, and columnist for more than twenty-five years. She studied professional writing with Carolyn G. Hart and Jack Bickham at OU.

She is the author of the Nell Matthews–Mike Svenson mysteries, featuring a newspaper reporter and her cop boyfriend, and of the Nicky and Sam Titus mysteries, centering on a rancher/sheriff and his photographer wife. Her short story "Bugged," in Malice Domestic 5, *was nominated for an Anthony and an Agatha, and the third Nicky and Sam Titus novel,* The Down Home Heifer Heist, *won the Oklahoma Book Award.*

The worst part was that Rogar was trying to be kind. "You must see that there is no other way," he said. "The baby has to die."

Amaya pulled her legs up against her chest and laid her head on her knees, shaping her body into a coconut. She had no more words. If she spoke again, the tears inside would spill onto the hut's sandy floor, and the hard coconut husk she was using to conceal herself would crack. All her fears and her griefs and longings would be revealed to this man she did not understand and to the strange people of his clan.

She turned her face away from Rogar. She stroked the back of the tiny girl sleeping on the grass mat.

Rogar spoke again. "It's not just my people who do this. It was the same on your island."

Amaya didn't move, but she felt the air pass over her, and she knew Rogar had gestured angrily.

"Elosa says there is not enough for my clan to eat," he said. "If we had plenty, we could keep your sister's child. But we don't have food for her."

"She can share my food," Amaya said softly.

"No! You would become weak. You should bear our own child. And we need you to work. You must remain strong." Rogar put his hand on her arm. Amaya did not pull away. She barely felt his touch on her coconut-shell arm. Did the arm feel rough and hard to him?

"Is it kind to keep the little one if we cannot feed her?" Rogar said. "Is it kind to keep the little one if the other women here hate her? If she will be an outcast in this clan? No! It's better to put her in the water now. Better for her. Better for you. Better for all of us."

He paused, but Amaya still hid behind her hard, outer husk. The silence grew between them.

Rogar sounded despairing when he finally spoke. "We cannot oppose Elosa. She is the one who decides."

Amaya spoke then. "And Elosa hates me."

"Don't be foolish!"

Amaya did not answer. What purpose was there in arguing with this man whom she knew so little, yet who had power over her, over the little one? She had thought she loved him. But he would not listen.

After another long silence, Rogar stood up. "I'm sorry,

Amaya. It's decided. I'll take the baby into the water as soon as it's light."

He walked softly from the hut into the darkness.

Amaya sat motionless. If she moved, her husk would crack. She kept her hand on the sleeping baby. Little Tani, all Amaya had left of her sister, of her own clan, of her own home on the westward island. If only, if only she had not left there!

Amaya had liked Rogar's looks as soon as he and his friends had come to her island, bringing fish and cloth to trade. He was strong and well-made, with broad shoulders. He had smiled at her. She had been flattered that such a handsome man had liked her. And he had come from afar. If she went with Rogar, she could see other islands, meet new clans.

She had been pleased when he offered her uncle a bride price. Her uncle hesitated, but Amaya made it clear that she wanted him to accept Rogar as her husband. Her uncle had said yes, and she had willingly gone with Rogar to his own island.

Then she had met Elosa. Elosa had hated Amaya from the moment she stepped on the shore of the lagoon. And as shaman, Elosa was one of the most important members of Rogar's clan. Her hate was serious. It had meant Amaya was shunned by all but Rogar's close family.

Rogar's mother had welcomed her as a mother-in-law should. Amaya had even thought she saw a slight feeling of exultation in her greetings. But most of the other women had been unfriendly—or perhaps fearful. They had spoken to her, but only sometimes. If they met alone in the forest, they would stop and talk. But if she met the women in a group, they would lower their eyes and pass by.

Amaya had asked her mother-in-law about it. "Why? What have I done?"

"You've done nothing, Amaya. They are afraid of Elosa."

"But she is the shaman. She is responsible for the clan's welfare."

"But the clan has had problems since Elosa became shaman. Our harvest has failed. The fish have been few. The tribe has become divided."

"But I have done nothing to cause the division."

Rogar's mother looked away. "Elosa wanted Rogar for her own daughter. When he took a bride from far away, it made Elosa fear that the people would think her foolish."

She put her arm around Amaya's shoulder. "Don't worry! Rogar wanted you! He is smart, that son of mine. Elosa will become interested in something else. Already she is looking for another husband for her daughter. The trouble will go away."

But the trouble did not go away. It grew and it grew, until it was not only between Amaya and the other women of the clan but between Rogar and Amaya, as well. They had not known each other well, Amaya realized. They'd only had a few days together without the interference of Elosa. Now Rogar grew impatient, hard to please. Their lovemaking grew more awkward instead of more comforting. Amaya felt she had ceased to please Rogar. And she had wanted to please Rogar. She wanted to love Rogar.

Amaya had hoped the ritual trip back to her own clan would help. But there they found greater disaster. Disease had come, and her uncle had died, and her sister and her sister's husband. The only one left was Tani.

The baby had grown since Amaya had left with Rogar.

Now she was walking. She was staying with the great-grandmother, but the great-grandmother could not run after her. Tani would hide. When the great-grandmother called, she would laugh. But she would not come. Amaya saw that the great-grandmother could not take care of her.

Rogar had hesitated when she asked if she could bring Tani back to his clan's island. "She is a fine, strong baby," he said. "But she is just a girl. And our clan's crop was small this year."

Amaya had not pleaded. But Rogar had also seen that the great-grandmother could not care for Tani. And perhaps Tani had won him over herself, with her baby smiles and games. He had grown fond of playing with her, taking her into the lagoon to splash.

"We will take her back," he had said finally. "She is a brave little girl. She laughs when water splashes her. She will be adopted by my tribe."

But that did not happen. Elosa had hated the baby, just as she hated Amaya. She had refused to take Tani into the clan. Then she had decreed that the clan did not have enough food, and she said that the child must die.

"It is not right for this stranger child to take food from the mouths of our clan," she said. "Rogar must put her in the water."

Amaya's heart broke, but her hard outer shell remained solid. She had hidden behind it all afternoon.

Rogar had argued with Elosa, tried to convince her that the clan's resources were not so few that one tiny girl would cause others to starve. But Elosa was firm.

"You must put the girl in the sea tomorrow—as soon as the sun rises," she said.

Amaya could not argue. Rogar had spoken truly. Her own clan followed that custom, too. If food was scarce, the oldest and the youngest among them must die. It was best for the weakest to die, to allow the strongest to live.

But Amaya did not want Tani to die. She was her sister's child. She was the final link with her own clan, her own island. If Tani died, Amaya would be left among a strange people, subject to a strange husband, with no one to care about and no one to care for her. And Tani was a strong child. She would grow into a strong woman who would help her clan.

But what could Amaya do?

Amaya nestled behind her hard coconut shell and thought.

Wildly she thought of killing Elosa. She could take the club she used for breaking coconut shells. She could creep up upon Elosa's house. She could hit the witch in the head. The shaman would die.

A feeling of pleasure swept over Amaya at the thought, but it was closely followed by a shudder that shook her whole body and rattled her teeth.

No, she could not kill Elosa. Even if she managed to creep into Elosa's hut undetected, Rogar's people would guess who had done it. She would be killed. Tani would still die. Killing Elosa would accomplish nothing, except that Amaya would herself die and her spirit would be condemned to roam the sea forever, never finding rest on the heavenly island.

Could she run away? Could she steal a canoe and go back to her own clan?

Amaya could paddle a canoe, of course. Everyone could do that. But only men, men like Rogar who had been taught to read the stars and the currents, could go so far as her native island and be sure of finding it.

Could she run away to the forest? She could take Tani and hide. She could find food for them there.

But Amaya knew that would give her only a few days.

Rogar's island was not her native place. She knew only parts of it. She might be able to hide from a stranger, but she could never hide from Rogar and the men who had hunted all over that island and the women who had gathered food all over it. She would have to sleep. Rogar's people knew where the water was, and she would have to have water. If food was scarce, the women would be looking for it everywhere. They would soon find her.

A sob bubbled up from Amaya's soul, like water bubbling from a spring. It almost cracked her coconut-shell coating. She choked it back, and she did not move. But she saw no way to save Tani.

Was Rogar right? Was obeying the shaman the right thing to do? Did she have to let him take Tani into the water?

Oh, she knew it was the law, the way of the people. As Rogar had said, it was the way of her own island. Her mother's mother had become ill in the year the crop had been so bad. When she had become too sick to work, she had stopped eating. The family had grieved, but the old woman had turned away from food. She had refused water. "It is time," the old woman said. Her tongue grew thick. Her daughters keened. And in three days she had died. Everyone had admired her action.

And when the wife of the headman's son gave birth to a child with a crippled foot, the mother had wept, but she had not argued. The headman himself had taken his grandson and put him in the sea to die.

Life on the islands was hard. The strong must not be held back by the weak. That was the ancient law. Amaya knew that. If the law was not obeyed, the island clans would not be strong and clever. They would not conquer their enemies: the other tribes who wanted their territory, the fierce beasts who lived in the sea and in the forests, the very hardness of life.

But Tani was not weak! Elosa had not said she must die because she was weak. That year's crop had been poor, but there was enough. Rogar said so. His father said so. But Elosa had not listened. She said Tani must die.

Tani was to be killed because she was a strange child.

No, Amaya thought, that was not true. Tani was to be killed not because the baby was strange, but because she—Amaya—was strange. Elosa hated Amaya, not Tani. But Amaya was married to one of the clan's young warriors. Elosa did not dare attack Amaya directly. She had decreed Tani's death because that was the cruelest thing she could do to Amaya. And this would not be the last thing she did to Amaya. Elosa might not dare condemn her openly, but she would find ways. Amaya's own fate would be like Tani's.

Already Elosa had threatened Rogar because he argued with her over the baby. Amaya's presence here on Rogar's island was all wrong. She was unhappy, and she was hurting Rogar by being there. She loved Rogar, and she did not want him to be hurt because of her.

Amaya, hidden inside her coconut shell, finally knew what she had to do.

She stirred, lifting the sleeping baby and holding her close, murmuring softly. "Little pet. Sweet one. I love you. We will always be together." Standing up, she went outside, into the dark. She took the path to the beach, where the waves were high, not to the friendly lagoon.

She stumbled once on the way, but her step was firm as she walked into the water. Soon it would be over. She and Tani would both die. Rogar would be rid of them and the problems they had brought him. Elosa would have won, true, but Amaya would have obeyed the law. She and Tani would reach the peaceful island. The gods would bless her action.

She pictured the peaceful island as the waves reached her waist. She clutched the sleeping baby against her breast. Soon the cold water would waken Tani, and she would cry. Amaya knew she must be ready to hold her tightly then, even to hold her under water, to make sure that the baby died first, that she wasn't left alone in the water, frightened.

Amaya paused, embracing the child more firmly.

Suddenly, she was grasped roughly from behind.

"What are you doing?" Rogar's voice was harsh. "You do not have to take the child into the water! I will do it!"

"No! No! I will take her! She must not be frightened!"

"I will not frighten her! And it must be done as the sun comes up!" Rogar tried to take Tani out of Amaya's arms.

Amaya clutched the child. "No! Let me take her! We will die and leave you in peace!"

"You die? You must not die!"

"It's best, Rogar! Elosa will never allow me to be part of your clan! She will not forgive you for marrying me! There will be more trouble! It's best if I die with Tani!"

Rogar held her and Tani tightly. His grip woke the baby, and the little one began to fuss and cry sleepily. When Rogar spoke, his voice was low and desperate. "No!" he said. "No! Amaya, you must live. We must live together."

The waves broke around them and the sand shifted under Amaya's feet. She felt as if she were falling, but Rogar held her up.

"We must live on together," he said again. "I love you, Amaya."

Amaya felt the coconut husk break. She was in Rogar's

arms, with nothing to protect her, with no shell to hide behind. Tani was crying, and Amaya was sobbing mighty sobs. And Rogar's arms, Rogar's love surrounded her. He led her slowly back to the beach, and there Amaya collapsed in the sand, still sobbing.

It was many minutes before she was able to speak. "Is there no way to save Tani?"

"We have to obey the law," Rogar said. "Amaya! Can you trust me?"

"Trust you?"

Rogar laid his cheek against her hair. "Yes, Amaya. Trust me."

"I can do nothing by myself," Amaya said dully. "This is your island, your people. I know you do not want Tani to die. But if she must—I trust you not to let her be afraid."

Rogar helped Amaya up and led her back to the house. Amaya did not put Tani down but held her the rest of the night, just as Rogar held her. Finally she fell asleep.

The stirring of birds woke her, and she realized she was alone.

Rogar and Tani were gone.

"No!" Amaya jumped to her feet. "No! No!"

It was still dark in the hut, but outside the light was coming. Rogar had already taken Tani away, to put her in the water.

Amaya ran along the path to the beach. She could hear the waves pounding loudly. The tide was coming in. Ahead she saw a figure silhouetted against the morning sky.

"Rogar!"

Rogar paused, but he did not stop. Amaya ran on, until she was beside him. "Please, Rogar! There must be another way."

He walked on. "Go back, Amaya," he said. "You said you would trust me."

"Please! Please!"

Rogar did not answer. Instead, Amaya heard the cackle of Elosa's voice. "The strange child cannot take food from the children of the people! Rogar knows the law, strange woman! He obeys the law of his people."

The voice brought Amaya to her knees. "Please," she said again. But this time she whispered.

"You have brought disgrace to Rogar and our people!" Elosa's voice gloated. "The way of the people must be followed!"

Amaya formed her body into its coconut shell. Rogar's mother and sister knelt beside her.

"Be quiet, Elosa!" Rogar's mother said. "Amaya is obeying the law. But a woman who likes seeing a baby put to death is no real woman!"

Surprised by her mother-in-law's sharp words to Elosa, Amaya looked up at the shaman. Elosa did not reply to the criticism, but she pointed to the surf with her heavy staff. "Rogar obeys the law!"

Amaya's eyes followed the staff, and she saw that Rogar was walking into the water. Tani was not frightened. She was laughing and clapping her hands. To her it was just another of the games Rogar had taught her to love.

Rogar did not go out very far. The waves were rolling. It would not take a lot of water to drown a tiny girl.

He seemed to be playing with Tani, and Amaya remembered he had promised to keep her from being afraid. He held her close to his body, and he ducked under the water.

But when he arose, the baby was gone.

Rogar stood motionless, the waves beating over him. Then he walked back to the beach. When he reached the edge of the water, he turned and looked back. His father joined him and placed a hand on his shoulder. Together they looked down the beach, and Rogar's father pointed.

Were they thinking where her tiny body would wash ashore? Amaya hoped so. To think of Tani not only dead, but lost in the sea—it was more than she could bear.

Then Rogar's father called out! "There! There!" He and Rogar ran down the beach.

And Rogar knelt down and scooped up a tiny bundle. He held it above his head. Amaya saw dark hair and legs. And the legs kicked!

"She is not dead, Elosa! The sea has refused her!"

Amaya jumped to her feet and watched in amazement as Rogar walked toward them. Tani was squirming and angry. But she was alive.

Elosa shook her staff furiously. "Put her in the water again! It is the law!"

Rogar stood silently for a moment before he turned once more toward the water. Amaya again sank into despair. She watched Rogar walk through the surf, the waves breaking over him and Tani. Again he sank beneath the waves with the child in his arms. Again he rose without her and slowly walked back to the beach.

And again he and his father watched down the beach until a tiny bundle washed ashore. Once more they ran down to pick up Tani's body.

And once more Rogar brought the child to Elosa alive.

Elosa pounded her staff on the beach and screamed. "She's a demon! She must die! It is the law!"

Tani was very angry now, but Elosa's fury frightened her. She clutched Rogar around the neck and shrieked. Rogar patted and soothed her until she became quieter. And when the baby became quiet, Amaya heard other sounds. Looking behind her, she saw that many people were standing behind her. They were buzzing with talk. And they were all looking at Rogar and Elosa, who stood facing each other. Neither of them looked around at the others.

Elosa spoke, and her voice was not loud, but it crackled angrily. "Put her back in the water, Rogar, and take her farther out."

"Are you sure, Elosa? Are you sure this is what the law commands?"

"Do you think that I—your shaman—can mistake the meaning of the law, the law that has governed our people for generations?"

"Twice the sea has refused to take Tani. A third time—"

Now Elosa's eyes flickered right, left. Amaya knew she was considering the people gathered behind her. She took a deep breath and raised her staff. "Take her out, Rogar. Leave her for the water to take."

She swung the staff around, but Rogar did not flinch away from the stick.

"Take her out!" Elosa's final words were a shriek. "It is the law!"

Rogar turned and walked back to the water. Amaya still knelt on the sand, with Rogar's mother and sister beside her. Tears were running down her cheeks. Tani saw her there and waved, a baby wave. Then she turned to look at the approaching water—still unafraid and still trusting Rogar.

"Trust me," Rogar had said. "Trust me."

If Tani can trust him, Amaya thought, *I must trust him, too.* And she stood up proudly, staring after her husband.

Now the sun had moved over the horizon, and it was hard to see what was happening with her eyes dazzled by tears and by the sun.

Again Rogar walked through the surf. Again he ducked into the water, playing a game with Tani. Amaya even thought she heard the child's laughter over the sound of the waves. Then Rogar ducked beneath the water, and when he arose, Tani was gone.

Amaya did not allow herself to hope that the child would survive. No, the small one could not be lucky enough to be washed ashore three times. This time, she knew, Tani was dead. And that was good. If the child had to go into the water one more time, Amaya's heart could not continue to beat.

Rogar came through the surf, and Amaya went to meet him. She put her arms around him and laid her head against his chest.

"You tried, Rogar. You faced Elosa, argued with her. You tried your best." She looked into his eyes. "I love you."

Rogar smiled. "And I love you, Amaya. Now, we had better go to Tani."

He gestured behind her, and Amaya turned to see the same brown bundle tumble from the waves.

Tani!

She and Rogar ran down the beach, and she scooped the little girl up.

Tani coughed. She sneezed. Then she screamed.

Suddenly Amaya and Rogar and Tani were surrounded by excited people.

Rogar's mother was embracing Amaya and Tani. "The witch is beaten!" she said. "This little one and my son have taken her power away!"

"What?" Amaya was amazed.

"Three times! Three times!" Rogar's sister yelled it out.

Rogar was smiling, and Amaya turned to him. "What do they mean, Rogar?"

"If the sea rejects the child three times, then the interpretation of the law is wrong," he said. "Elosa condemned the child wrongly. So Tani will live, and another will be selected as shaman."

An hour later, Tani had been fed and was asleep. Other women had come to marvel at the strong little girl who had survived the sea three times. They brought gifts to the child the sea loved. Now alone, Amaya stared in awe at the little girl.

The others were taking Tani's survival as a miracle. Were the gods of the sea showing that they loved her niece? Oh, it was easy to say that Elosa had condemned her wrongly and that the sea had rejected her. But it was hard for Amaya to believe Elosa had not condemned others wrongly, and her other victims had died. Amaya did not understand.

Outside, she heard a deep voice greeting Rogar, and she heard Rogar's respectful reply. The headman had come. Would even the headman want to behold the miracle child?

But the headman was talking to Rogar.

"The elders are going to ask you to join their council," he said.

Join their council? Amaya took a quick breath. But Rogar was young! Too young to be an elder!

Rogar sounded wary when he answered the headman. "That is too high an honor for me. The elders must command canoes. I do not have the years—"

The headman chuckled. "But you have the head, Rogar. And you have the knowledge."

Rogar did not answer.

"And you used that knowledge to benefit your people. We are rid of Elosa."

"If she had admitted she was wrong after the second time the sea refused the child—"

"But she did not." The headman's voice was brisk. "You gave her the chance to back down, to save face. She did not take it. You handled her wisely. The little one will be lucky to have you as a father."

"The little one is already lucky."

"Yes. She was lucky to have a man taking care of her who taught her not to fear the water. That is one reason we wish you to join the elders."

"But—"

"Do not say no, Rogar! The other reason is more practical."

He dropped his voice to a whisper, and Amaya barely heard his final words.

"We need all the men who understand the currents and tides as you do to command canoes."

LOVE AT FIRST BYTE

Kathy Hogan Trocheck

Kathy Hogan Trocheck is the author of ten mystery novels, including the Callahan Garrity and Truman Kicklighter mystery series. Her eleventh book, Body Slam, a Callahan Garrity mystery, is forthcoming from HarperCollins. A former journalist, Trocheck is a native Floridian. She now lives and works in Atlanta. Her books have been nominated for the Agatha, Anthony, and Macavity Awards. The inspiration for "Love At First Byte" came during a week Trocheck spent writing at a small tourist motel on the Florida panhandle.

Andy Kenneally aimed the gun carefully, held his breath, and squeezed the trigger.

Damn.

The staples were too short. He'd meant to use five-eighths inch, had somehow picked up the shorter ones. He tossed the roll of wire mesh screening aside, picked up the now warm Dr Pepper, drank, and considered his handiwork.

High winds the night before had blown out every screen on every porch of every concrete-block cottage at the Whispering Sands Motel. Replacing them would take all day, maybe tomorrow, too.

Well, Andy thought, it's a job. And where would he be without rotted screens and high winds?

Not at the bank in Birmingham, Alabama. All the mid-management there had been let go after the merger with ChemBank of California. Not at a consulting firm. No, people didn't hire consultants who'd spent six months in a court-ordered drug rehab after a highly visible flameout.

He'd left the drug rehab on a Friday in early January. It didn't dawn on him where he was going until he was crossing the bridge over Saint Andrew's Bay. The coast. It was as good a place as anywhere else.

Just before Destin, in the town of Santa Rosa, he'd stopped for gas at a convenience store, overheard an elderly woman asking the attendant if he knew anybody good with his hands.

"I'm good with my hands." Andy put his money on the counter.

The old woman turned and looked him over. She was tall and bony, white-haired, with a beak nose that made her look like one of the egrets that tiptoed through the roadside ditches on the coast highway.

"You a smoker?"

"No."

"Drinker?"

"Not anymore," Andy said.

"You'd be the maintenance man," Marguerite Geary said. "Pay's two hundred dollars a week, plus your room."

The place was called the Whispering Sands. It was the last mom-and-pop tourist court left on the panhandle, she said proudly, pointing at the high-rises that lined the coast to the north and the south. Marguerite Geary had rules. No smoking. No drinking in front of guests. No loud music, no pets, no grills on the deck. No women in his room.

"Other than that, you mind your business, I mind mine," Marguerite said. She lived in a two-story cedar cabin at the entrance to the tourist court with her granddaughter Caitlyn. Marguerite kept the books, Caitlyn cleaned the rooms, and Andy was the maintenance man.

The part about being good with his hands was a lie. But Andy Kenneally learned fast. He found he liked being outdoors, the sun on his back, a sweat-soaked shirt pinned to the clothesline every night. His efficiency was two rooms—a combination kitchen-sitting room-bedroom, and a bathroom with a toilet that ran all night. He had a portable radio to listen to the ball games, and guests left paperback novels behind when they returned to their city lives.

Marguerite never told him he couldn't hit on Caitlyn. It was understood, that was all.

But there was no rule against looking. Caitlyn Geary was easy to look at. He'd see her sometimes, pulling the wagon full of linens and cleaning supplies along the brick walkways that ringed the court. She was tall and slim and wore threadbare blue jeans and clean cotton T-shirts, her tan neck brown above the pristine white cotton. She'd pile her honey-colored hair on top of her head, or tie it back in a ponytail, and it would bob in the breeze from the Gulf.

She was clean and new and wonderful, Andy thought.

One Friday, payday, he was in Destin, eating alone at the counter at Captain Tony's, when Caitlyn Geary came in. Andy said hi, went back to his own plate of fried oysters. Caitlyn came up, sat down beside him at the bar. She noticed the Dr Pepper.

"My grandmother says you're probably a dried-out drunk," she said.

"Nope," Andy said. "Drugs. But like they say in treatment, alcohol is a drug."

"She says you're too smart for the job you're doing."

"Not smart enough," Andy said. "But I'll learn."

"You're probably too old for me, too."

"Probably," he said. "Nearly thirty."

"Well, how old do you think I am?"

"I never guess a lady's age."

She smiled. Her teeth were fine and even, dazzling white against the tan of her face, but there was a chip in the front tooth, and she had a tiny, entrancing mole beneath the left corner of her mouth. "I'm twenty-one. Old enough to know better, my grandmother says."

After that, they were friends. Friday nights, if she wasn't busy, it was understood they'd meet on the deck overlooking the seawall and watch the sunset together. The winter sunsets were spectacular, when the sky would go all violet and streaky with oranges and crimsons and yellow.

Near the end of February, a silver Lexus pulled into the oyster shell drive of the Whispering Sands. Andy was painting the trim on cottage three. He turned and watched the driver get out and make a show of standing a fancy leather golf bag against the side of the car. He was short, with a shock of wavy dark hair and mirrored sunglasses. He wore a white polo shirt with some kind of country club crest over the breast, black knit slacks, and black and white saddle oxfords. *Sporty,* Andy thought. That was Monday night.

That Friday night, Andy took his Dr Pepper out to the seawall, along with a couple of Cuban sandwiches he'd picked up in town. Just as the sun was sinking low in the horizon, he saw Caitlyn come out, by the silver Lexus. Dressed in a white sundress that bared her shoulders and back. Wearing strappy high-heeled sandals. It took his breath away.

Brett Sayre came out of cabin two, locked the door behind him, and tossed the key in the air. Like he was somebody. He sprinted over to the Lexus and opened the car door for Caitlyn. He threw a great spray of oyster shells as he peeled out of the parking lot.

Andy emptied the Dr Pepper onto the sand and went inside to listen to the ball game.

After that, he watched Brett Sayre carefully.

Sayre was a busy boy. He was in and out of the Whispering Sands all day long, always dressed casually but expensively. He saw Andy around the complex, gave him a conspiratorial wink, a "hihowyadoin'" kind of look just once, then ignored him as part of the scenery after that.

Once, just once, Andy tried to approach the subject of Brett Sayre with Caitlyn. It was early on Friday; they were driving into Destin together to buy supplies.

"This Brett guy. What's he do all day long?" Andy asked. "Why is he here?"

Caitlyn gave him a cool look. "He sold his software company. To MicroMega. Now he's looking for investment opportunities. He's really brilliant, Andy."

"Brilliant? I've seen that kind before. All hat and no cattle. And if he's so brilliant and successful, why's he staying at the Whispering Sands? He could be down at Sandestin, or Seaside, someplace like that. We don't even have a pool, for Christ's sake."

"Well, if you're so brilliant Mr. College Man, what are you doing at the Whispering Sands?" Her face was white with fury. "I don't think a recovering drug addict has any room to talk, Andy."

He made another stab at it. "We're not talking about me. I've made a mess of my life. I just don't want to see you make the same mistake."

Her smile was arch. "I know exactly what I'm doing."

When they got back from town, Caitlyn left him to unload the supplies by himself.

Marguerite watched her flounce off, clucking her tongue in disapproval.

"I tried to talk to her about Sayre," Andy said. "She won't listen to me. Maybe you could try?"

Marguerite turned and faced the Gulf, shading her eyes. It was late in the day, overcast, and the waves came limping in, glassy and pale grayish green. A pair of sea-birds were diving at something in the shallows. "Might as well try talking to those seagulls," she said. "There's no talking to 'em when they're that way about a man."

Another afternoon, Marguerite and Andy watched the stranger emerge from his cottage in yet another country club golf outfit. "Says he's in software. Just sold his company to some big outfit, wanted a little rest and relaxation," Marguerite commented.

The tags on the Lexus were Dade County. "He couldn't relax in Miami?" Andy wanted to know.

"Credit card's good," Marguerite said. "I ran it soon as he checked in. He's paid up till the end of March. He don't get a lot of calls and he don't make a lot of calls, I'll tell you that. Caitlyn says he spends money like it's water. Took her to dinner over there at Finizi, at Seaside. It ain't cheap."

Software. Wasn't everybody in software these days?

Brett Sayre didn't need the pile of receipts on his dresser to tell him he was nearly maxed out. The gold card had a limit of $2,000, but with the lease on the Lexus, restaurant bills, the clothes he'd needed, and incidentals, he was close, very close.

As usual, he had money on this mind. A deal, he thought. One deal. A few weeks ago, he'd been close. But the hatchet-faced old lady in Sarasota had neglected to tell him she had a nephew who was a wiseass lawyer. When Brett showed up at the old lady's condo with the time-share papers, the lawyer-nephew demanded the deposit check back—that or he'd call the sheriff.

He'd been able to talk his way out of that one. Be right back, he'd promised the nephew. And he'd hit the road, cashing the deposit check at the branch bank close to the mall.

His luck had turned when he'd taken the wrong turn in Santa Rosa, passed the crude wooden sign for the Whispering Sands. It sat there, like an ugly brown wart, smack on eight hundred feet of gleaming white Gulf beach. Condos on both sides with pools, tennis courts, Jacuzzis, dinner clubs. And right in the middle, the Whispering Sands, twelve dumpy concrete-block cottages on what, an acre?

Brett walked it off the first night he'd checked in. An acre and change. Plenty of room for two towers, eighteen stories each. He'd checked the prices at the nearest real estate office. Gulf-front units, two-two, were bringing an easy $250,000. Laid out right, you could get two pent-houses on each tower, ask $750,000 apiece.

When he saw the owner, old Marguerite Geary who was eighty if she was a day, he knew it was his lucky day. "All right," he told himself. "This could be good."

How good he hadn't realized until Marguerite had sent her granddaughter, Caitlyn, over to his cottage with an armload of towels and an extra blanket in case he got cold in the night. Right then, Brett Sayre took a long, lazy look at Caitlyn and drawled, "It's not a blanket I need to keep me warm at night."

She'd taken it exactly right, laughed, like he was kidding. But she'd gotten a good look at the luggage, the golf clubs, the leased Lexus. He felt her watching him when he was out walking on the beach, working on his tan, working on his plan, adding up all the numbers.

Caitlyn Geary was an attraction he hadn't planned on. But yes, it made sense. That first night at dinner, he'd ordered the most expensive bottle of Chardonnay. She'd lapped it up, talked nonstop. She was Marguerite's only family, parents divorced when she was a kid, both dead five years now. Santa Rosa was a boring, hick town, Caitlyn said, but she couldn't leave Marguerite.

No, honey, Brett thought. *We'll stay right here.* Money spent nicer at the beach, he'd decided.

B ut it cost money to make money. Brett got the Costa Rica time-share brochures out of his briefcase. One deal, just one, and he'd have some moving-around money.

Something banged hard against the door of the cottage. He threw the brochures in the drawer of the nightstand, bounded to the door, threw it open.

"Sorry," Andy Kenneally said. But he didn't look sorry. He had a load of cedar planks laid across a wheelbarrow, a toolbox balanced on top. "Gotta fix these chairs," he said, pointing to a pair of rotted-out Adirondack chairs on the brick patio at the front of the cottage. Andy took a hammer to one of the chairs, knocking the ruined board loose.

"Fix somebody else's chairs," Brett hollered. "I'm trying to get some work done in here."

"Won't be too long," Andy said, ignoring him. He wanted to get a look inside that cottage, see just what it was the brilliant Brett Sayre was working on.

"I said," Sayre started, but stopped at the sound of . . .

"Ah-hem." It was a polite, not-so-subtle throat clearing.

They both turned to see the woman standing on the brick walkway.

"Are one of you boys named Andy?" The woman had shoulder-length red hair, she was wearing a skimpy little skirt and an even skimpier little top, and her big eyes were taking everything in, including and especially Brett Sayre's well-muscled bare chest. She was petite, but built, and she knew it and liked it.

Andy put down the hammer he'd been clutching in his hand, wanting to hit Sayre with it, knowing he needed to walk away. "I'm Andy."

"Well," she said, sticking out her hand in the friendliest kind of way, "I'm Sherry Westphall. Mrs. Geary said you'd help me put my things in my cottage. Number eight," she said, emphasizing the number so Brett could get it right.

Brett held onto her hand a second longer than was strictly necessary. The band on her ring finger held a two-carat diamond. Big diamond studs at her ears, too. And she smelled expensive. "Let me give you a hand," he said. "Andy here's got a lot of hammering to do." He took her hand in his. "I'm Brett. Your new neighbor."

She gave a contented little sigh, and Brett's plan changed, right in that instant. Caitlyn was a sweet, desirable kid. Fun. And once he got his hands on that acre of Gulf-front acreage, they would have a lot more fun. But this here, this was a woman. A woman with immediate possibilities that would need exploring. Maybe she would be needing a time-share in Costa Rica. Or maybe she'd like to buy into a little real estate investment trust he was putting together to snap up some apartment complexes down in Lauderdale.

Sherry Westphall saw the way Brett Sayre eyed her diamonds. Good. She liked to be noticed, now that Harris was dead and in the ground. Poor old GoodOleBoy. That was his screen name, the one he'd used in Love-Lines, the Internet chat room where they'd met. He was GoodOleBoy; this time around she called herself SherFair. She loved making up screen names.

Oh, it was love at first byte.

Poor old Harris left a well-off widow. He would have liked that idea, if he hadn't had to die so painfully from a freak snakebite. The snakebite was her favorite so far. Before Harris, she'd helped four other men along to early graves. Five husbands. Five deaths. None of them the same. Five bank accounts. Five diskettes with the details mapped out, for review.

After the funeral, she sold the Explorer Harris bought her, traded it in on a new Mercedes convertible. She listed the ranch with a real estate agent, took the insurance money, and put some of it in mutual funds and some short-term high-risk bonds and T-bills. She packed her little laptop computer in the trunk of the Mercedes and shook the dust of Peavine, Texas, from her shoes and never looked back.

She had plenty now. She could stop, maybe go to Europe, the Caribbean, and take a cruise. She'd never learned to swim, though, and the idea of being on a big boat out in the middle of the ocean unnerved her. She couldn't even watch that movie *Titanic*. It made her feel all panicky, all that water, everywhere. The beach might be nice, though. She liked the feel of sand between her toes. Liked the way men looked at her in a bathing suit. She'd drive over to the Florida panhandle, drive south a ways, and cross over to the Atlantic Coast. Palm Beach was someplace she'd been thinking about. Older men, older money, it had a certain amount of appeal.

Brett Sayre pulled Sherry's luggage out of the trunk of the Mercedes. He had a thing for convertibles, and this one was brand-new. "Nice," he said, running his hand across the front bumper.

Sherry took the laptop from him. She shrugged. "My late husband picked this out for me, just before his last illness. Warren left me quite a lot of money. He wanted me to enjoy myself. It's my first trip after Warren's death."

This man, she thought unexpectedly, was simply too yummy. Swarthy almost, bulging muscles, deeply tanned, barefoot. She felt like a starved tiger eyeing its first T-bone steak in a long, long time. She could see the line of dark hair extending down his chest, below the waistband of his shorts. Maybe she would stay around for a while, Sherry decided. Palm Beach and the withered flesh of withered old men could wait. Right now, she was ready for something lively, maybe something a little dangerous.

She tilted her head and looked at Sayre through lowered eyelashes. He had a game, she was sure of it. Nothing about him was straight or honest. But that was okay. She would enjoy watching him play his game, allowing herself to be reeled in.

"Come for a ride," she cooed. "I'd love some company."

Caitlyn watched the two of them drive off in the Mercedes, Brett behind the wheel and that woman—Sherry Westphall? In unit eight? Laughing, her head thrown back, big sharp teeth bared. What was so funny?

At eight o'clock, she changed out of the new dress, threw the heels against the wall. He wasn't coming back. Not tonight. She changed into shorts and a T-shirt, went into the living room where Marguerite was watching television.

"Thought you had a date," her grandmother said.

"Something came up," Caitlyn said, a catch in her voice. "I'm going out."

It was warm out. She could hear the waves lapping at the sand below the seawall and music drifted out of one of the cottages. Her hand brushed against the shrubbery in front of the cottage, and the scent of beach rosemary wafted up to meet her.

It was Friday night, and she was alone again.

She wandered up the path toward unit eight. She put her hand on the cool metal of the passkey in her pocket, then decided against it. Suppose they came back? Suppose Brett caught her snooping in that woman's cabin?

Caitlyn sagged down into one of the Adirondack chairs in front of Brett's cabin. She would talk to him, try to make him understand. Make him realize that she was not the kid he thought she was.

The crunch of oyster shells awoke her with a start. And voices, faint. Brett's voice. She started to stand up. But another voice chimed in. A woman's. Caitlyn scrunched down in the chair.

"Shh," Sherry Westphall cautioned. She lurched against Brett, and he caught her in his arms. "Don't wanna wake up the neighbors," she said, giggling. She reached up and kissed him hungrily.

"Your place or mine?" Brett asked. Sherry giggled

again. *It was obscene, that giggle,* Caitlyn thought.

"I've got a bottle of Tanqueray in my room," she heard Sherry say. "And a couple other things I think you might enjoy."

They both laughed and staggered down the path toward unit eight. No lights went on in the cabin.

Brett snuck out of cabin eight early. He sprinted down to the water, letting the cold Gulf waves wash over him, washing off the scent of her. This morning the rays of the early sun shone across her face, asleep on the pillow beside his. He saw the puffiness around her chin, tiny lines radiating at the corners of the eyes, the brassy red hair splayed out against the white linens. It was so easy. Why was it bothering him? Nothing this easy had ever bothered him before. It was going to be a very sweet deal. The wine made Sherry talk about her dear departed Warren, who'd left her a couple mil.

Brett looked up and saw Caitlyn on the seawall, pulling the wagon full of linens behind her. She was coming out of his cottage. She would have seen the bed, the sheets untouched from the day before when she'd changed the linens. And she would know.

He felt a pang. God, had he developed a conscience? Why should he care what the kid knew? Unless it soured her on their arrangement. He'd talk to her, Brett decided. Let her in on the game, tell her how it would be, how it had nothing to do with them, just a little business deal he had going. A quick marriage, an unfortunate accident. He knew just how it would go down. Last night, when he'd proposed a midnight swim, she'd drawn away from him. Swim? No, Sherry didn't like the ocean. He could see into the future, see a wave sweeping her up and under, catching her and tossing her cruelly, unexpectedly.

*   *   *

The wagon bumped along behind Caitlyn. She kicked at a broken clamshell. It skipped along, and she walked forward and gave it another vicious kick, sent it sailing.

"That shell do something to offend you?" It was Andy, up on a ladder, scraping the eaves on unit seven. He climbed down, wiped his paint-spattered hands on a rag. He gestured toward Sayre. "Never saw him up and about this early."

Caitlyn stared over at the door of unit eight.

"Oh," Andy said, slowly. "So it's that way?"

"Looks like it."

"I'm sorry, kiddo." His voice was kind and his eyes sad.

"Shut up," Caitlyn said. She yanked the wagon handle so hard it toppled over, dumping out her load of clean linens.

Sherry stood in the doorway of unit eight, watching Brett cavorting in the waves. He was so alive, so brown and young and warm. And obvious. Last night at dinner, when she'd ordered the forty-dollar bottle of wine, she'd seen his eyes widen.

When the check came, she'd swept it off the tray and made a show of taking out three fifties and placing them on the tip tray. "Now Sherry," Brett had started, but she'd quickly shushed him. He'd been full of big plans and big talk at dinner, all about his software company and how much the stock would bring, once he liquidated.

"Software?" she asked innocently. "What type of software, Brett?"

He'd known so damn little about computers it was laughable. "It's software I developed for the real estate industry," he'd said, all puffed up.

Every lie he told, every pathetic swagger and boast, she found entrancing. She knew his type—greedy, self-involved, with a hard, cold center to that warm, dazzling exterior. And the more she recognized it, the more she wanted him.

Desire. Was this what it was like? An unexpected care-lessness? A loosening and then a quickening? And the more you got, the more you needed? This was it?

Her cheeks flamed hot, and that amused her. What was Brett? Maybe twenty-five, twenty-six? Old enough to be her son. And how old was she, really? The identities she'd created so carefully over the years had taken over. She believed in the moment. And at that moment, she was Sherry Westphall, a rich, twenty-eight-year-old widow with money to burn.

B rett waited for her inside the laundry room, grabbing her as she rounded the corner.

"Caitlyn," he breathed, and he kissed her hard, and at first she melted against him, then pushed him away.

"What about your girlfriend?" she said coldly. "Mrs. Westphall. I saw the two of you last night, Brett."

"I know what it looks like. But it's just business," he said, lowering his voice. "She's got a lot of money to invest. She's lonely, that's all. It's got nothing to do with you and me. Just hang in there. You're the one I want. We just have to wait a while. And you have to trust me. So I can fix it so you and me can be together."

Caitlyn's upper lip trembled. "I can't stand thinking of you with her. In bed. I can't stand that, Brett."

"Then don't," he said, and with his pinky, he wiped away the tear tracing its way down her cheek.

A ndy climbed heavily down from the ladder outside the laundry room. He'd heard more than he'd wanted to. Goddamn it! He put the paint can and the drop cloth in the wheelbarrow and trundled away toward the next cabin. It was hot, and the air was still and damp, and the beach below smelled of dead fish and rancid oil and rotting seaweed. He had stayed too long, seen too much. He had to get out.

Brett Sayre watched Andy through the laundry room window. This guy was everywhere, in his face, watching him, like he knew what Brett was thinking before he'd thought it. He asked Caitlyn about Kenneally, why was an educated guy like that bumming around the Whispering Sands, hauling garbage, hacking weeds? What was his story?

Her face softened when she talked about Andy. "He's all right. He's had a tough time. Lost his job, had a breakdown. He went to jail, then to drug rehab."

Jail? He'd tuck that little detail away for the right moment. *So Handy Andy was an addict. A head case. An ex-con.* That was something useful.

Later, he was in the office, supposedly getting change for the dryer.

Marguerite was at the desk, doing paperwork.

"Say, Mrs. Geary," he said, offhandedly. "What's with that Andy guy?"

"What's that?" she said, looking up from her ledger.

"Well, he talks to himself a lot. And last night, he was outside that room of his, I walked by and I thought I smelled dope. You know, marijuana? The guy was stoned out of his mind. And you know what he was doing?"

"What?" Marguerite's eyes narrowed.

"He was watching that woman over in unit eight, Mrs. Westphall. Maybe somebody should warn her to draw those shades when she gets out of the shower at night."

Sayre found a jewelry store in Panama City that didn't mind taking an out-of-state check. The ring was showy, carat and a half. He stopped at a liquor store in Seagrove and got a bottle of chilled champagne.

Brett and Sherry drank the whole bottle on the short trip over the state line to Alabama. No wait in Alabama, Brett explained to Sherry. He was a man who didn't like to wait.

She couldn't believe it was real. Five weddings, five husbands. She'd banked all those feelings down inside. Yet, somehow, this two-bit Romeo had gotten to her. He was running a con, all right. Already he'd talked about the new software he was developing, he just needed some start-up money. God, it was so clumsy. And so endearing. She'd already handed over $10,000 to him, half the cash she'd brought with her. He was like a kid, touching the money, stroking it, patting the suitcase she'd packed it into. And when she'd hinted about the other funds, his reaction had been comic, the double take, and the faked indifference.

But it was real, all right, the way he made her feel. She wanted to melt when he said her name, touched her, looked at her. It was a con, she knew, but a con this delicious was worth the price. Besides, with what she really did know about computers, maybe they could make a go of Brett's game together. She decided to let it play out.

They found a motel in Fairhope, Alabama, for their wedding night. It was exhausting, exhilarating; she was dizzy and unquenchable, alternately shy and shameless. She found herself detached, looking down at the two of them, locked in the sweat-soaked sheets. Who was this dewy bride?

Sherry Sayre. She liked the sibilant sound of it.

When she was finally asleep, he eased away from her, extricated himself from the octopus hold of out-flung arms and legs that tried to wind around him and squeeze and suffocate. He wanted to cut and run, never hear the voice again, the coy "Bre-e-e-t!" The suitcase of cash was there. His for the taking. But there was more, so much more.

He found his mind wandering down U.S. 98 to a scrubby patch of sand on the Gulf of Mexico and a grubby clutch of concrete-block cottages with the improbable name of the Whispering Sands.

"You hear about the newlyweds?" Andy drawled.

Caitlyn looked up from the sheets she was fold-ing. "It makes you happy, doesn't it? Being right about him."

He'd been tinkering with the water hose on the wash-ing machine when she'd walked in to take the clothes out of the dryer. Her eyes were dull and red-rimmed.

Andy put the wrench down carefully, chose his words the same way.

"I don't like seeing you hurt," he said finally. "Those two—Sayre and that Westphall woman—they deserve each other. So yeah, I'm glad. Glad he can't hurt you anymore."

"He doesn't love her," Caitlyn said, the words tumbling out. "He told me. It's just business. That's all. When he finds out who she really is, he'll leave her."

Andy took her wrist, turned the hand over. Fine blue veins showed through on the back of her hand. "His business is hurting people. Ripping them off. You want a man like that? Come on, Caitlyn, you're too good for that."

She laced her fingers in his. "That's the problem. I'm too good for him. Who am I good enough for, Andy?" She gave him a searching look.

He blushed. "I gotta go."

Brett waited until he'd seen Kenneally leave the laundry room. She was in there, alone; it might be his only chance. Sherry didn't let him out of her sight, not a minute. She was at him, touching, pawing, patting, every minute. He felt as though he were boxing with flypaper.

"Caitlyn," he'd whispered, slipping into the laundry room, closing the door behind him.

"Oh. It's the happy honeymooner. Congratulations, Brett. I hope you'll be very happy."

He tried to pull her toward him, but she shoved him away. "Don't touch me."

"Just listen," he begged. "It was a mistake, all right? I admit it; she talked me into it. Sherry thinks she can buy people. She promised me a lot of money. But it's not worth it, Caitlyn. Listen. I'm going to leave her. I don't want the money. I want you, baby."

"You married her," Caitlyn pointed out. "And you don't know a thing about her. I could tell you some things."

He shuddered. "I know all I need to know. I can't live with her. Look, it won't be long. You'll wait, won't you?

I'll get a lawyer, get a divorce, an annulment. And then it's us. Promise."

Sherry stared out at the dazzling sunlight. It was a sickness with her, an all-consuming disease. She wanted to follow Brett into the bathroom, out to the car when he went to get gas, into the store when he stopped for a Coke or some gum. She sensed he was pushing her away, and it made her more desperate to pull him to her. She stood at the window of unit eight and watched while he went to fetch the fresh towels. She saw him come out of the laundry room, shoulders slumped, saw the girl, Caitlyn, follow. Brett turned, took her hand, his face soft, expression pleading.

Sherry felt the warm flame inside her flicker, felt it sputter and go cold and die. The Brett Sayre walking slowly toward unit eight was the real man she had made a fool of herself over. In the harsh light of day she saw the cheapness of his haircut and the ruthless, calculating eyes. She had gone soft for only a little while, but in that short time, she knew, she had lost what was at her core, the power she had held over all men.

She went into the bathroom and took a long look at herself in the tiny mirror. Sherry Sayre was gone. There was only one way to redeem herself. Immediately she felt lighter, surer, stronger. The others had all been made to look like accidents. Death had come quickly. It would be different this time. It was the only way to exorcise the thing she'd become.

She'd have to work quickly, though, and that part was troubling. She didn't like improvisation. She shut her eyes, concentrated, was reassured by the little clicks and whirs, impressions, flickers, and sensations.

Two nights later, when Brett came into the cottage from his swim, she emerged from the bathroom wearing only a towel.

She came over to him, put her arms around his neck. "I've been thinking," she said, nuzzling. "Today's our one-week anniversary. Don't you think we should celebrate?"

"Definitely." His voice was dull.

"Let's go somewhere wonderful. All right? Really live it up?"

"Whatever you say."

"How about Finizi?" She'd found the matchbook in the pocket of his pants. He'd been there. With that girl.

"Not there," Brett said quickly. "It's full of phonies. No wine list at all."

"Where, then?" She'd hit a nerve.

"Anyplace else. Just not there."

More improvising. It wasn't so hard, really. She had the knife she'd stolen from that handyman's tackle box. It could be made to look like a robbery attempt, in a dark restaurant parking lot.

"Back to Fairhope, then. This dump is depressing."

Brett swallowed hard. Leave the Whispering Sands? Tonight? It would spoil the setup. It had to be here, here or nowhere. He fought back the feeling of panic. "We've already paid for the cottage till the end of the week. I tell you, what about that French restaurant in Destin?" He was stroking her hair, kissing her neck, choking back the feeling of revulsion.

"Well," she said, softening, "I do love French food."

"Fine," he said, shrugging. "Just let me get a shower, and we'll pack up."

"Leave the door open," she called. "I can't get enough of that body of yours."

He saw her in the bathroom mirror, sitting there at the dressing table, filing her nails, smearing makeup on her face. He let the hot water run full-blast, sending clouds of steam out into the bedroom, feeling his resolve grow.

He worked quickly. She'd left the hair dryer in the bathroom. He stretched the cord taut between his hands. He saw his hands trembling. *Now!* he told himself. *It has to be now.*

He padded into the room with the cord. She looked up from the mirror, saw his face etched in fury and determination. With a single movement he looped the cord around her neck and twisted, pulling, yanking against the sagging white flesh.

Her scream of terror was cut short. A hand lashed out, scratching him, digging nails into his upper arm. He felt a burning pain in his thigh, looked down, saw hot blood streaming down his leg.

Impossible. She'd stabbed him. He wrenched the cord tighter, his face muscles strained, he heard himself groaning. Still she struggled, kicking out at him. The two of them fell to the floor. He pinned her on the sand-crusted carpet, kneeled with his knees on her heaving chest, pressed down with the electric cord.

Her eyes bulged, spittle flew from her mouth, her head twisted once. Then she went limp and still, the knife still clutched in her right hand.

He got up, gasping for breath. His leg burned. He looked down. Two vicious rips in his thigh.

He made a crude bandage for the wound, turned off the light in the cottage, showered in the dark, dressed in his running clothes, went to the screened door of the cottage, and kicked it in.

He was nauseous. His leg throbbed from the stab wound. Half a mile, he told himself. Half a mile. He ran down the road in front of the Whispering Sand. To the end of the block and back, stopping once to fling the knife into a storm drain. *The knife. Why? Could she have known? Impossible.* Then into the cottage. Flick on the lights.

The scream was no fake. God, it was awful. The purple face, the bloodstained robe. He ran from the cottage, stumbled, shouting. "She's dead!" he screamed. "My God, he's killed her."

Marguerite Geary, grim-faced, was stalking toward unit eight. Right behind her were two uniformed cops, and trailing behind them came Caitlyn.

How? Brett wondered. How had they gotten here so fast? And what had they already seen?

"Caitlyn? You called the police? Thank God," he croaked, his voice hoarse. He turned and pointed toward the cottage. "Back there. Unit eight. My wife. She's been stabbed. I think she's dead."

The first cop was tall and lean, and he wore some kind of fancy lizard-skin cowboy boots. "Your wife?" he asked, hurrying toward Brett. "Gerilyn Varnedoe?"

Brett stared. "Who? No. My wife's name is Sherry. Sherry Westphall Sayre. She's dead. I think she's been stabbed. Blood all over the place."

The cops followed him into the cottage. Marguerite came, too, but Caitlyn stayed outside. Marguerite didn't blink at the sight of Sherry, lying there in a pool of her own blood. Brett pointed at her body, looked away, shuddered, terrified. What did these two hicks know? They kept asking the same questions, circling the body, kneeling down, poking at the body. The tall one had a lazy drawl and he made a lot of notes.

Where had Mr. Sayre been? What did Mr. Sayre see?

"I went out for a run before dinner," Brett said, letting his voice catch. "I got back and noticed first thing, the light was off. Sherri had been inside, getting dressed. Something caught my eye. A movement. I crouched down behind that thicket of palmetto near the porch. He came out. It was dark, but he was wearing a white shirt, and when he turned around, I saw his face in the moonlight."

He looked pleadingly at Marguerite. "It was Kenneally. Andy Kenneally. The handyman. He'd been watching Sherry. Stalking her, peeping in windows at her. I told you, didn't I, Mrs. Geary? About his watching her? And being stoned?"

"You told me," Marguerite said, tight-lipped.

"It was Kenneally?" The first cop asked. "You're sure? You got a good look at his face?"

"It was him," Brett said angrily. "He's an ex-con. Did time in drug rehab. Why aren't you people out looking for him? Why all these questions?"

The second cop yawned lazily. "Say, Marguerite, how'd you figure out Sherry Westphall was really Gerilyn Varnedoe? Those fellas out in Texas been trying to track her for six months now. That poor SOB she was married to? Harris Stubbs? He ran into her in one of them Internet chat rooms. Love Lines." The cop snorted. "That's a good one. Two months later, Gerilyn Varnedoe was Sherry Stubbs. Another two months after that, Harris went out to his dog pen to see what was frettin' his favorite bird dog, and he got bit by a rattlesnake. Freak accident." The cop snorted again. "We figure she banked seven hundred thousand dollars off that snakebite."

Brett looked at Marguerite. "Who? What are you people talking about? My wife was Sherry Westphall. She was a widow. But her husband's name was Warren. And they lived in Oklahoma."

Marguerite Geary shrugged. "It wasn't me figured it out. It was Caitlyn. You know how girls are. Jealous. She couldn't see through this pretty boy here, but she spotted Gerilyn Varnedoe the minute she laid eyes on her. Caitlyn had the passkey, took a look around the cabin while these two were getting hitched over in Fairhope."

"Caitlyn?" Brett looked up sharply. "That pervert Kenneally was watching her, too? My God, she could have been his next victim."

"Don't think so," the first cop said. He pulled a chair up, sat backwards on it, his broad, stupid face inches from Sayre's. He fanned five brightly colored plastic diskettes like a deck of cards.

"Darryl Strickland, Bakersfield, California. Oliver Sorensen, Saint Paul, Minnesota. James Moody, Bainbridge, Washington. Louis Greenfarb, Kansas City. And Harris Stubbs, Peavine, Texas. All heavily insured. Married briefly to Gerilyn Varnedoe. Recently deceased. Looks like you were number six, Mr. Sayre."

Brett's eyes bulged; he looked wildly about the room. "What are you people talking about? Kenneally's getting away."

His mind raced. Words tumbled out. "It was dark. He, the man, it was the same build. I just assumed . . ." Talking, he stood, gestured wildly, paced the room, closer toward the door, his hand on the knob, the Lexus parked just outside.

The first deputy closed his own callused hand tightly over Sayre's, wrenched it hard. He pointed toward the damp spot on Brett's slacks. "You're bleeding, Mr. Sayre," he commented. "We'll get you patched up, once we get to the jail."

The door popped open, and Caitlyn stepped inside, followed by Andy Kenneally. They were holding hands. "It's all on the diskettes, Brett," Caitlyn said. "I found her computer, but it was Andy who found the diskettes. He was the one who figured out how to read it."

She gave Andy a loving glance, made little tapping motions with her fingertips. "He's really good with his hands."

THE COLLABORATION

Marilyn Wallace

Marilyn Wallace is a founding member of Sisters in Crime and has served Mystery Writers of America as president of the Northern California chapter, as a national board member, and as General Award chair of the 1999 Edgar Allan Poe Awards. The daughter of a former New York policeman, she has worked as a high school English teacher, a silk screen fabric printer, a potter, a pastry chef, a waitress, and a computer programmer, all of which continue to provide material for her fiction. Her three-book series featuring Oakland, California, detectives Jay Goldstein and Carlos Cruz includes A Case of Loyalties, *a Macavity Award winner, and* Primary Target *and* A Single Stone, *both Anthony Award nominees. The focus shifts to psychological suspense in* So Shall You Reap, The Seduction, Lost Angel, *and* Current Danger. *Editor of the five-volume award-winning* Sisters in Crime *short story anthology, which highlights the work of American women mystery writers, and co-editor with Robert J. Randisi of* Deadly Allies, *she has led numerous writing workshops and classes across the country.*

In the fall they'd look like ants scurrying around on skinny legs, struggling under the load of their pathetic bits of leaf, crumbs of stale bread. In a July heat wave the faceless, frantic crowd would resemble maggots, pale with exhaustion and overwork, barely enough energy left to crawl to the platform in the airless hole under the ground. But it was February, and Gloria Simone thought the huddled mass of humanity struggling down the grimy steps and into the subway station looked like furry, robotic drone bees.

Which was good, because in New York City, you could still get lost in that swarm. Be anonymous. Go unnoticed. Anthony was counting on that. His plan depended on it. And because she loved him, loved the way he laughed suddenly at things like rainbows and babies learning to walk, loved his brown eyes, his broad shoulders, the curve of his forearm when he reached out for her, because of all the magic he wore about him like a cloak, she had agreed to be part of his plan.

"The target has to be near a subway line," he'd said that night six months ago when he first mentioned the idea. *"Details are important. That's what a Steven Spielberg would say, or a George Lucas, am I right?"*

Shivering, she bumped the stroller down the stairs. If only she didn't have to balance the bulky shopping bag, stuffed with her wool jacket and the baby's blue parka. Raymond squealed, turning his head on his baby-fat neck to share his fun. His brown eyes, curled up at the outer edges like Anthony's, were flecked with amber lights like his father's, too. Well, this was no game, and fun wasn't part of the story.

She paused to catch her breath. It would be over soon. One more hour, and the whole, ridiculous nightmare would be done.

The stroller nearly tipped forward, but she righted it in time. *Mustn't spill the precious cargo,* a silent, mocking voice warned. Screw up Anthony's plan big time if that happened.

How had she ever allowed herself to go along with his idea?

"Here, let me give you a hand with that."

The voice was way too cheery, and Gloria looked up into water-colored eyes fringed with heavily mascaraed lashes. The woman's purple beret sat, calm and serene, on the back of her head, and her black quilted jacket puffed out so you couldn't tell the shape underneath. But her smile was broad, and she reached a gloved hand to lift the front of the stroller.

Cold air pressed on Gloria's lungs, squeezing the breath out of her, wringing sweat onto her face. She shouldn't let anyone help her, shouldn't let anyone get this close, make this much contact. If the woman recognized Raymond later in a newspaper photo . . . if this Good Samaritan with a Coach purse slung over her shoulder recognized *her* . . .

Arms aching with the strain of controlling the teetering carriage and the shopping bag, Gloria nodded and mumbled her thanks.

"Oh, listen, it's nothing. This city is hard enough. I mean, other places, you just get in your car and go wherever, but here, schlepping down subway stairs, up escalators, taxis that pass you by, it's so easy to forget the person next door is, well, a person. Trying to live a life, am I right?" She stopped when they reached the bottom of the stairs. "What beautiful eyes she has. Those lashes . . ."

"He." Gloria reached into the diaper bag, fumbled for a baby wipe, and pressed the cool cloth to her cheeks, her neck, her burning forehead. The citrusy, chemical smell clung to her hands. *The very image of his father,* she thought, as she watched the woman's pale cheeks flush with embarrassment.

As though it mattered whether she'd guessed correctly that the baby was a boy or girl. The clerk in the token booth squinted at Raymond, nodded at Gloria, and then buzzed them through the latched gate. The woman in the black jacket appeared from the throng and picked up the front end of the stroller and started down the second staircase. At the platform, the woman smiled and then disappeared into the crowd. Where were all these people going, anyway? It was two in· the afternoon and—

An elbow jabbed Gloria's spine. She tripped, grabbed hold of a startled boy who couldn't have been more than twelve. Furious, she whirled and glared at the bug-eyed man behind her, rejecting the apology that spilled, soundless, from his lips as a train rattled to a stop.

Please, Lord, let me get on this train, she prayed as she righted herself. She pressed forward, trying to avoid the heels of a man in front of her, but something was wrong. The stroller wouldn't budge.

Damn! She'd told Anthony this flimsy piece of junk would tip over, would jam up, would fall apart, would somehow cause an accident. *"He'll outgrow it so fast, why do we need to go spending like we're Leona Helmsley just for a piece of equipment that's gotta last, what, maybe a year?"* he'd said.

Gloria clenched her jaw. Serve him right if he had to trash his whole plan because of this chewing gum and paper clip affair.

The heavy subway doors started to close, but she wedged her body against the thick rubber gasket that rimmed the door and pushed the stroller hard. Raymond wailed.

"Stand clear of the closing doors." The disembodied voice shouted above the din of a train arriving on the opposite platform.

If she was late, Anthony would be furious.

She knelt and tried to free the wheel. The brake—that was the problem. Someone had stepped on the little piece of metal, and the skinny rubber wheels wouldn't roll. She lifted the latch and pushed the stroller into the packed car. The doors shut, and the train lurched forward.

Nearly panting with relief, Gloria maneuvered the stroller to the center of the car, gratefully sat when a young girl offered her a place, and bent to undo the strap that held Raymond in place.

"Okay, sweetie, stop crying." Her jaw hurt from the effort not to yell at him. If he kept up all this noise, everyone would look, would remember the woman and the screaming baby. Would memorize his beautiful face, round cheeks, and brown eyes with those lashes, lashes so long that the lady in the black jacket had mistaken him for a girl.

A bubble clung to the tip of Raymond's nose and he swiped at it with a mittened hand. She dabbed at his nose with a tissue as he resumed his wailing. Her fingers wouldn't work properly. Instead of undoing the strap, she was making it tighter. Raymond screeched with frustration and twisted in the stroller.

"Here, let me help you."

It was the same damn woman, the one with the new purse, good shoes, nice watch, pleasant smile, nosy attitude. Who asked her to be so helpful?

This was not in the script Anthony had written. Should she just smile, accept the woman's offer, and then get off at the next stop? She could hardly pretend she didn't hear. The woman had already decided to get in Raymond's face. And that was very, very bad news.

"Thanks." Gloria smiled, stroked the baby's soft cheek, held the tissue to his nose and wiped the dampness, all the while talking, words streaming from her lips like water from a tap that wouldn't shut off. "Shh, baby boy, it's all right, you're just hungry and cold and I'm gonna give you a cracker, all right, as soon as we get you unstrapped, these contraptions, they make them so that you need six pairs of hands to get it to work right and then, oh, no, baby, don't pull the woman's earrings, don't do that, Raymond, that's a good boy, here, here's a cracker, you hold onto this and I'll—"

He was free, and she nearly fell backward into the hard plastic seat. The woman reached out and steadied her.

"Thanks again," Gloria said, before she'd realized she was looking at the other woman full-face, as though this were just another afternoon subway ride.

"Oh, you know, it's nothing. This is how people used to act to each other when I was a girl, and then something changed. Don't you think? I mean, you're really too young to remember how it was then, before things got mean, but I think if we each make an effort, it really is a nicer world." The woman smiled at Raymond as though he were some kind of enchanted creature. "Yes, baby, that good?"

Raymond examined the cracker and pushed the end of it into his mouth. That dreamy expression—just like Anthony when he was sitting in front of a bowl of steamed mussels. He'd close his eyes and lean over and inhale, and his whole body would soften, as though the smell of garlic and tomatoes and oregano was the most interesting, satisfying thing in the universe. He made love that way, too, his absorption with every nook and curve of her body so intense he never heard ringing phones or the baby crying.

Gloria held Raymond loosely while he squirmed around until his little legs stuck straight out on her knees.

No more excuses. She would not make conversation or eye contact with the woman standing in front of her.

Intoxicating, that's what it was, to be the object of Anthony's attention. The giddy anticipation when he looked at her as they were clearing the dinner dishes; the languid climb to the moment when he stretched his long legs and nodded his head, just the barest gesture, hardly more than a blink, toward the bedroom.

Damn him.

To give her all that, and then use his love to convince her to go along with his plan.

"Sweetheart, you think Lee Iacocca's wife and child have any worries? This is for you and Raymond, for our future, for all of us."

If we don't get caught, he forgot to add.

"You gotta know people, gotta understand what they feel, like Oprah does. Just meet me at the bank with the baby. No one's gonna shoot a man holding a cute little kid in a tasseled hat, right? Him and my gun in one hand, the bag they're gonna stuff with all that pretty green money in my other. Then I'll step outside. You grab him and disappear down the rabbit hole, right? Soon as you hit the platform, you quick dump the old jackets in the trash can, put on the ones in the shopping bag, and go to that little Greek restaurant in Queens. I'll meet you there by five. That's all. Right? Nothing hard about that."

Nothing but the terror that was churning in her stomach, and the rage. A perfect plan? He wouldn't listen when she tried to point out flaws in his logic. Pretended not to hear when she'd told him all the ways it might go wrong. Stubborn, stone-headed man, he insisted he'd make sure everything worked out right in the end.

"Oh, don't!" The woman's sharp voice startled Gloria.

As she snapped her head down, she felt a hard thwack against Raymond's back.

A huge piece of gummy cracker flew out of his mouth, and he let out a horrible, frightened wail. Gloria held his rigid body against hers as his cries pierced the air.

"I'm sorry. I . . . he was choking and . . . that cracker was . . ." Pale, her voice barely more than a whisper, the woman shook her head and fell silent.

Gloria sank back, eyes closed, panting for breath. She'd been so preoccupied that she hadn't known her own baby was choking.

"Thank you." Gloria clutched the woman's hand. That woman was her guardian angel. "You saved my baby. Thank you."

This time, the woman didn't try to shrug off what she'd done. She met Gloria's gaze straight on, blinked slowly, barely nodded.

The train clattered around a curve, and the standing passengers grabbed hold of bars to keep from falling into the laps of those who were seated. Gloria kept stroking Raymond's face, as though her life depended on touching this sweet, innocent child. He had stopped coughing, had stopped crying, and now looked soberly into her face for some explanation of the panic that had gripped him moments earlier.

He frowned, a small squeezing of the space between his eyes, and in that moment, Gloria saw Anthony.

"I don't believe you'd think I could harm you or the baby. You're just stressed, that's why you can't see how perfect this is. This is a visionary plan, honey, a Bill Gates kinda plan. I never thought I'd hear that from you, that doubt in your voice, that scorn. I'm hurt, honey, really hurt you don't trust me enough to go with me on this."

She'd gulped back her words and sipped at her cooling

tea. Trust required proof, didn't it? What evidence did she have that he would keep his promise? She wanted to believe Anthony would take that job her brother had offered him, but as her mama used to say, wanting wasn't getting. He would have to get up at six to travel to the Jersey warehouse by eight, then get back home at six, if he was lucky. Didn't everyone arrange their life to take care of business first? Then, comfort and pleasure followed, after the hard work was done.

"Why do you think someone like Donald Trump, some no-talent sleazebag of a human being, makes billions of dollars? You think it's because he's afraid of taking a chance? You think it's because he wakes up when it's still dark outside and gets on the subway and busts his back humping marble slabs so that some Wall Street whiz kid can make his bathroom more expensive than his father's whole house ever was, you think that's how he made it? You think it wasn't because he had a good idea, and the guts to take the risks to see the whole story through to the end?"

And then he'd slammed the door and stormed out of the house and stayed away for three days. Three days of waiting for the phone to ring, of scrambling to come up with enough money to get Raymond's vitamins and milk and orange juice. Three days of feeling lost without Anthony sleeping beside her in the bed, his even breathing lulling her back to sleep. And when he'd finally come back, hidden behind an armful of the most beautiful flowers she'd ever seen, full of concern and apologies, she'd said, "Maybe, maybe you're right; I'll go along with your plan."

Raymond's body softened against her, his head lolling and his arms limp against his sides. Just like a baby to recover from a shock by drifting off to sleep in a crowded, overheated subway car. How nice to be taken care of by someone bigger, stronger, smarter.

Smarter?

Gloria stuck her thumb into Raymond's palm and his fingers curled around it gently.

Not very smart for a woman to let herself be talked into this crazy scheme. For what? She was risking everything: her freedom, her baby's future, for what? Because Anthony had promised to marry her when this was over? Damn, that was anything but smart. Smart would have been to take the postal worker's exam. Smart would have been to sign up for a couple of programming classes. Smart was not part of the story here, she was sure of that.

She bent her head, kissed Raymond's soft cheek, and his eyes flew open. He grinned, and his grip tightened on her thumb.

"Those fingers . . . he's going to be tall. And maybe even be a piano player." The woman in the black jacket reached her hand out as though she were about to touch Raymond, but then she frowned and pulled back. "Does he like music?"

Despite herself, Gloria answered. "He loves Ricky Martin, dances up a storm whenever he hears that old song from a couple years ago. We got him a little xylophone, you know, just a plastic one but . . ." She frowned and reined herself in. This was not a normal day, and she could not have a normal conversation with this woman.

Could she?

Maybe things had already gone too far. She had joined Anthony in his madness the moment she'd agreed to his plan, and now here she was, sitting next to a smiling woman who couldn't take her eyes off Raymond, a woman who had no idea about how your whole life could turn upside down, like a cake dumped onto the floor before it was done. A runny, puddled-up mess. That's what their lives had become.

As the train picked up speed, the dirty tiles of the Chambers Street station became a blur. Next was Fourteenth, then Thirty-fourth. Two more stops before she would take her child up the stairs and expose him to danger. The express hurtled past Franklin, past Canal and Houston, slowed as it approached Christopher Street.

"Hmmm hmmm la vida loca . . ." the woman sang, and Raymond's eyes widened, a smile bursting across his face. He bounced and twisted, his winter jacket too bulky to allow his hands to meet as he tried to clap in time to the woman's half-humming, half-singing rendition of the popular song.

With a woman like that, someone with a little money, someone who obviously loved kids, a child would be safe.

The train rumbled toward Fourteenth Street.

Gloria looked at her baby. His face beamed with the pure pleasure of the music as his head bobbed from side to side on his chubby little neck.

Oh, Lord, how was this going to end?

The first of the station lights gleamed ahead. People pushed toward the doors, shifting parcels, pulling on gloves, adjusting coat buttons.

". . . la la inside out," the woman sang, and Raymond rocked with the music as the train shuddered to a stop. "Hmmm hmmm la vida loca."

She laughed in delight as Raymond closed his eyes, bowed his head, and then tried to clap again. The doors slid open. "Oh, he's just so cute," she exclaimed.

Gloria leaped to her feet and shoved her baby into the woman's arms. "You take him," she said, as she shouldered past a slow-moving man and ran through the crowd toward the exit.

*   *   *

" la la inside out," the woman sang, and Raymond
. . . rocked with the music. No, Gloria Simone wouldn't
give her own child away. That wouldn't solve anything.
Besides, she'd go crazy knowing he was out there where
she couldn't see him. Growing. Learning to talk, to read,
to add. Figuring out how to balance on a bike. Making
friends. Discovering his special talents. All the things she
dreamed about for her sweet Raymond.

It was all Anthony's fault, this whole mess.

First he lost his temper when he was fired as head-
waiter at Caprainha, the upscale Brazilian restaurant that
had become the darling of the dot.com barons in TriBeCa.
Flew into a rage and threatened everyone from the bartender to the maitre d' to the busboy, never once admitting
that he'd screwed up three big parties in two days. One
of those fiascos had actually made the Gotham section of
New York Magazine. Which resulted in his earning a place
on the blacklist, the do-not-hire roster that circulated in-
formally among the restaurants in the city. Which meant
that six years of working hard to get to a big-money restaurant position were down the drain.

All Anthony's fault, including and up to this very terrible moment that found her on this express train to hell
as it rattled toward Fourteenth Street.

". . . hmmm hmmm la vida loca," the woman sang, and
the train shuddered to a stop.

The woman laughed in delight as Raymond closed his
eyes, bowed his head, and then tried to clap again. The
doors slid open. "What a good boy you are," she exclaimed.

Gloria paid no attention as passengers poured out of

the car. *La vida loca.* That's what Anthony had dragged them into. And it was up to her to get them out of this. The train rolled forward again. Eighteenth Street flew by, then Twenty-third.

Fingers trembling, she zipped his jacket, tied the strings on Raymond's hat, and stood as the train sped past the Twenty-eighth Street stop. Blindly, she pushed the stroller toward the door, steadying herself against the rocking motion with one hand on the cold metal pole as the train pulled into the Thirty-fourth Street station.

She turned to look at the woman, whose intent gaze was fixed on Raymond, then pushed through the doors and onto the platform.

No way was Anthony going to keep putting her—and her baby—in danger. Demanding that they take part in his scheme, using Raymond as a shield. Never again would a plan of his put her in such a position. She couldn't let him do this to her.

Not to anyone.

She cursed this stupid idea, and the logic of whoever had planned this station. When they did the trial run a week earlier, she should have realized the station design was weird, different, not like all the other stations. She had taken the local then. That's what she should have done today. From the express, she had to descend one level, walk through a passageway, then go up a flight of stairs to the platform where the local stopped. Then she had to climb another flight to reach the street.

Gloria felt as though she'd stuck her finger in a socket. A buzz traveled through her arms, her legs, a trembling so fine she could feel it behind her eyes.

Who did he think he was, putting a sweet child between him and some cop's bullet so he could play rich man?

Suddenly, she realized she was standing at the entrance to the bank. How she had gotten there, she wasn't entirely certain. She knew what she had to do, and she was ready.

She pushed the outer door open, barely noticing the white-haired man who held the inner door for her. There he was, third in line, the brim of his baseball cap putting his face in shadow. Anthony acknowledged her arrival with a slight dip of his cap. Otherwise, he stood slouched and relaxed, his shoulders drooping and his right hand crammed into the pocket of his leather jacket.

His plan called for her to hold Raymond in her arms. She would walk up beside him. He would grab the baby from her.

She knelt, undid the strap with a single motion, and lifted the baby from the stroller and into her arms.

She had to move quickly.

She could do it. Her timing had always been good.

She had to take him by surprise.

Anthony glanced at her, his big brown eyes lingering on hers. Those lashes, just like Raymond's. For a moment she faltered.But a new wave of anger coursed through her, and her resolve returned.

Anthony snatched the baby from her arms.

Gloria grabbed the gun from his hand.

His eyes widened in surprise. The woman behind him gasped.

"Give my baby back," Gloria demanded.

Anthony appeared to be frozen in place.

"Now!" She pointed the gun where his legs met.

Anthony held out his son, and Gloria grabbed him up, the smell of his baby skin all she needed to help her make the next move.

Eyes open wide, she pointed the gun at the second button on Anthony's leather jacket and squeezed the trigger.

Muttering, she bumped the stroller, one step at a time, down the stairs, then yanked a startled Raymond into her arms and pulled the empty stroller up, counting each step as she marched. Fourteen, fifteen, sixteen. Her age when she first set eyes on Anthony and succumbed to his laughter, the way his skin smelled, the strong hands that lay quietly folded in his lap as he stared at her. Twenty-one, twenty-two, twenty-three. The number of hours from the very first twinge of labor until Raymond finally made his appearance. Anthony, beaming, sweating, breathing with her, holding her hand every step of the way. Not betraying his worry when the doctor's face screwed into a frown as he leaned over the mountain of her belly with the stethoscope pressed against it.

She couldn't kill him. She loved him, that much she knew. She paused at the top step, the cold wind already biting at her skin. Joining him in his mad plan wasn't really proof that she loved Anthony. That was even clearer.

The clamor of noise from cars, buses, taxis, trucks melted into sudden silence. The sun burst through the thick gray sky and the crowd seemed to part as Gloria approached the bank. She glanced down at Raymond, at the top of his head, his jaunty red tassel bobbing as he danced to some inner music.

The white-haired man standing just inside the second set of doors smiled at her baby and pulled the door open for her. She nodded, glanced at the line waiting to reach the teller cages, spotted Anthony.

His chin nearly touched his chest, his shoulders were pulled down. One hand hung at his side, the other was jammed into the pocket of his black leather jacket. Beneath the brim of his baseball cap, his eyes stared at the floor.

God help her, she really did love the man.

The man he had been.

The man he might still be if he hadn't gotten it into his head after he was fired that he deserved to be rich and that he should find a way to do it quickly.

Now she heard every sound, the toe-tapping of the woman in front of her, the damp cough of the teller in the far booth, the whir of the heating system pumping oppressively hot air into the room, her own blood coursing to her brain. She took a slow, deliberate breath and then walked to the line, stopping beside Anthony.

"You have to come with me right away," she said, her voice ringing through the hush of the bank. "We have a problem. You have to come."

He stared at her as if she'd lost her mind.

She forced her voice louder, higher. "It's about the baby. You have to come with me right now. Now, Anthony."

As if he'd been shaken out of a deep sleep, his entire body twitched. He grabbed her arm.

"What are you doing? You lose your mind?" His mouth tightened and he glowered from beneath his cap. His hand came slowly out of his pocket, and he dabbed at Raymond's drippy tears with his index finger before he stepped out of the line.

As soon as he did that, she knew. It was going to be all right.

She had done the only thing she could, even though neither of them had been able to see it that way when he'd spun out his plot.

Now, his arm around her and his eyes blinking back the stunned knowledge of what he'd almost done, she knew what would happen next. He would follow her onto the street, back down into the subway that would carry them to the apartment, where he would finally understand that he'd suffered from some kind of temporary insanity when he'd proposed this awful scheme.

They would both work on a new plan. They'd figure out how to make a good life, a safe place for their child and their dreams, all three of them helping to define it. What did it matter if it was la vida broke-a for a while?

Together, they would write a much better ending.